Linda Regan is a successful actress having worked ⟨...⟩
from television to film, radio, and theatre. She ⟨...⟩
eight crime novels, all critically acclaim⟨...⟩
set in London, where she was b⟨...⟩

Praise for ⟨...⟩

'Regan exhibits enviable com⟨...⟩ in
this skilful and fascinati⟨...⟩
Colin Dexter

'One of the best up-and-coming writers'
Peter Gutteridge, *Sunday Observer*

'Regan continues her sure-footed walk on the noir side.
Entertaining stuff, but not for the faint-hearted'
Kirkus Reviews

'A sound debut; I look forward to Linda Regan's next book'
Tangled Web

'Extremely well written'
Encore Magazine

'This is a book you can't put down'
Eastbourne Herald

LINDA REGAN

KILLER LOOKS

ACCENT

First published in 2009 as *Monroe Murders* by Accent Press

First published in 2023 by Headline Accent
An imprint of HEADLINE PUBLISHING GROUP

1

Cataloguing in Publication Data is available from the British Library

ISBN 978 1 0354 0585 5

Offset in 11/15.2pt Times New Roman by Jouve (UK), Milton Keynes

Printed and bound in Great Britain by Clays Ltd, Elcograf S.p.A.

HEADLINE PUBLISHING GROUP
An Hachette UK Company
Carmelite House
50 Victoria Embankment
London
EC4Y 0DZ

www.headline.co.uk
www.hachette.co.uk

ACKNOWLEDGEMENTS

There are many people without who this book really would not have come together. I cannot thank them enough for their input and expertise, and I would like to acknowledge here their generosity in giving their time and knowledge:

My friend and editor Lynne Patrick, whose expertise on crime writing and love of chocolate had made my life much happier – not to mention the loan of her daughter's teddy bear!

DC Paul Steed for keeping me on the right side of the law, and putting up with my endless questions, and righting me when I venture into criminal mistakes.

The charming PC Cindy Dobberson, for generously giving her time and helpful advice, and for her knowledge of South London policing – not forgetting the excellent coffee.

Robbie Gentry for his fire expertise – this time I made the coffee!

The support from all my chums at the University of Portsmouth. Thank you for the pep talks, the train timetables, and especially for handwriting expertise from Kate Strzelczyk.

And as ever, to my wonderful husband – for everything.

I was inspired to write this book because my late father, Peter Regan, so loved Marilyn Monroe. Sadly he never made it to see me play her in the story of her life.

This book is dedicated to him.

It is also dedicated to my own favourite sex symbol – my wonderful husband Brian Murphy.

CHAPTER ONE

Sadie Morgan could have been Marilyn Monroe. The blood-red dress was an exact replica of an iconic one. It clung to Sadie's curvy figure and opened from her ankle all the way up her long shapely legs to the top of her thigh, allowing a glimpse of black seamed stockings, a hint of thigh and a cheeky red marabou garter to peep through. She stood with her back to the audience, wiggling her hips in time with the CD track of *Diamonds Are a Girl's Best Friend.* Then she walked up the steep stairs.

She reached the top, flicked the red marabou boa over her shoulder and turned her head, resting her chin on her shoulder and shaping her mouth into Marilyn's famous sultry pout before stretching her shiny scarlet lips into an innocent smile.

She was the best Marilyn Monroe impersonator this tribute club had.

The room span. She momentarily lost concentration, but carried on, bobbing her bottom in time with the music and stretching her arm, pointing a gloved index finger to the dazzling rings on her other hand. Normally in this part of the routine the audience were going wild, but tonight they felt distant; she heard only murmurs, and now she was struggling to remember the words.

She had worked here at Doubles for a year, earning almost as much for her three spots a week as she did as a

1

full-time staff nurse at the local hospital. She always mimed to this song – and suddenly she couldn't remember the words. Something was wrong. It felt like a bad dream.

The room span again and she had to grab the banister to stay upright. It took all her energy to carry on.

She'd only had the usual single shot of whisky before her performance, and it never affected her. What was happening?

She looked out into the audience. Eddie Chang stood in his usual place, arms folded, diamond signet ring glistening on his little finger. He wore a made-to-measure purple suit with matching lining, with a lilac silk tie and a handkerchief in his top pocket. He was easy to spot: his hair was black on top and completely grey underneath, styled and lacquered so not one hair was out of place. He always watched the Marilyns – not just because he owned the tribute club, but because he was obsessed with the Hollywood goddess. He demanded perfection: the dress and wig had to be exact replicas of the ones the star had worn, the walk identical, the infamous pout rehearsed endlessly. Mr Chang had to be satisfied the impersonator could pass for Marilyn Monroe.

His face blurred, then cleared. Was he smiling at her – or scowling?

She realised she had missed her cue. She should have started to walk down the stairs at this point in the song – and he noticed everything. He was blurred again, but she could still see him watching her. So was Johnny Gladman, doorman and jack of all trades for the club, standing next to a life-size cardboard cut-out of Marilyn in that famous white dress, pushing the pleated skirt down, giggling as gusts of wind threatened to reveal her knickers. Johnny's dark-skinned hand covered his mouth, a sure sign she was messing up.

She didn't want to lose her reputation as the best of the many Marilyns working in this club. Being the top impersonator meant not waiting on tables or serving drinks, and she earned more money, which she desperately needed to finish paying her way out of her marriage and keep her flat. She enjoyed the attention and compliments too; she'd never experienced either in her six-year marriage.

Had someone spiked her drink? She was a nurse, so she knew the signs. Was it possible Eddie Chang had found out what she was planning?

Suddenly she was frightened.

Someone laughed. Were they laughing at her? Eddie had turned his back on her; his attention was now on the Marilyn Monroe film running silently on a screen in the other side of the club. That was a very bad sign.

The walls were covered in pictures of Marilyn, from every production, at every age, at every stage of her career. Other celebrity impersonators worked here on other nights, but Eddie Chang was obsessed with Marilyn Monroe.

She clung to the banister miming, '*We all lose our charms in the end.*' She glanced over to her friend Johnny Gladman again. His hand was still covering his mouth; she wasn't imagining it, she really was out of time with the music. Something was wrong.

She carried on as best she could.

She saw Terry King. Terry never ventured out of the dressing room. He said he was too busy combing wigs or sewing dresses to watch the show, yet here he was in front of the stage. And it was definitely Terry. He wasn't tall, but

3

he was very broad in the shoulders, and still looked masculine even dressed as a woman. Everyone knew he wanted to be a Marilyn impersonator, and Eddie found it laughable.

Had Eddie called him because something was going on?

She reached the bottom of the stairs just after the music ended, and didn't wait for the smattering of applause; she hurried to the dressing room as quickly as her unsteady legs would allow. She needed to get out of the club.

Detective Inspector Alison Grainger woke to tangled limbs and the aroma of sex. Sleep had been a long time coming for her but when she had finally, briefly, dropped off she'd dreamed of Paul Banham, and the fulfilment of years of yearning.

Now she felt the hair on his legs sliding from under her, and the smell of his naked body untangling itself from their embrace. As he paused to kiss her tenderly on the forehead, his tummy touched hers and his spent penis gently brushed against her thigh.

He climbed over her and headed for the shower, and she lay staring at the side of the bed where he'd slept, listening as he washed last night's lovemaking from his body. The clock's luminous hands pointed to five-thirty. He hadn't said a word as he slid from her bed. What was she supposed to gather from that? She knew he had arranged to take his nephew to the zoo today, and try to talk to him about his refusal to go to school; and she knew he had promised to get there before the boy got up. Paul Banham would never let his twin sister or her children down. Nor did Alison want him to. But it was five-thirty in the morning, and he was leaving her bed.

She swallowed down the musky, morning taste in her mouth. Was he regretting it? They'd agreed so many times that mixing work and pleasure wasn't on. And they did still have to work together, even though they had both climbed to the next rung of the ladder. She was now detective inspector in the murder division, and he was DCI; he would still be her immediate senior officer. She would be heading up the next murder case, but he'd be with her, guiding her and giving her confidence before he left her on her own to run the next one and the many that would surely follow.

Frustration and anger welled up. He clearly wasn't keen to stay in bed with her; was he going to pretend it never happened? After seven years working closely with him she still had no idea what was going on in his head. The unsolved murder of his young wife and ten-month-old baby all those years ago had affected him very deeply – but was it going to haunt him to his grave? It wasn't that she didn't sympathise and care, but if he didn't feel ready to move on after nearly eleven years, why had he made love to her?

Perhaps it was just sex – just one of those things. It wasn't planned; they hadn't agreed to go out on a date. They were just celebrating their promotion, a spur of the moment thing. But to Alison it felt like they had made love. He was tender, considerate and caring, and to her that didn't seem like a one-night stand.

Yesterday had been a good and bad day. A victim in their last case, a pretty actress who had reminded Banham of his murdered wife, had died after a month in a coma. It had hit Banham very hard; he still took things personally after eleven years in CID. He believed if he'd got there sooner he

5

might have saved her. Alison knew they had done everything in their power. She hoped she wasn't callous, but deaths went with the job.

The news of their promotion had come through a few hours later, and they decided it would be a good idea to go out and get slaughtered. It hadn't occurred to her it might end up like this. Deep down she'd wanted it to happen for years, and now it had she was half regretting it. Had he used Alison for comfort, to ease the guilt about the actress who reminded him of his wife? Or had he too wanted it to happen? He'd had enough chances, and never taken them up in the past.

Most likely it was just a spur of the moment thing: they would never talk about it again, and she would be expected to pretend it hadn't happened. She combed her fingers through the tangled mane of mouse-coloured hair he called her squirrel's tail. He said the dark flecks in her greyish-green eyes reminded him of a cross squirrel too. She wasn't sure if he meant it as a compliment – but that was one of the things that she found endearing about him; a smooth-talking guy he was not.

She took a deep breath, suddenly feeling sober and confused. This wasn't going to be easy, whichever way it went.

The sound of the shower continued. She thought about joining him, but he might not welcome that. She sat up and hugged her knees. Yesterday her promotion to DI had fuelled her with ambition; now she felt empty. She decided to hit the gym as soon as it opened, to work her frustration out. The sound of the water running over him was really beginning to upset her.

Eddie Chang kept his back to Sadie as she hurried unsteadily past him. One of the other Marilyn girls looked concerned; another, the cocktail waitress, turned away. Johnny Gladman watched her every move, and helped her get through the crowded club to the dressing room.

She downed a glass of water and was struggling to get the wig off as Terry King followed her in. Terry nagged the girls about hanging their clothes up but no one took any notice. It was common knowledge that his ambition to be a Marilyn impersonator had come to nothing; he had to make do with maintaining their costumes. He was Chang's other half, and Sadie knew he reported back on everything he heard in the girls' changing room. At the best of times she avoided saying much in his presence; right now he was the last person she wanted to see.

She changed as fast as she could, struggling hard to focus and stay upright. Hairpins scattered as she tugged to free them from her wig.

'Are you all right, love?' Terry sounded concerned, but Sadie wasn't fooled.

'Just tired.' The words came out in a slur.

'Do you want some more water?' Terry bent to pick up Sadie's discarded clothes. Normally he shouted at anyone who dropped their costume carelessly, and that unnerved Sadie more.

She struggled into her jeans and thick jumper. 'No, I'm going. I'll see you next Tuesday.' She pushed her arms into her black padded anorak, zipping it up as she made for the exit.

Johnny was waiting for her outside, his concern evident.

7

He handed her an envelope and she struggled to push the contents into her red clasp bag. She wondered whether to wait for the night bus or walk down the hill. She often walked. It wasn't far, and the night air would help to clear her spinning head. If this was a bug, she could shake it off. If someone had spiked her drink it would be better to walk it out of her system. As she stood pondering the decision, Terry King came out of the club reminding her she was still wearing one of the long diamante earrings; he reached out and snatched it from her ear. That decided her; she wanted to get away. A few seconds earlier and he would have caught her talking to Johnny. She set off down the street.

She didn't see the parked car less than a hundred yards away, its light off, its occupant watching her.

Her stiletto heels clacked down the deserted street; they were uncomfortable, and she began to regret having worn them. Had someone slipped something in her drink? She hoped no one had noticed she had messed up tonight; Eddie Chang was fastidious and would sack a Marilyn for the slightest mistake. He hadn't said anything. Was it possible someone had told him what she was up to? That thought really frightened her. But, she reasoned, Eddie wouldn't mess up her act; he would just shoot her. Besides, there was no way he could know. Still, best not to take the chance. Tomorrow she would deliver.

She crossed the street, unaware that she was zigzagging, or that she was being watched.

She paused briefly at the end of the road. There was a short cut; halfway down the hill she could turn into the alleyway that led to the park, then walk past the duck pond and cut across the field. She loved that walk, watching the

8

night change into morning. The dew in the air always felt fresh after a night of inhaling fumes from the smoke machine at the club. She often finished work just as the birds began their breakfast chorus. It was too early for that tonight.

The field was quicker than the road. She turned to check no one was around, and entered the unlit alleyway, away from the safety of the CCTV cameras. She was totally unaware that someone else entered too, very quietly and only seconds after her.

The cry of an animal in the distance unnerved her and she stopped to listen.

The follower stopped too.

As she turned her head listening, the figure quietly stepped sideways into the shadow of the bushes.

The branches over the fence rustled a little. Sadie told herself the noise was just a hungry fox or a randy cat, but she felt for the reassuring shape of the hand-gun in her red satin handbag. She reached the other end of the alley and turned to look back. Nothing. She stepped out and crossed the road toward the open field, where the only light came from the stars. Nearly home. She closed her eyes for a moment and breathed the fresh smell of dew.

Something touched her neck, and her heart shot into her mouth. She instinctively turned her head toward it – then it was over her face, pressing against her, sucking her breath away.

She kicked out wildly and scrabbled at whatever was covering her face. She touched what felt like an arm, but the increasing pain and desperate need to breathe took all her attention. Her leg kicked out instinctively and she lost her

9

balance, then a sharp kick behind her other knee brought her down, tearing and ripping at whatever was over her face.

She hit out with feet and fists, then… the gun! Could she get the gun? Did she still have the bag on her wrist? She fumbled for it, but something hard hit her hand and her head exploded and white stars danced in front of her.

She felt and heard the thud as her knees hit the ground, and a shot of adrenalin gripped her. Her fists flew and her legs kicked out, but they missed their target like a marionette with an inexperienced handler.

Pain shot through the top of her head like an exploding pressure cooker. Her body felt as light as a rag doll, and time stood still. Coloured stars danced around her brain and disappeared into blackness.

She no longer needed to breathe.

After a quick check, her assailant pulled the pillow away. The handbag flew through the air and landed a good hundred yards down the field, scattering Tampax, cosmetics, and the hand-gun and bullets.

The attacker turned to leave the scene, but had second thoughts and walked back to the slumped body, lifted it by the legs and dragged it the few yards to the pond, over uneven paving which scraped away the skin on her face.

The corpse dropped almost soundlessly into the filthy slime-ridden water, but the squawks from indignant ducks panicked the killer: what if someone in one of the neighbouring houses awoke and looked out the window?

The water was shallow, and Sadie's face slowly sank beneath it. Her bleached-blonde hair darkened as slime, reeds and water crept over her broken face and finally covered her sightless eyes until just the tip of her nose remained above the surface.

Good, thought the killer, staring through the black night into the pond; that was a job well done. Then suddenly her face bobbed above the surface. For an instant it was as if she had come back to life, but it was the movement of the water as the inquisitive ducks swam in to see what had invaded their home.

The face was dirty, stinking and very dead, and the job finished.

The real Marilyn had died in her bed and looked beautiful.

CHAPTER TWO

It was just before six a.m, and Alison was pacing up and down outside the gym waiting for it to open. Last night's events were whirring around her head and the craving for a cigarette was making her edgy. The running machine always quelled the nicotine craving, and she could use the time to think through what had happened and how best to deal with the consequences.

They'd both had a fair amount to drink though neither of them was completely out of it. They'd shared a taxi, and he came back to her flat as he had on many occasions; it wasn't unusual for him to crash at her place. She'd offered him the sofa – then as she handed him a spare duvet and watched him snuggle into the sofa, she had surprised herself by inviting him to share her bed, mumbling feebly that he looked neither warm nor comfortable. Even more surprisingly, he had accepted.

He had slept in her bed before – literally fallen asleep on it, after a long day. So what was different last night? Was it the alcohol? And was he now regretting it? She had believed it was the start of something, but at five-thirty – *five-thirty* – he got up, showered and dressed, then made her tea and cornflakes. When she refused them he had kissed her on the forehead, picked up his keys and said he'd call her later. But he always called her later; she was his second in command! Of course he would call – but would he mention the fact that they'd had sex?

She pulled her fur-hooded anorak close around her neck against the early morning dampness. It was early March and not yet six o'clock – still dark, and very cold.

Had she just made a huge mistake? Had he? Yesterday had been a strange day. Promotion for them both, following the news that a victim they had tried to protect during a horrific kidnap had died from knife wounds. And Banham had blamed himself for not getting to the victim in time. Alison punched the palm of her hand. Why did he think he could save a victim? He wasn't God. The truth was he was an emotional mess. It was eleven years since the murder of his wife and baby; by now most people would have moved on. He couldn't. He blamed himself for not being there to save them. The death of that female victim yesterday had let his personal ghosts in all over again.

She really needed a cigarette, but she had given up a few months ago, the same time as she gave up men. She had broken one resolution, but she was determined to hang on to the other. She would work this excess energy off in the gym and then spend the rest of the day catching up on paperwork in the department.

She started pacing again. She was going to be thirty-six in three weeks, yet right now she felt like a silly, insecure seventeen-year-old.

She had wanted to go to bed with him, no doubt about that. She'd had one night stands, but Banham was different. She had wanted to touch him and hold him and make love with him so much and for so long, it almost hurt to think about it. A lump rose in the back of her throat as she recalled the tenderness: his hands exploring her body, and

13

the gentle way that his tongue teased, then pleased.

She squeezed her lips together to stop the emotion welling up. Was he thinking about her right now, she wondered. No; what a ridiculous notion. He was with his twin sister and her children at the zoo, trying to find out why Bobby wouldn't go to school. Of course he wasn't thinking about her.

The sound of the gym door being unlocked made her swallowed down the turmoil inside her. She needed that work-out.

As Alison pushed her bag into the changing room locker, Paul Banham was sitting on the end of his nephew's bed. It was a quarter to six in the morning, and Bobby was sobbing into his pillow. Banham wanted nothing more than to give his nephew and niece a fun day out, but he needed to have a heart-to-heart with the little boy. Lottie, his twin sister, had told him about the crying bouts, the nightmares, the refusal to go to school; he even picked fights with his younger sister, Madeleine.

Banham thought the problem was that Bobby was missing his father. Derek had gone off with a barmaid two years ago, and broken Lottie's heart. Banham still wanted to punch him; every child needed a dad. Banham had lost his own chance of being a father when his ten-month-old baby Elizabeth was murdered; he was glad to step in when Derek left. But uncle wasn't the same as dad.

Bobby was nine, and normally a plucky little chap. Now he was sobbing into his pillow, and Banham felt helpless.

Lottie was standing in the doorway. Banham gestured silently, asking her to leave them on their own.

She left.

'Mum's gone, Bobby,' Banham said. 'It's just you and me now. What is it, mate? Are you missing your dad? It's OK to tell me, you know.'

The boy shook his head, but kept it buried in his pillow.

'Well, something's up. I can keep a secret. I won't tell your mum.'

'S'nothing.'

'You know I'll do all I can to help.'

'S'nothing.'

'OK.'

Silence.

'Do you still want to go to the zoo today?'

A muffled 'Yes.'

'Good.' Another pause. Banham unfolded his arms and interlocked his fingers, then leaned his chin on his hand, a habit he had acquired interviewing witnesses. 'Did you have another bad dream?' he asked very quietly.

A beat passed. Banham waited. The boy's face stayed buried in the pillow, but he nodded.

'Do you want to tell me about it?'

'I was killed.'

Banham ruffled the back of Bobby's hair. 'Well, you know that was only a dream. You're here, safe in your bedroom, with me to protect you. OK?'

'OK.'

But Banham was convinced there was more. This was so out of character. Bobby rarely showed his feelings and almost never cried. Alison always said he took after his Uncle Paul.

He pushed away the image of Alison which rose in his

15

mind. He would call her later; this was Bobby's time. He watched the boy rub his eyes and start to get up.

'I'll go and wake Madeleine,' he told him, 'then I'll help your mum with breakfast and we can make an early start.'

'OK.'

Banham stood up. Usually if Bobby had a problem he confided in his uncle, but he wasn't saying anything this time. What was going on? Banham didn't need to be a detective to work that out that it wasn't just bad dreams.

He stared at his nephew's slight nine-year-old frame as Bobby opened his wardrobe to get his clothes out. Had he done something wrong and was afraid to own up? Banham so wanted to help him. He never had the chance to protect his own daughter from anything that scared her; he hadn't even been there for her when she and her mother were attacked. But he was going to be there for these two children, come what may.

'See you in the kitchen in five?'

'OK.'

Banham he paused outside the door to listen. Bobby had started sobbing again.

Alison worked up a sweat on the rowing machine, then moved to the treadmill, set it a little faster than her usual pace, and started running.

She was just getting into her stride, starting to sweat in earnest, when the gym door opened noisily and Colin Crowther sauntered in – newly promoted Detective Sergeant Crowther, she remembered. His dark curly hair was sticking out in all directions, and clearly hadn't seen a comb this morning. His unaccountable and bizarre dress sense was always a talking point among the murder squad, but this morning he had excelled himself. He wore a t-shirt that read *Blackpool Pier Wet T-Shirt Competition* Runner-up in large shocking pink letters, and the baggy shorts that nearly reached his knees had an abstract pattern of green, gold and white. The t-shirt obviously belonged to whoever he'd spent the night with. His regular live-in lover forensic officer Penny Starr had too much style, thought Alison; and DC Isabelle Walsh, with whom he'd recently had a fling, was definitely not the wet t-shirt competition type.

She didn't know whether to laugh or ignore him. What was he doing here at this time anyway if he'd spent the night with someone? There was no one else in the gym save one overweight man in the corner. It would have been difficult to pretend she hadn't noticed him.

Crowther looked surprised and a little embarrassed to see her, but he sauntered over and climbed on to the next running machine. 'Morning, ma'am to be,' he winked.

Though she wanted to be alone to think things over, she was always pleased to see Crowther. He always cheered her up – and anyway, he wasn't easy to ignore, especially dressed like that.

Crowther was an excellent detective. Born the son of an East End scrap metal dealer who dealt with local villains, he had grown up perceptive and sharp. He knew all the right people and wasn't afraid to use those contacts to lead the team to an arrest.

He had just been promoted to Alison's old job, and she was glad he'd got it. Isabelle Walsh had applied too, but Colin deserved it more. Alison liked and respected him –

17

though she couldn't understand his phenomenal success with women. Perhaps he appealed to the mother in them; she couldn't think what else it could be. He certainly wasn't her type; she was two inches taller than him in her bare feet, and possessed not a single maternal instinct. She knew she wasn't obviously sexy; the men in the squad saw her as one of the lads. She was always ready to jump into a fight with the most hardened criminals, and could hold her own every time. Physically she was tall and very slim, but her wide hips and a small bust put her out of the running for a wet t-shirt competition; and though she would never admit it, she would have liked to buy a bigger size bra than a 32A.

The knots tightened in her stomach as last night flooded back.

Crowther clocked the speed she was running at. She stared straight ahead, but knew he was looking at her. Nothing slipped Crowther's notice. He wasn't nicknamed Know-all Col for nothing. He knew something was up with her. He set his own machine at the same fast pace and started running next to her. Every few seconds he threw her a questioning glance, waiting to see if she wanted to tell him what was the matter.

She wondered if she could; he wasn't a gossip, and under the macho front he was a decent bloke who cared about his friends. But she could hardly say, 'Actually I slept with the boss last night and now I think he's regretting it.'

They carried on running, panting heavily and every now and again catching each other's eye.

Laughter suddenly burst out from Alison. She had to press the Pause button on her machine to stop herself choking, then bent forward trying to catch her breath and stop herself laughing at Crowther's ridiculous get-up.

Crowther pressed his own Pause button and looked at her. 'What?'

She picked up her towel and wiped the sweat pouring down her face and neck

'I'm presuming that t-shirt isn't yours.'

He tapped the side of his nose.

'It's not Penny's either,' she persisted. 'She's too classy.'

He lifted his eyebrows, but said nothing.

Penny was Alison's friend too. As assistant head of Forensics she had helped them both out many times, working all hours for no extra pay to get a result that would lead to a conviction. She had probably helped, indirectly, to get their promotion.

'I thought it was over with Isabelle?' she pushed.

Crowther again raised his untidy eyebrows and grinned, but remained silent.

'So who did you spend the night with?'

'Who did you?'

That took her by surprise. How did he know?

His eyes didn't leave hers. 'It's the guvnor, isn't it?'

Was there nothing he couldn't suss? She blushed, and swiftly bent to pick up her bottle of water while her burning cheeks cooled.

'About bloody time too...'

Her head shot up. 'It's not like that. And I don't want anyone to know.'

An urgent bleep sounded from her phone, and Crowther's warbled the theme from an old Clint Eastwood movie.

'OK?' she said before she pressed the call answer button.

19

'Of course.'

Banham walked down the stairs and into the kitchen where Lottie, still in her dressing gown, was making porridge.

He couldn't bear her to be upset. They were twins; he hurt when she did, and he understood everything she had been through when her husband left her with the two children and no money. At first she had been too proud to allow her brother to help, but now she had let him in, and he wasn't going to let them down.

'I'll talk to him again during the day,' he said, taking porridge bowls out of the cupboard. 'Has he ever mentioned a class bully?'

She shook her head. 'Nothing like that. He used to love school.'

Banham rested a hand on her shoulder. 'It'll be OK. I'll sort it. I promise.'

'Do you think he's missing Derek?'

Banham decided to lie. 'No. He's a Banham. He's too intelligent for that.'

The door opened and six-year-old Madeleine came in, dressed in her party dress and pink ballet shoes.

Lottie looked at her in exasperation. 'I said jeans and wellingtons. We're going to the zoo.'

'But Uncle Paul said we can go to tea with the chimps.' Madeleine appealed to her uncle with the blue eyes that Banham couldn't resist. 'It's my tea-party dress, Uncle Paul.'

'Yes, but…' He didn't finish the sentence; his phone was trilling, and the look Lottie gave him meant she knew the day was spoiled before it had started.

CHAPTER THREE

As Alison and Crowther turned into the road a sea of flashing blue lights signalled the location. An exceptionally tall WPC stood guarding the cordon; she immediately lifted the blue and white tape to allow their car access. Alison shivered with anticipation; clearly she had been recognised as the officer in charge of the case. Then she saw that the lanky woman constable was smiling so warmly at Crowther that she was almost alight. Crowther returned the smile with one of his winks. That said it all.

Alison suppressed a smile. The woman's feet were nearly as long as Crowther was high – but then the last thing newly promoted Sergeant Crowther noticed about a woman was her feet.

She pulled up close to the alleyway that led to the open parkland. Crowther opened the door open and jumped out, and was comparing sightlines at the edge of the alleyway almost before she had turned the ignition off. He had thankfully changed his clothes and now sported a pair of ill-fitting jeans and a brown anorak with the sleeves rolled up so many times it looked like a Cossack hat on each skinny wrist. Alison was just grateful he wasn't out on the first murder scene since their promotion with WET T-SHIRT COMPETITION written across his chest in fuchsia pink lettering.

'A lot of these houses have a clear view over the alley

21

and park land,' Crowther shouted. 'Someone just might have seen or heard something.'

He called a uniformed sergeant over, to order an immediate door-to-door.

Alison had noticed Banham's car. 'Guvnor's already here,' she shouted to Crowther.

She heard him instructing the uniformed sergeant to get the alleyway cordoned off as she walked into the park. Good old Col, always on the ball.

A crowd of officers dressed head to toe in bluebell-coloured plastic overalls, plastic shoes and white mouth masks milled around the pond on the opposite side of the wasteland. Banham was there, along with dozen or so of the forensic team, including Crowther's girlfriend Penny Starr and the head of Forensics, Max Pettifer. Some were on hands and knees, examining the area minutely.

She hovered, studying her surroundings. There was a fence around the perimeter of the park, and another padlocked entrance.

Crowther caught her up. 'Pathetic Pettifer is here,' she told him.

Pathetic Pettifer was Banham's pet name for Max Pettifer. Max was an excellent forensic investigator, but he got by making tasteless jokes, often at the expense of the victim. Mostly people were too busy doing their jobs to take any notice – but Paul Banham refused to put up with his crass remarks. Banham was ultra-sensitive around female corpses. It was common knowledge that eleven years ago he had come home and found his wife brutally murdered, her body unrecognisable and her severed arm still around their baby daughter, also unrecognisable from the attack on her tiny face.

So when Banham vomited if the victim was a baby or a blonde female, everyone sympathised and no one commented. No one except Max Pettifer.

Crowther was now examining the sightlines from the cluster of bushes that lined the edge of the fence by the alleyway.

'She had to enter from the alleyway,' Alison told him. 'The rest of the park is locked at night.'

Crowther bent down and picked up a lipstick rolling free on the path, its chrome container unscratched and free from rust. 'This was dropped recently,' he said, swivelling it open to reveal a bright red stick of colour.

'Could be anyone's,' Alison shrugged.

He nodded his agreement. 'Could be hers,' he said, dropping it into an evidence bag.

Alison pulled mauve forensic gloves from her pocket and joined Crowther, squatting to peer under the bushes lining the pathway. He pushed his gloved fingers through the damp, cold foliage and pulled out a mess of fast food containers, mouldering food, rusting beer cans and cigarette packets, all crawling with insects.

Alison came across a black and white rubber football and threw it out into the parkland in case a football-mad youngster, like Banham's nephew, was desperately searching for it.

Crowther was holding up his next find – a small, red satin handbag.

'It's a known muggers' dumping ground,' she said handing him another evidence bag to wrap it in. 'But you're right. You never know.'

The clasp was loose. He emptied out the contents: Tampax, keys, a purse containing money and credit cards and a name and address. 'Not a mugging,' he said. 'Sadie Morgan, 3 Fox Meadow.' A frown creased his forehead; he pushed a hand into the bottom of the bag. and pulled out a bullet.

'Definitely not a mugging.' Alison passed him yet another evidence bag. 'Better look for a gun.'

Banham was making his way over to them. He looked ashen. As DCI he wouldn't have to attend all murder scenes, she thought; a good thing too.

'Good morning,' he said. 'Welcome to your first murder enquiry, Detective Inspector Grainger. You too, Sergeant Crowther. Max thinks the victim was killed over there.' He pointed to the path. 'Then dragged along the footpath, and thrown in the pond. She was dead before she hit the water.'

Crowther preened. 'We may have her identity, guv.' He handed the evidence bag containing the red handbag to Banham. 'We think this could be hers. It's not been here long, no rust or scratching, material hasn't seen much weathering.' He paused. 'And it had a bullet in it.'

'Penny's just found a gun over there.' Banham pointed to the ground near the pathway. 'See if they're a match.'

Penny Starr was standing at the edge of the pond wearing long waders over her forensic suit. Crowther headed towards her.

'We're hoping there might be some light sleepers out there,' Alison said. 'Crowther's ordered an in-depth house-to-house on the houses that overlook the park.'

Banham nodded. 'Good.'

'Who found her?'

'Two support officers at the end of their night shift; they're both in shock.'

'Have you spoken to them?'

'No, I left that for you. It's your case – Detective Inspector Grainger.'

'You organised forensics, though.' The words came out a little too sharply.

'I thought we should get things moving as fast as possible,' he said quietly.

Not your call any more, she almost said, but bit it back. He was right, of course. The important thing was that the investigation was under way.

They looked at each other for a moment, then Banham took a deep breath. 'Look, I'm sorry I left so early. You knew I'd promised to get to Lottie's before the children woke. I need to find out what's wrong with Bobby.'

She nodded. 'We'll talk later. I need to focus on this for now.' She set off in the direction of the pond. If she was honest, it was a relief not to have to think about last night.

Banham caught her up. 'Are you annoyed that I left early?'

'No. I'm thinking about the woman in that pond.' She turned to face him. He was smiling, one of those smiles which made the sides of his eyes crinkle and her tummy think it was in competition with the Red Arrows.

He put a hand on her shoulder. 'I promised you a slap-up Italian meal when you crack your first case, remember?'

'You've been promising me a slap-up Italian meal for years.'

'Well, I've chosen the restaurant.'

She looked at him.

25

'Italian as agreed.'

She sensed there was more.

'I think you'll like it. It's in Venice.'

The victim's face was just visible through the moss-muddied slime. The eyes were blurred, and an arm, stiff with rigor, pointed away from her body as if she was directing traffic. Alison willed the corpse to tell her what she was doing in the park in the small hours of the morning.

'Welcome and good morning,' Max Pettifer chortled from the pond. 'Come in and join us, we're having a quacking time.'

For once Banham ignored the tasteless humour.

The area was crowded with uniformed police and forensic officers. The exhibits officer was videoing the scene and two forensic officers stood by, a black body bag at the ready, next to the mortician's black van which had reversed to the pond, its rear doors open.

'Has the FME been?' Alison asked. The duty forensic medical examiner had to pronounce life extinct before the body could be moved.

'First person I called,' Banham said.

'But…' As senior investigating officer all this was up to her. Irritation welled in Alison's chest; didn't he trust her to do the job properly?

No point raising it now; there was too much to be done.

Penny Starr had a white breathing mask over her face, a stark contrast to her toffee-coloured skin. She stood with one foot in the water, comparing the gun with the bullet Crowther had found.

Max Pettifer was still in the shallow water shouting his

orders. The ducks kept their distance, squawking their protests on the far side of the pond as they swam around an upside-down rusting supermarket trolley. Alison zipped herself into a forensic suit and pulled the white mask over her mouth, then stepped into a pair of waders and into the water, to get a good look at the victim before she was taken away. For once she was grateful she had such long legs; the water looked disgusting and smelled worse.

Max watched her with amusement. 'You'll need a sense of humour as well as your thermals in here, ducky,' he shouted, his short stocky frame vibrating as he laughed at the feeble joke. Alison's teeth clenched; she understood exactly why he got on Banham's nerves. 'Can we get on with it?' she snapped. 'It's freezing.'

'Oh, not in the mood for joke quacking!'

She let out an irritable sigh. Max she could cope with, but the water would wash away any DNA clinging to the body, making their job harder. They'd need a lot of luck to get a quick result.

'Let's bag her up and move her out,' Max shouted.

'Check her clothes first,' Banham shouted to Alison. 'Is she fully dressed?'

'Oh, I'd never have thought of that,' she muttered under her breath.

'Must be,' Max shouted. 'None of the ducks are peeking. Peeking – Peking. Get it?'

'Give it a rest, Max,' Alison snapped. She checked the body and climbed out of the pond. 'Hey, there's a footprint here, on the path.'

Max Pettifer was behind her. 'We know,' he said patronisingly. 'I think you'll find it belongs to the clown of an officer who discovered the body.' He inclined his head towards the two PCSOs who sat on the far side of the pond.

Alison closed her eyes. 'Don't they get any training?'

'They're both new, and greener than pond slime,' said Max.

'They walked towards the pond, saw the body in the water, and waded in to investigate.' That was Penny Starr.

'What?'

'It gets worse,' Penny said, shaking her head. 'When she realised it was a body the female PCSO threw up, actually on the crime scene.'

Alison rolled her eyes. 'Get their shoes.'

'We've got them.'

Crowther was talking the PCSOs. The female was a pretty blonde; Alison and Penny exchanged glances. Alison shouted, 'I want their clothes, too. Get someone to drive them home and then bring them straight back to the station to make statements.'

She turned back to Max. 'Anything at all to go on?' she asked hopefully.

'The skin is missing from one side of her face.'

'We're looking for particles of that on the pathway,' Penny told her. 'So far nothing, but we'll keep at it.' She gave Alison an encouraging smile. 'We'll get you something, never fear.'

Alison smiled back. Penny was a godsend to the team. She knew everything about forensics and never minded working all hours to get results. She was also strikingly beautiful, and even made the shapeless blue plastic overalls look elegant. And she was totally besotted with Crowther; Alison couldn't understand why he strayed.

'Looks like Col's bullet matches the gun I found,' she told Alison. 'It's a .22 Astra Cadix.'

'Where was it exactly?' Banham asked.

'Over there, just off the pathway.' She pointed to a spot near the entrance, not far from where the bag was found.

'There was a fight?' Banham suggested to Alison.

'The killer took the gun and threw it,' Alison nodded.

Banham's face brightened. 'Could be our first piece of luck. Let's hope he wasn't wearing gloves.'

'Why didn't they dump it with the body?' Alison mused.

'Couldn't find it?' Banham shrugged. 'It was dark.'

'Not very experienced then,' Alison said.

'Or he panicked,' Banham suggested. His face became a mask, and he turned quickly and started walking. They were bringing the body out of the water, and zipping it into the black bag to be taken to the morgue.

Alison followed him over to Crowther, who was talking to the PCSOs. Both were visibly shaking.

'We're going to send you home with a forensic officer,' Alison told them 'We need you to change out of your uniform and give us the clothes you're wearing.'

'I'll go with them,' Penny offered.

'Then we'll bring you back to the station to give full statements,' Alison told them, 'but tell me now, briefly, what happened.'

'In your own time,' Banham added, a little too sensitively in Alison's opinion.

PCSO Andrew Fisher's clothes were grubby and his complexion pale. His uniform looked a size too small. His fingers covered his mouth; he moved them, and spoke with a slight northern accent. 'I thought it was… well, I'm not sure what I thought it was… but I didn't think it was a body.'

PCSO Millie Payne spoke in a monotone. 'I know her. I… er… I threw up. It was such a shock. I think I've messed up the DNA tests.'

Banham shook his head sympathetically, but Alison was unimpressed. PCSOs were trained to be the eyes and ears of the force, not to go investigating on their own. This woman might have been new to the job, but she should have known enough to call it in. 'Who is she?' she asked Millie.

'Her name's Sadie Morgan. She works at a club called Doubles. I work there too. It's the Marilyn Monroe club. She was their top impersonator.'

Crowther looked at her sharply. 'Doubles, opposite the supermarket?' He exchanged glances with Banham. 'Eddie Chang's den of iniquity.'

Millie blinked her large blue eyes. 'I've been working there, with her.' She looked at Alison and took in her shocked expression. 'It's not against the rules of this job,' she said. 'I checked before I applied. My actress friend Lily Palmer worked there as a Marilyn Monroe impersonator too, then she got a proper acting job, playing Marilyn in a touring play. She introduced me to the owner and suggested I take over her nights until her play finishes. He auditioned me and took me on as a trainee Marilyn.'

'Eddie Chang?' Crowther asked.

Millie nodded.

Crowther blew out a breath. 'He's a villain, Millie, and highly dangerous. We're talking drugs, arms and woman-trafficking.'

Millie looked nervous. 'No one told me.'

'How well did you know Sadie?' Banham asked her.

'I met her when I went for rehearsals. She was so like Marilyn Monroe – the punters loved her.'

'Someone didn't,' said Andrew Fisher.

'I know where she lives,' Millie offered.

'Good,' Banham said. 'Tell me about her.'

'Married – well, separated. He's Italian. He turns up a lot at the club, shouting. No one likes him.'

'What does he do?'

'I think he's a chef.'

'Where?'

'I'm not sure. A local Italian I think.'

'What's his name? Alison asked.

Millie wrapped her chin length blonde hair around her finger, like pastry around a sausage. She frowned thoughtfully. 'Bruno, I think.' She looked at Crowther for reassurance and he responded with an encouraging smile.

It didn't need a detective to see what was going through Crowther's mind.

'What time was it when you found her?' Alison asked.

'About five-thirty.'

'At the end of our shift,' Andrew added.

'Will I be in trouble for working at the club?' Millie asked Crowther naïvely.

'As you say, sweetheart, it's not against the rules.'

'You should have cleared it with your duty sergeant first,' Alison added sharply, flicking an angry glance at Crowther. 'You are allowed to do other work, but there are limits. If you'd asked if you could work there, you'd have been refused permission.'

Millie nodded, and lowered her eyes.

31

'Best thing you can do is offer your knowledge of the club to help the investigation,' Banham said gently.

'I'm happy to help any way I can.' 'Good,' Alison said flatly. 'Go home with Penny and change your clothes, then meet us at the station for a statement.'

Unable to trust herself, she set off down the path. Banham caught up with her after a few moments. 'Go easy on them. 'They're very new officers, just out of training, and they've had a shock.'

'Sadie Morgan's family will get a bigger one.'

'All I'm suggesting is that we tread gently. We'll get more out of them that way.'

'For God's sake, they've just contaminated my first crime scene!'

'Haven't you ever made a mistake?'

She paused. Her eyes held his for endless seconds. 'Yes. I have.' She turned and walked towards her car. There was no time for this.

'OK, so what have we got?'

Alison stood in front of the whiteboard in the incident room with Banham beside her. A second board held photos of the dead woman, her eyes glass-like and open, wet green slime clinging to her bleached hair, and one side of her face looking as if a rabbit- skinning knife had been at work on it. The peeled skin had crusted in caked blood, and the broken nose and cheekbone dragged one side of the face down.

Alison addressed the dozen or so murder squad detectives gathered in the hope of cracking the case in the first twenty-four 'golden' hours.

'We believe she was killed near the bushes, then dragged

across the pathway.' She pointed to the close-up of the face. 'Hopefully we'll find some of her skin on the pathway, and may get DNA from that. For now, we'll work with what we know.'

'The post mortem will be Monday morning,' Banham butted in. 'But this could be straightforward. We may even have the killer by then.'

'Door-to-door is ongoing,' Isabelle Walsh informed them. 'But so far no one saw or heard anything.'

'The two support officers who found her, Millie Payne and Andrew Fisher are here and waiting to give their statements,' Crowther added. 'Millie has already mentioned a jealous ex-husband.'

'Millie Payne knew the victim,' Banham told them. 'She also has been working at the Doubles club with the victim.' Crowther opened his mouth to speak, but Banham put a hand up to silence him. 'Not now, Colin.'

Crowther subsided, then began again, with a quick shake of his head in Banham's direction. 'The victim had a .22 calibre bullet in her bag. And an Astra Cadix gun was found nearby. The odds are high that this will lead us back to Doubles.'

Eric, an older detective with a cigarette behind his ear, pushed his body off the wall and stood up straight. 'Oh, come on, guv, we all know about the CO19 operation.'

The room fell silent, and everyone's eyes were on Banham. Alison saw a smile twitch the corner of his mouth. 'Talk about jungle telegraph,' he said. 'Just keep your mouths shut, that's all. One word in the wrong ear and it could all fall apart again.'

Heads nodded and a rumble of agreement went round the

room. Eddie Chang was the slipperiest villain on Banham's patch. Drugs, firearms, under-age girls for the sex trade – there was little he wasn't involved in. The Serious Crimes squad had so far failed to pin anything on him; covert surveillance produced plenty of information, but hard evidence eluded them.

'OK, Colin, you'd better tell us what the position is.' Banham used a foot to hook a chair towards him and sat with folded arms, looking expectantly at Crowther.

The young sergeant was in his element. He walked to the front of the room, pushing up the folded-over sleeves of his anorak. To Alison it looked like one a mother would buy for a child, hoping he'd grow into it. Crowther's dark brown curls stood away from his head like a little corkscrews, and he looked as if he'd slept under a bridge. No one who didn't know him would guess he was one of the shrewdest detectives on the force – something she was sure he used to his advantage.

'According to our informant,' he began, 'Chang is waiting on a supply of Mac 10 sub-machine guns. There's a bunch of girls expected too – Ukrainians, all under-age, for prostitution. There's talk of a consignment of crystal meth as well, but that's not the main focus this time.

'The girls are going to be moved in next Wednesday. Surveillance is in place, and if they arrive as scheduled the club will follow two hours later. So if Eddie Chang's club is part of this investigation, we'll need to keep CO19 in the loop.'

Banham stood up, rubbing his fingers over his mouth. 'The fact that the victim was carrying a gun and worked at Doubles certainly takes us back there as a starting point,' he said. 'But we don't want to get in CO19's hair with a raid imminent. No one needs reminding what could happen if Mac 10 sub-machine guns make it to the streets of south London. And it's taken Serious Crimes six months to get this far. Nevertheless, we're investigating a murder. So we need to find out, and quickly, if there is a link between Doubles and the death of this woman. As I'm sure Detective Inspector Grainger will agree.'

Alison was beginning to feel out of her depth. Leading a murder enquiry was one thing; getting involved, or rather, trying not to get involved, in a major Serious Crimes operation was quite another.

Crowther was talking again. 'I'll talk to my snout,' he said. 'We got him a job at Doubles, to help with the CO19 operation. Let's see what he can tell us about the victim.'

Alison took a deep breath; time she asserted herself as senior investigating officer. 'I want you with me to interview PCSO Millie Payne,' she told Crowther, 'I think she liked you. And we need to bring in the victim's husband; that's top of my list of priorities.'

'Let's hope Penny can up with something that will give us a lead,' Banham said.

'She will,' Crowther assured them, crossing his arms confidently in the oversized sleeves.

'She will as long as you behave yourself and don't upset her,' said a voice from the back of the room. It was Eric, the older detective. 'Better put your Y-fronts on the wrong way round with that pretty blonde support officer.'

Crowther looked at the floor and said nothing.

'That pretty blonde support officer walked on the crime scene then vomited on it,' Alison reminded them. The room

35

went quiet.

'She knew the victim, though,' Crowther pointed out. 'And she found the body.'

If Eric's remark had embarrassed him, Alison, thought, it didn't last long.

'Any chance it could have been an accident?' Isabelle asked.

Crowther laughed. 'Try to keep up, Walshie.'

'She could have been drunk,' Isabelle argued. 'Praps she dropped her bag and crawled around looking for it, then fell in the pond and hit the bottom. It's shallow, she could have knocked herself out. It's possible.'

'She lived very near the park,' Crowther said flatly. 'We've got her address from her bag, and the keys. So she knew the area, she'd have known where the pond was. Drunk or not, she wouldn't have fallen in.'

Isabelle was loud-mouthed, tough and ruthlessly ambitious, but Alison and the whole department knew that much against her nature she'd fallen for Crowther. He had taken advantage of it; where women were concerned he couldn't help himself. Their affair had been shortlived, but there was still a spark between them.

Alison still wondered if she should pull Isabelle off the case, but she was pretty sure the young DC would set aside her personal feelings and make it work. Isabelle was determined, and would pull out all the stops to get a result and prove her worth. And Alison knew they needed a quick result.

Besides, what right had she to tell Isabelle and Crowther to keep their personal life out of the incident room? That was the pot calling the kettle!

'Max is sure she was dead when she hit the water,' she told Isabelle. 'If he commits himself it has to be right.'

'We've made a good start,' Banham said. 'We've identified the victim – her address was in the handbag we found, and PCSO Millie Payne has confirmed it.'

'After we've taken Payne's statement,' Alison said to Crowther, 'I want you and Isabelle to go to the victim's flat. If no one is there, we have keys. See if you can find a next of kin, then bring in the ex-husband.' Eric was still by the door. 'You'll be on family liaison duty,' she told him.

'Yes, ma'am.' He gave her a mock salute.

'Alison and I will pay Eddie Chang a visit at Doubles,' Banham said.

'I'd like a chance to go in the club,' Crowther chipped in. 'I've been working with CO19, and it will give me a chance to look round. I'm also curious about the hand-gun found in the victim's handbag. Penny says it's an Astra Cadix. That's a Spanish gun. Chang may be dealing in Mac 10s, but we know he's got a villa in Spain. There may be something coming out of there.'

'I understand,' Banham told him. 'But we have to concentrate on finding who murdered this woman, and right now it's the golden hours; every second is vital.'

Alison felt control slipping away again. 'And unlikely though it sounds,' she said firmly, 'it might not have anything to do with Eddie Chang. I think the ex-husband is our first suspect.'

CHAPTER FOUR

Millie Payne was now dressed in tight denim jeans and a figure-hugging t-shirt horizontally striped in different shades of blue. Her large, wide-set blue eyes, slight ruddy complexion and round full lips reminded Alison of Christmas card pictures of young cherub angels; but Alison suspected there was more to this woman than she was letting them see.

They had agreed Crowther would lead the interview; he was good at winning young women's confidence. Alison knew she'd have little patience. She was edgy, and she wanted a result. This woman seemed to be treating the whole thing like an acting role, and both Crowther and Banham were sympathetic towards her. Banham had even suggested Alison was being too hard on her.

Millie clearly liked Crowther. Her eyes lit up when he walked in the room.

As Alison slipped a disc into the recording machine the smile on Millie's face faded. 'Just routine,' she assured her, switching the machine to *Play* and waiting for Crowther to start the interview.

At first he made small talk, asking Millie if she wanted more tea, or even a proper cup of coffee from the newly installed machine in the murder investigation room. Alison had to make a conscious effort not to tap her fingertips on the table. When Crowther added that it would be no trouble for Alison to go and get her some coffee she decided that was a step too far. Alison had a famous temper. Banham always said the black flecks in her green-grey eyes literally expanded when she was about to explode, and right now they felt as if they were about to break into flames.

Crowther got the message. 'OK, Millie. Tell us everything that happened last night, from the time you came on duty until we arrived on the scene.'

'I should have been on duty at ten,' she said. 'I was late, remember? So you drove me in?'

Alison slowly turned her head. So that's who Crowther was with last night. The wet t-shirt competitor was Millie Payne. And Crowther grew restless waiting for her to come back, and decided to do an early morning workout. He hadn't expected to meet Alison in the gym – and he certainly hadn't expected Millie to find a dead body. But Crowther hadn't bothered to tell Alison.

'We walked through into the open parkland at about four-thirty a m,' Millie continued.

'Do you often go into the parkland at that time, on your shift?' His voice was gentle, coaxing even. Alison wanted to slap him hard.

'Yes, when I'm on nights. It's the route we cover.'

'Do you see many people around?'

'The odd drunk, or a couple having it off, or drug users. It's a bit of a drugs haven – I think that's why it's on the route. But we didn't expect...' Millie looked from Crowther to Alison, then put her hand to her mouth.

'Go on,' Alison encouraged her, managing a minimal smile. 'In your own time.'

Millie fiddled nervously with the tissue in her hand. 'We

39

saw the arm first, in the duck pond, all stiff and pointing.' She looked up at Crowther. 'I said I thought it was a body.'

'Then why didn't you call for back-up?' Alison asked her. 'Isn't that what they taught you in training?'

Millie squeezed her cherub lips together and curled a finger in her hair. 'We didn't want to look silly.' Her brow furrowed. 'It might have been a joke or something, so we decided to investigate first.' She paused, and her forehead wrinkled again: 'It was hard to see. Only the arm was above the water. I got a bit spooked, so Andrew went into the water to make sure.'

She looked appealingly at Crowther. 'Neither of us wanted to appear stupid,' she said.

'You've contaminated a crime scene,' Alison said quietly. 'That's hardly very intelligent.'

'I'm sorry,' said Millie. It was addressed to Crowther.

Alison sighed; time to move on. 'Tell us about the victim, Sadie Morgan.'

'I didn't know her very well.'

'How long had you known her?'

'Only a couple of weeks, since I started rehearsing at Doubles.'

'Why did you take a job there?' Alison asked her.

'My actress friend Lily Palmer.' The blue eyes appealed to Crowther again. 'The one I told you about?'

Crowther nodded.

'She worked there. She's going on tour in a play about Marilyn's life.' She smiled proudly. 'She's actually playing Marilyn. She introduced me to Mr Chang, and suggested I worked there while she was away.' The eyes opened wide. 'I didn't know it was such a bad place.'

Crowther gave her another encouraging nod.

'We'll need your friend's address and phone number,' Alison said.

'Of course.' Millie looked Alison in the eye and added, 'I am allowed to do other work. I checked the rules. I'm an actress as well as a PCSO.'

Alison opened her mouth to deliver a short lecture on loyalty, but closed it again without saying a word. Someone else could sort this woman out; she had a murder to solve.

'Tell us what you know about Sadie,' she said.

'Sadie was a brilliant Marilyn impersonator, the top one at the club.' She suddenly blushed. 'I only met her in passing in the fitting room, with Terry King.'

'Who's Terry King?' Crowther asked.

'Terry works at Doubles as the wardrobe mistress and wig-dresser. He's a bit strange. He's a cross-dresser.'

Crowther scribbled something in his notebook. 'How did Terry King and Sadie get on?' he asked.

'I think Terry is jealous of all the Marilyn girls.' Her eyes flicked to Alison. 'That's what Lily told me, anyway. She thinks he wants to be a Marilyn impersonator. He is always telling us off about petty things like hanging our dresses up, and generally being picky with us.'

'Do you like him?' Alison asked.

'Dunno, I haven't really formed an opinion. He seems OK. A bit odd, that's all.'

'How did you get on with Sadie?'

'I liked what I knew.' Her voice became quieter and she blinked away the moisture in her eyes. 'She gave me a couple of helpful notes about being Marilyn Monroe.' She stared at the table and became quiet again. Crowther and

41

Alison waited.

After a few seconds she looked up. 'You should talk to the ex-husband. He turned up at the club shouting and threatening her. He got thrown out.'

'When was this?'

She reddened again. 'A few nights ago. He has a horrible temper. You should talk to him.'

'We will,' Crowther told her.

'Do you happen to know where he lives?' Alison asked.

Millie shook her head. 'No, I don't, but I know where Sadie lives.'

'We have her address,' Alison said, failing to hide her irritation.

'Someone at the club might know where he works,' Millie suggested. 'His name is Bruno and he's a chef.'

'Did Sadie have any close friends at the club, or enemies beside the ex-husband?'

'She was friendly with Johnny Gladman, the doorman. He's the black guy with the long dreadlocks.'

'How friendly?' Alison asked.

'He always watched her perform. He liked her a lot, that much was obvious.'

'Were they a couple?'

'I'm not sure. Lily might know. She's worked there on and off for about six months.'

'There was a key in Sadie's bag,' Alison said. 'It has H14 painted on it in red nail varnish. It looks like a garage key – do you know if she had a car, and where she kept it?'

Millie shook her head. 'She didn't have a car, I'm pretty sure of that. She talked about being late for work and how it's quicker to walk because the buses aren't reliable.'

'When did she say that?'

Millie reddened again. 'Oh, one night last week, I think, in the dressing room. She was talking to one of the other girls and I overheard her.'

She looked away, still blushing.

'What is it Millie? What are you hiding?'

Millie looked up, her complexion even redder.

Alison pushed on. 'I shouldn't have to remind you that this is golden time in a murder enquiry. If you lie to me or withhold something that could prove vital in this enquiry, I'll charge you with obstruction.'

Millie's chin trembled, and Crowther blew out a breath. 'Millie, you have to tell us if there's something else,' he coaxed gently.

Millie's forehead furrowed again, but she swallowed her tears. 'Tonight. No, last night.' She shook her head. 'Sorry, my mind is a bit scrambled.'

Alison thought that was the most honest thing she'd said all night.

'I'm so sorry,' Millie said, sounding like a guilty child.

'What for, Millie?' Crowther pushed.

'I went into the club while I was on my shift.' She turned the blue eyes on Crowther again, but this time there was no reassuring smile.

'Just briefly, for a dress fitting,' she pleaded.

Alison was astounded. 'In your uniform?'

'I know I shouldn't have, but I was only a few minutes. I had to have a fitting. I am so sorry.'

Alison and Crowther exchanged looks. Alison was suddenly furious, with Crowther because he was sleeping with this woman, and with herself because she could hardly

43

haul him over the coals when she had done the same with Banham.

She glared at Millie instead. 'In your police uniform?' she repeated.

'No. I changed in the street to civvy clothes before I went in, and I changed back again when I came out.'

'Where? Where did you change?'

'In a doorway. A group of guys on their stag night passed by. They thought I was a singing telegram girl.'

Alison took a sharp breath. Why had time and money been spent to train this woman as a PCSO? It was plain she was totally wrong for the job.

'What time was this?'

'Around three am.'

Alison lifted her eyebrows. 'A bit late for a dress fitting.' Millie shrugged.

'Where was Andrew Fisher?' Crowther asked.

'He waited for me, outside. It's in our patrol area, so he wasn't doing anything wrong.'

'Yes, he was,' Alison corrected. 'Community support officers, especially new community support officers, are told to stay in pairs. Do you remember *any* of your training?'

'It's not his fault,' Millie pleaded. 'I asked him,'

Alison didn't trust herself to pursue the subject. It was the critical twenty-four hours after a murder, and here she was sitting opposite a part-time police community support officer who knew no better than to waste her time. 'Let's go back to Sadie,' she said curtly. 'Did you talk to her tonight?'

Millie nodded. 'She was about to go on for her final spot when I came into the changing room for my dress fitting.'

'With…' Crowther looked at his notes. 'Terry King?'

'Yes.'

'Go on,' Alison snapped.

'She seemed quite distant. I put it down to performance nerves. I get nervous too when I'm working. As an actress, I mean.'

'In what way distant?' Alison said sharply.

'She seemed wrapped up in her own thoughts. She was rambling about the buses. Terry gave her a glass of water.'

'Are you sure it was water? Did you see him pour it?' Alison questioned.

'Yes, I think so.' She looked to Crowther. 'No, I'm not sure. My mind has gone all vague.' She looked down and suddenly started to sob.

Alison sighed and pushed her chair back. This was going nowhere.

'Let's get someone to drive you home,' Crowther said. 'But we'll need to talk again later.'

'*I'll* need to talk to you again.' Alison said tightly, handing her a card.

Millie nodded and pocketed it. 'You said you wanted Lily's details.' She dug in her pocket for her mobile phone. As she scribbled the number on a slip of paper from Crowther's notebook, Alison studied her. She was very pretty but not very bright; very much his type.

Andrew Fisher smelt of stale drains.

Isabelle had pulled a face as she and Banham entered the interview room, but Banham ignored the stench. He sympathised with the young PCSO officer, who was weak at the knees after finding a murdered woman, and hadn't noticed the stale water and pond slime in his hair. Andrew was in his late twenties, stocky with a square face. He was broad across the shoulders, Isabelle thought he probably worked out. There was a flourish of acne across his cheeks, and a tattoo on each of his fingers that spelled out LOVE.

'You should have radioed for back-up,' Isabelle told him as soon as the recording machine was running. 'If anything seems suspicious, you call for back-up. It's not your job to get involved.'

'We weren't sure what it was at first,' Andrew said apologetically. 'If it was a prank we would have looked stupid.'

Banham changed the subject. 'What time was it exactly when you found her?'

'Almost the end of the shift, so about four forty-five a m.'

'You always cover that area?' Banham asked.

His fingers intertwined on the table in front of him. He untangled them and pulled them into fists. 'Yes. We caught a flasher in there last week. We radioed that in, and he was arrested.'

Isabelle stifled a giggle. It was highly likely that the flasher wasn't flashing at all, but had been caught short and had gone to the open wasteland to relieve himself. There wouldn't be many people to flash at at four-thirty in the morning.

'How long does it take you to walk down the hill and around the parkland?' Banham asked.

'About thirty minutes. Actually, we probably got to the park nearer five o'clock.'

'Then what happened?' Banham asked gently.

'We walked toward the pond and...' He swallowed hard.

46

'There was something floating on the water, a bundle of some kind, then as we got nearer we saw what looked like an arm sticking out. We thought it might be a body, but we weren't sure.'

Banham and Isabelle looked at each other.

Andrew looked apologetic. 'I'm sorry, I just thought it was a prank. Like a guy on bonfire night or something.'

'It's early spring,' Isabelle said.

'Yes, but you know what I mean.'

'No, we don't,' Isabelle said.

Banham helped him out. 'You didn't expect to find a dead body? You'll probably come across a lot more if you stay in this job.'

There was a knock on the interview room door and Alison's head appeared. 'Sorry, guv,' she said.

Banham stopped the disc.

'Has he mentioned that Millie Payne went into Doubles last night and saw the victim?' Alison asked outside the door.

'What?'

'She works there. She went to have a dress fitting during her shift.' Alison shook her head, still unable to believe the girl's stupidity. 'She spoke to the victim. She said Andrew Fisher waited outside for her. That was around three a.m. Ask him about that, will you?'

Banham was hardly inside the interview room door when he shouted at Andrew, 'Why didn't you tell us PCSO Payne was in that club tonight?'

Isabelle quickly pressed the *Play* button on the CD machine.

Andrew went scarlet, and his pimples stood out. He said

47

nothing.

'Detective Chief Inspector Banham asked you a question,' Isabelle snapped.

'I didn't want to get her into trouble,' Andrew said, hanging his head.

Banham was furious. 'This is a murder enquiry, not a game of Cluedo. Withholding vital evidence is a serious offence, and you are an officer of the law.'

'Everything else I have told you is correct.' Andrew's voice had gone up an octave. 'I didn't want to get Millie into trouble.' He scratched his forehead with his tattooed fingers. 'I stayed on duty. I'm really sorry.'

Banham calmed down. He realised the lad was being loyal. Loyalty was a good trait, and he was inexperienced, and in a quandary.

'OK,' Banham said quietly. 'Go home and get some rest. We know where you are, and we will want to talk to you again.'

'She changed out of uniform in a doorway. And she should have known she wouldn't get permission to work at that club. Was her duty sergeant asleep or what!'
They were walking along the corridor to the back stairs which led to the car park, and Alison was ready to explode.

'Let's get it in proportion,' Banham reasoned. 'They're inexperienced PCSOs and they screwed up.'

'It's outrageous,' Alison ranted on. 'She could have cocked up the entire CO19 operation with her stupidity. And to top it all Crowther's having it off with her.'

Banham stopped in his tracks and turned to look at her. 'It's not against the rules.'

48

'It's a bad call for an ambitious new sergeant.'

'Maybe it isn't.' Banham set off again. 'Maybe we can use it to our advantage. And the fact that she works at the club.' He opened the door to the car park and stood back to let Alison walk through.

'You are joking. She's not even very bright. She told Crowther she's using the PCSO training to help her get into a television police series.'

He clicked his key to unlock his car, and opened the passenger door for her. 'Why tell that to Crowther?'

'Because he's sleeping with her.'

Banham leaned across to help Alison with her seat belt.

'I can manage,' she snapped.

'I know you can.' He pushed her hand away and clicked the belt into place. 'It's an excuse to touch you.' He brushed her cheek with his hand, and she heard herself sigh. 'And you know what? I wish we weren't on our way to interview Eddie Chang.' His eyes looked straight into hers. 'You need to wind down. A massage would help.'

She turned away, unable to deal with this. She had wanted him for seven years, and now it had happened it was overwhelming. She felt his eyes on her, but she didn't turn around. He started the engine and drove towards the car park exit.

'You got up so early, I thought you were having regrets,' she said quietly.

His head spun around, and he braked hard.

'Watch the road,' she smiled.

'I'd already said I was taking the kids to the zoo. And I wanted to see Bobby before he got up – I had to leave early.'

49

'I know. It's just… Last night was a bit… unexpected, that's all.' For the first time in the seven years they had worked together she felt uneasy. Last night had changed everything. 'It all happened so suddenly,' she said quietly. 'How are Lottie and the kids, anyway?'

'Bobby is still having nightmares. He cries a lot and won't talk to me or his mum.'

'That's so unlike him. He was always the outgoing one, off playing football with his mates. Lottie could never keep him in.'

'Now he won't go outside the door unless he has to.'

'Not good,' Alison said. 'He needs a father influence. You should try to spend more time with him.'

'Like this job lets me.' He brushed her cheek with his open palm. 'I want to spend quality time with you too.' She froze, and he pulled his hand back. 'Are you having regrets?'

She shook her head, took a deep breath and turned to look out of the window. The truth was she really didn't know.

Was she regretting sleeping with him? Or was it just that everything had changed in a few short hours: her promotion to DI, her relationship with Banham, and now heading her first murder case.

As they approached the club she did a double-take. 'That's Andrew Fisher. Over there.' Banham looked in the direction she was pointing. 'Walking along the road.'

'He's going toward the bus stop.'

'Why didn't he get the bus from near the station?'

'He's got a bag of shopping. He's allowed to walk to the supermarket.'

'Interesting that he chose the one near Doubles.'

50

CHAPTER FIVE

After Isabelle Walsh had leaned on the bell long enough to satisfy them both that no one was in, she used the keys from the victim's handbag to open the front door. Crowther stepped inside into a long hallway festooned with photographs of Marilyn Monroe.

'Police!' Isabelle shouted. No one answered.

'No arguing that she lived here,' Isabelle said, as Crowther studied the pictures.

'Are these Marilyn Monroe or Sadie Morgan?' he asked.

'Marilyn, I think. Hard to tell.'

There was a picture of the star in a white, silky low-cut dress, hands pressing down the pleated skirt against the gusts of wind that threatened to reveal her shapely thighs. She tapped the photo. 'This is definitely Marilyn standing over the wind machine. *The Seven Year Itch*, remember?'

Crowther moved to a picture of Marilyn in a long, tight, backless red dress with a split up the back and a red marabou boa draped over one shoulder. Her head was turned back over her shoulder, smiling into the camera; one of her legs peeped through the split in the dress, displaying a black seamed stocking. 'They're not all the same woman,' he said.

'Dunno,' Isabelle answered. 'I've only seen Sadie dead.' She pointed to another picture. 'This one isn't Marilyn Monroe. It must be Sadie.'

There was a signature under the photo. 'Lily Palmer,' Crowther read. 'Millie Payne mentioned her. She's another Marilyn Monroe impersonator who works at Doubles. That one's Sadie Morgan.' Her name was printed in tiny letters below another picture of a Marilyn in a long red dress.

Isabelle shook her head in disbelief. 'How do you tell? They could all be the real thing.'

'Isn't that the whole point?' Crowther said.

A wedding photo hung at the end of the Marilyn gallery. 'This is definitely Sadie,' Crowther said. 'We need to talk to the husband. They only recently split; his address will be here somewhere.'

Isabelle walked into the first room off the corridor. It was the kitchen, and a walkabout phone lay on the table. She scrolled down, checking the texts and making a list of the numbers in her notebook. 'Nothing under *Bruno* here,' she muttered.

'Try *husband*.'

Crowther walked away. 'No garages in the grounds of this block of flats,' he called from the other room. 'That's one unexplained key on her ring.'

'She might rent one somewhere else.'

'Millie Payne doesn't think she drives.'

Isabelle had taken a dislike to PCSO Payne. She was a new recruit with a lot to learn, but she had ideas above her station. She was also far too friendly with Crowther.

Right now Isabelle was kicking herself for sleeping with Crowther. She'd only done it to distract him, when they were both up for the sergeant's post, and it hadn't worked. But now, much as she tried to persuade herself otherwise, she was still attracted to him – but he had made it very clear the feeling wasn't mutual.

She noticed the answerphone flashing and pressed the Play button. There was a call from the dead girl's mother, asking her for a lift to the supermarket. She dialled 1471, made a note of the number and phoned it through to Eric, who was on family liaison duty.

A thought struck her. 'Col,' she shouted. 'Her mother's left a message about taking her to get the week's shopping. She must drive.'

Crowther was on his way back down the hall, carrying something wrapped in newspaper.

'Look what I found, in the cupboard at the end of the hall!' He held up the bundle. It contained a stained knife, and a diary full of handwritten entries.

Isabelle stared at the knife. 'That's blood, Col!'

It was a pleasant morning, and the cast of *The Legend* had finished their rehearsals. Lily Palmer gave her order of a latte with extra milk to one of the other actors, taking it for granted he'd go in and order it for her. It looked as if she thought she really was Marilyn Monroe.

Lily leaned back to take in the early spring sunshine, and pulled her red lipsticked mouth into a false Monroe smile.

She didn't know someone was watching her.

The figure hovered by the shop next to the café, pretending to read the notice-board displayed in the window but observing her every move.

Mouth. The nickname had seemed appropriate for this job. Mouth wore a dirty old raincoat, the kind of thing seedy perverts and stalkers were meant to wear, and also sunglasses and a very strange wig that looked as if it had

53

been scraped from the corpse of a large dead rat. Smelt like it too, but it did the trick.

Lily had noticed. She looked across a little nervously. So she should be: Mouth had been around since she left rehearsals and wasn't being very subtle. Her fear was a perk of the job. The real Marilyn had to put up with all those perverts and stalkers; now it was Lily Palmer's turn. She couldn't have all the fun without the other side of it. And if Lily Palmer knew there was a theory that Marilyn Monroe was murdered, that would heighten her fear.

It was turning out to be a fun morning.

Mouth watched closely. Only half of Lily's attention was on the conversation with the other actors; every now and again her eyes flicked sideways. She was wondering whether to confide that she thought she was being watched, but Mouth knew she wouldn't. She was too unsure of herself. And what would she say? *Have you seen that strange person staring at me?* How pathetic would that sound? You couldn't get someone arrested just because you suspected they were following you; the police wanted proof of harassment. Mouth was too clever for that. Why would anyone follow her anyway? Only famous people had weird stalkers and she was a no one: just a two-bit actress who wanted to be Marilyn Monroe.

She nervously lifted her latte to her lips, missed, and gave herself a moustache of froth. Mouth had to quell the urge to laugh. Not exactly sexy, was it?

Then she did a Marilyn: 'M'mm that's good,' followed by a lowering of her eyelids and a pout just like Monroe. She licked the froth from around her mouth and giggled that familiar Monroe giggle.

54

'You are so like her,' said the actor who had brought the coffee. 'And your accent is spot on New York.' His was genuine.

'Marilyn wasn't from New York though,' disputed the other actor. 'She came from Los Angeles.'

'She went from foster home to foster home all over America,' the first man responded.

Lily joined in. 'I've read a lot about her. I used to work in a club, impersonating her. Her mother worked for one of the studios in Los Angeles, but the woman was mentally unwell. She tried to suffocate Marilyn with a pillow when she was only a year old. Marilyn, Norma Jean was her name in those days, was taken into care because the mother couldn't cope, and she was sent from home to home. She had a very tough life.'

She began to hum *Candle in the Wind*, and flicked her eyes in Mouth's direction. Mouth watched, transfixed.

Lily turned her attention back to her coffee, scooped a spoonful of froth from the top and put it in her mouth. 'Have either of you noticed that strange person outside the newsagents?' she asked her companions.

But before they turned to look, Mouth had darted away round the corner.

Alison glanced at her watch. 'Someone's always here, according to Crowther,' she told Banham.

They had rung the bell in the wall outside Doubles three times.

'They're sure to have CCTV,' Banham said. 'I expect they're watching us.'

'They've got three minutes,' Alison snapped, 'then I'm

55

having the door broken in.'

'Stay calm,' Banham said. 'We're keeping this low key, remember? Every time the place is raided, they never find anything.' He examined the door handle and the spy-glass. 'There has to be a hidden surveillance system. I'll bet good money that Chang's watching us right now.'

Alison leaned on the bell again.

'Can you get to the courtyard at the back without going through the club?' he asked her. Around the corner a high wall concealed a cottage at the rear of the club.

Alison shook her head. 'Only by going over that wall.'

'Go round and pretend you're going to climb the wall. If there's CCTV on us, they'll be out in a shot.'

'They'll know it isn't a routine enquiry if I do that!' She stepped away from the door.

Banham took a deep breath. 'OK, it's your call. How do you want to play this – DI Grainger?'

She hid a smile and thought for a second. 'Let's run with what we've got. The gun Sadie was carrying was a .22 Astra Cadix, and we need to find out where it came from. He's aware that we know he deals in firearms; that makes it a bit more than a routine enquiry on an employee.'

'He also knows we can't prove anything,' Banham told her. 'That puts the ball in his court.'

'OK. I'll climb the wall and go into the courtyard.'

'Without a search warrant?'

'Like you said, if they come out, then we know there is hidden surveillance. If nothing else, we can let CO19 know – it'll be useful when the raid goes off next Wednesday.'

Alison had only started to hoist herself up on the wall when the front door opened.

A black guy around thirty years of age stood on the threshold. He was dressed untidily in denim, and had a six o'clock shadow and long dreadlocks. Alison recognised him right away as Johnny Gladman; his drugs record went back some years.

'I'm glad to see you've found yourself a job, Mr Gladman,' she said sarcastically. 'I hear the perks are pretty good.'

Johnny Gladman took a step backward as Banham flashed his ID and walked into the doorway.

'What's up?' he asked.

'I ask the questions!' Banham snapped.

'We need to talk to Eddie Chang,' Alison said.

'I'm not sure he's in.'

'Don't play games with us.' Banham stared into Johnny's eyes, and the doorman's gaze dropped. Chang was in all right.

Alison pushed past Johnny and into the club. She headed for the door in the corner, Eddie Chang's office, and entered without bothering to knock.

The club owner was sitting behind his desk, pretending to sort through some papers. He didn't seem surprised to see her. He was impeccably dressed, a lean man with narrow, dark, oriental eyes and a curving scar to the right of his mouth. The fringes of his hair were grey, but the centre and top were still black. Alison couldn't tell if it was natural.

'What's the problem?' His accent betrayed his Peckham origins.

'Do you know Sadie Morgan?' Alison asked, holding his cold, cruel stare. He placed two fingers against his cheek, and she clocked the large solitaire diamond ring and the

57

Cartier watch. A gold chain hung from his neck, bearing a dragon pendant. The scar beside his mouth, a souvenir from a knife fight many years back, was fainter than Alison remembered. Over the years its curving shape had earned him the nickname of Snake. These days if he dealt with knives, it was to hire other people to bring him souvenirs of his enemy's faces or sexual organs.

The club was a cover. His real business was trading in drugs, firearms and under-age women, all of which he smuggled at regular intervals through customs at Dover. The women were sold into prostitution until they were worn out or died of drug overdoses.

The club advertised a different lookalike act each night. A poster by his desk advertised Over The Rainbow Night on a Wednesday; an asterisk at the bottom denoted Lisa Minelli impersonators that night as well as Dorothy lookalikes. There was an Elvis night, and another devoted to Frank Sinatra.

The whole of the club was covered in pictures of Marilyn Monroe. It was common knowledge that Chang hated women, and regarded them as a saleable commodity, like firearms and drugs. Yet Marilyn Monroe was his idol.

'Sadie Morgan?' Alison repeated. 'Did you know her?

'Yes, I know her. Constable.' One side of Chang's mouth curled into a smile as he leaned on the first syllable of *constable*. 'Is something wrong?'

'It's Detective Inspector.' Alison raised her ID card. 'Sadie Morgan's body was found in the pond on the open ground next to the Rose Estate early this morning. When did you last see her?'

Surprise flashed momentarily across Eddie Chang's

eyes, then they dropped back down to the papers on his desk. 'She worked here last night,' he said. 'But she wasn't on form. I sensed she'd taken something. Was it an overdose?' He paused. 'Detective Inspector.'

'Got it here, did she?' Banham had walked in. 'Care to give us the names of the dealers?'

Eddie Chang's snake-like black eyes narrowed, and he lifted his diamond-clad hand defensively. 'You should know me better, Mister Banham. This place is clean. You've raided it enough times and found nothing.' He smiled, but only with his mouth. 'There are no drugs here.'

'Don't be too confident, Mr Chang,' Banham said flatly.

The mouth pulled into a tight smile again. 'I can only be what I am. Can I offer you a drink?'

'No, but you can tell us where you were between midnight and six a m,' Alison said.

'Here. It was a busy night. We had a packed club. A new Monroe in training. We worked late.'

'Were you here all night?'

'All night.'

'Someone verify that for you?' Alison pursued.

'Ask Johnny.' Gladman was hovering a little way behind Banham. 'He's my caretaker. He works and lives here, in the cottage in the courtyard.'

'I seem to recall we found women's underwear in that cottage on one occasion,' Alison said. 'Do you wear ladies' underwear, Mr Gladman?'

Johnny threw a horrified glance at Eddie Chang.

'This is getting tedious, Detective Inspector,' Chang said. 'I told you at the time, sometimes the Marilyn girls stay over.'

59

'Actually, you told us at the time that you knew nothing about it.'

Chang's face remained expressionless, but Alison persisted. 'Still trafficking under-age women from eastern Europe?'

'This is harassment.' Chang threw his pencil down 'Prove it, can you? My memory says your last raid turned up nothing.'

'That was then,' Banham said fixing his eyes on Chang. A couple of seconds passed. 'I'm on your case, Mr Chang. If something is going on, I am going to find out.'

Eddie Chang sighed. 'I run an honest lookalike club. If there is any drug-pushing going on, I too need to know.'

'I'd like a word with Mr Gladman,' Alison said.

'Of course.'

'On his own. Can we use the club? Or shall I take him to the station?'

'I don't want to go to the station,' Johnny protested.

'I bet you don't,' said Banham.

'I haven't done anything, man.'

Eddie put his hand out. 'Use the club. I'll stay here in my office.'

'We also need a list of your staff and club members,' Banham said. 'And a separate list of everyone working here last night, and another of the guests.'

'My pleasure.' Eddie narrowed his eyes.

'And the CCTV tapes from last night,' Alison added
He gave a curt nod.

'All of it, including the camera at the front door.'

'I don't have one at the front door.'

'Do you know an Andrew Fisher?' Alison asked.

60

'Never heard of him.'

'Has anyone else been here today?'

'Not to my knowledge. I've been in here all morning, doing the accounts. Ask Johnny.'

Johnny shook his head. 'No, no one. Only you.'

Johnny was nervous, that was clear. It was mid-March, the club was empty and the heat was turned off, yet tiny rivulets of sweat were running down his temple. He lifted his arm to wipe his face.

They sat at a table in the far corner of the club. 'I presume you knew Sadie Morgan,' Alison said.

'Yes, I did.' He crinkled his forehead and swallowed. 'Is she really dead?'

Alison nodded. 'She was my friend.'

Alison studied him for a few moments. 'OK,' she said. 'Tell me all about her.'

He licked his dry lips nervously and his forehead creased again. 'She was my friend,' he repeated quietly.

'Do you know who might want her dead?'

He pressed his lips together and shook his head. When he looked up tears glistened his eyes. 'Was she killed?'

'We're trying to find out,' Alison said.

His plaits bounced against each other. 'She was trying to get free of her ex-husband.' He looked away. 'He was always in here, ranting at her. He wanted her back.' He fell silent and stared into space.

'Go on,' Banham coaxed.

'She's been here about six months. She was the best Marilyn. She just had what it takes. Everyone liked her, even the other Marilyn girls. She was a sweet girl.' He swiped at a droplet of sweat rolling down the side of his

61

face. 'She needed money to pay her ex- husband off. She wanted to buy him out of the flat their shared. She was a nurse – this was just a bit extra.'

He wiped his cheek again as more droplets of perspiration broke out. 'Her husband was a waste of space…' The plaits moved again as he shook his head. 'All she wanted was to get her independence back. She was my friend.'

He's said that three times in as many minutes, Alison thought.

'Were you working here last night?' Banham asked him.

'Yes, sir. I work every night.'

'How did she seem to you?'

There was a pause. 'Unhappy.' He paused again. 'Bruno, her ex, was bugging her yesterday. She was real afraid of him. She seemed distant last night. I think she was upset.'

'Do you know what time she left?'

'Well after two, more likely be three o'clock. Straight after her last spot.'

'Did you see Chang after that?' Alison asked.

'Oh, he's always here, but you don't see him all the time.'

'Thank you,' Alison said. 'Do you live alone?

He shifted uncomfortably. 'No, my brother Otis lives with me. He's only fifteen.'

'And someone can verify you were here all night?' Banham asked.

Johnny looked nervous again, then nodded his head.

As they stood up to leave Eddie Chang was standing in the doorway of his office, his arms folded across his chest.

'Have you got the CCTV tapes we asked for?' Alison

asked. 'And the list of members and guests?'

He nodded. Judging by the look on his face, he didn't like being told what to do by a woman. She was delighted. Whether or not he had anything to do with Sadie's death, she was going to make life as difficult as possible for him. 'That will be all for now,' she told him crisply. 'Don't leave the country, though.'

His cold eyes narrowed as he unfolded his arms. He walked slowly to his desk, picked up the papers and handed them to her. 'You have nothing on me.'

'No,' Banham said. 'But I'm sure you wouldn't like to have your club taken to pieces brick by brick.' He smiled without humour, exactly as Chang had earlier. 'It might be bad for business.'

'You have nothing on me,' Chang repeated flatly.

Millie was in the bath, enjoying a long, hot soak. She was exhausted, and very glad she could do as she chose for the rest of the weekend.

The phone rang, and she reached for it reluctantly.

'Hi, Millie! It's Lily.'

Millie thought quickly. Did Lily know about Sadie? Was that why she was ringing? If she didn't, it would probably be better not to say anything.

'Lily! How's the play going?' Millie tried to sound casual.

'It's good. I'm really enjoying it.'

'When do you open?' Millie knew the answer, but she needed to buy herself some time.

'We leave London on Monday, and rehearse in Birmingham for a few days, then there the tech and dress,

63

and we open next week. It's a big theatre, holds about eight hundred people.'

'Sounds good.'

'How are things going at Doubles?'

Millie's brain raced. 'OK.'

'When were you last there?'

Another pause. Did Lily know about Sadie or not? In the runup to opening in a play, the last thing she'd have time to do was read the paper. It wouldn't be in the paper yet anyway. So unless someone told her, she probably didn't know.

Millie decided to brave it out. 'Last night. I was there last night.'

'Who was doing the Monroe spot? Sadie?'

Another pause. 'I'm not sure,' Millie lied. 'I was on duty, and I only popped in for a quick fitting with Terry King. He's odd, isn't he?'

'Yes, he is. Watch out, though; he can be unkind. He wants to be Marilyn himself.'

'Really? He's been OK with me.'

'Terry hates Sadie.'

'Oh? Why's that?' This was getting very interesting.

'Because she is so good at being Marilyn.'

'Is that all?'

'Far as I know.' There was a pause. 'Millie?'

'Yes, I'm still here.'

'I need to tell you something. I'm telling you because you work for the police.'

Millie held her breath. 'What?'

'I think I'm being stalked.'

Millie closed her eyes. Her heart began to race as she

replied. 'Go on.'

'I keep seeing the same person. Wherever I am, he's there.'

'What does he look like?'

'I don't know, that's the problem. He wears dark glasses, and a mackintosh. And I'm sure his hair's a wig.'

'Are you sure he is following you?'

'Yes.'

'Lily, are you locked in your flat?'

'Yes, course I am.'

'OK, you're safe at the moment. No one has a key that you know of?'

'No, the only spare is with my neighbour.'

'And will you be travelling to Birmingham with the others?'

'Yes. They're picking me up on Monday evening and we'll all travel together.'

Millie's heart was still thumping. 'I'll call you tomorrow, Lily. Will you be at home?'

'Yes, I'm planning a day off to look at my lines.'

'You know I should tell the police about this, don't you?'

'Do you think they'll be interested? I mean, no one has approached me. It's just sort of a strange stalker.'

'I'll let you know what they say.'

CHAPTER SIX

It was the first time in a while that Banham had experienced one of his violent reactions to a young female corpse. He leaned against the glass front of the shop next to the morgue, slowly pulling himself together.

He'd thought he was dealing with it, until Mrs Morgan let out a wail as the attendant drew back the covers on Sadie's body. That took him back eleven years, to the day he had found his wife and baby, their blood soaked into the nursery carpet and the room smelling like an abattoir.

Alison had noticed as the colour drained from his face and he began to tremble, and quietly helped him over the embarrassment by suggesting he wait outside while she talked to Sadie Morgan's mother and father after they had identified the body.

As soon as he got through the door of the building he threw up his lunch.

Sweat trickled slowly down his face. The memory of that nightmare day was as clear as if it was happening right now. The wail Sadie's mother had let out was ringing around inside his brain, and he wanted to crumple into a heap and weep.

He leaned against the wall next to the window, shaking like an alcoholic. He understood only too well how the poor woman felt. The machete-wielding madman who had butchered his wife and baby was still free and walking the streets.

The questions refused to go away. Why them? Were they targeted? Or just unlucky, in the wrong place at the wrong time? Eleven years had passed and still he had no answers. The only thing that helped was solving other brutal murders. Perhaps it would help these parents if he could find their daughter's killer.

He took deep breaths, gradually steadying himself. He didn't want Alison to see him like this. It wouldn't be the first time, but it hadn't been this bad in a while. Things should be different now, after last night. Alison was his woman at last, and he wanted to be there for her.

He smiled. Alison would be the first to tell him she could take care of herself. When she was in one of her famous tempers, and those squirrel eyes of hers flared, she could take on the whole of the murder squad and come out on top. That was part of the reason he had fallen for her.

Maybe this upsurge of emotion was a mixture of memory and guilt. Last night had been the first time for him since Diane's murder. He had wanted to get closer to Alison for a long time, but had always ended up saying the wrong thing. He wondered how the sex had been for Alison. After such a long time it had been difficult for him to stay in control, though all he wanted was to hold her and please her. He had been nervous and fumbly, but she had been patient, and he knew it would get better between them, if he could just stop feeling guilty about Diane.

Diane had been his childhood sweetheart, and he couldn't help feeling he was betraying her. He had promised her that night, as he stared at her unrecognisable face, that he would find the person responsible, and he wouldn't move on until he had. Last night when he made love with Alison he had broken that promise. Yet, in his heart he knew Diane would approve; she would know that loving Alison didn't mean he had stopped loving her.

He wiped the perspiration from his forehead with his handkerchief. So why did he feel guilty and confused and emotional?

His mind began to clear, and he came to a decision. For the moment they needed to focus on finding Sadie's killer – but once that was done, he would take Alison to Venice. She deserved a holiday, and they could cement their relationship far more easily away from the prying eyes of the rest of the team.

The incident room smelt of burgers and curry. Phones trilled, warm paper was burring through the fax machines, and the murder division detectives were making the best possible use of the golden hours, talking on the phone – sometimes more than one phone at a time – or scrolling through pages of criminal records or witness statements on their computers, desperately looking for a lead to help crack the case.

Alison stood in the doorway and gazed around the incident room. Banham followed as she walked towards the whiteboard and stood with her back to the pictures: the grisly shots from the murder scene, and the poignantly contrasting ones of Sadie dressed as Marilyn Monroe, looking happy, gorgeous and vulnerable.

'Gather round, everyone,' she shouted.

The twenty-odd detectives put half-eaten sandwiches back in their wrappers and brought their phone calls to a halt; one left to finish an important call outside in the corridor. Some perched on the side of their desks, others took out notebooks. Eric, as always, put a pencil behind his ear. They all gave Alison their full attention.

'It's official,' she told them. 'We have identification from her parents. Her name was Sadie Morgan. She was a nurse and worked part-time at Doubles, as a Marilyn Monroe impersonator. Crowther has found a bloodstained knife, a bag of crystal meth and her diary, all wrapped in newspaper, hidden in her flat.' She paused, and looked round the room, noting with satisfaction that every eye was upon her.

'This could well be linked with Doubles,' she went on. 'Perhaps Sadie Morgan was acting as a mule for Chang? Or for someone else? But where does the bloodstained knife come in?'

'Knife is with Penny,' Crowther said. 'She'll get back with any DNA results as soon as she can.'

'Anything relevant in the diary?' Eric asked.

Alison looked at Isabelle.

'Nothing about the knife, but she did write that she was scared of her ex's temper. Two entries about him hitting and threatening her, and another where he tried to smother her.'

'We've got his address from Sadie's parents,' Alison said, waving a sheet of paper. 'He's living with his mother – and guess what? She lives within yards of the crime scene.'

'Sadie's mother has verified he was insanely jealous,' Banham said. 'She was trying to buy her way out of the marriage.'

Alison handed the address to Crowther. 'Take Isabelle with you and bring him in. If he's not there, try some local restaurants. Sadie's parents know he's a chef, but they don't know where – just that it's Italian and local, and owned by his cousins.'

'His mother will know,' Isabelle said.

'Anyone got anything else?' Alison asked the room.

'We've been going through last night's CCTV footage from Doubles,' Eric said. 'And interviewing the club members.'

A detective called Sam raised a hand. 'I'm getting through that, with help from uniform.'

'Good. So we're waiting on DNA tests,' Alison said. 'Hopefully they'll turn something up.'

'Penny is going to be working all night again,' Crowther told her.

Alison noticed Isabelle's eyes cloud when Crowther mentioned Penny. She wondered how she would feel when she found out he was playing away with the pretty new PCSO.

'What about the gun?' someone at the back asked. 'Can we link that to the club?'

'The one in the victim's bag was an Astra Cadix hand-gun,' Crowther said. 'We're pretty sure Chang was selling those a while back, but at the moment he's dealing in Mac 10 sub-machine guns.'

Banham ran a hand through his hair. 'Perhaps Sadie was working for someone else and Chang found out. There's still a suggestion that she'd taken something before leaving the club, and Chang denies all knowledge.'

'We won't have the toxicology results until Monday at the post-mortem,' Crowther said.

'It could still turn out to be a simple domestic killing,'

Alison said. 'I want to talk to the husband.'

'We'll bring him in,' Isabelle promised. 'We'll sit outside his house all night if we have to.'

Alison threw her a grateful look.

Eric took the pencil from behind his ear and used it to scratch his eyebrow. 'We've had so many tip-offs about Doubles. How many times have we raided the place? And Chang always comes up squeaky clean.'

'And Crowther's got an informant working in there too,' Isabelle reminded them.

'He's a good informant,' Crowther assured them. 'But Eddie Chang is a clever bastard, but his luck can't last for ever. This just may be the opportunity we need to trip him up.'

Alison put up a hand. 'Look, this is about Sadie Morgan's murder. We must keep our focus. If Chang is involved, let's get him – but Sadie is our priority. I want her killer found.'

A rumble of assent went round the room.

'Chang said she was doing drugs,' Banham said.

'I wouldn't believe a word he says,' Crowther replied. 'He's a vicious, lying killer. I bet he's behind this.'

'I'm not so sure.' This was Isabelle. 'Chang would have had her shot.'

Crowther shook his head. 'He knows we'd think that. He could be playing us. We'll pay my snout a visit tonight too.'

'Yes, do that,' Alison nodded. 'But bring Bruno Pelegino in first.'

Isabelle sniffed. 'We've raided that club twice on information from Col's snout. We've not found anything. I'd say that snout needs to earn his keep. Either that or he's

71

bent.'

Crowther didn't rise to the bait. 'He's not clever enough to be bent. We'll lean on him though. He'll do anything for the price of a fix. He found out about the shipment of Mac 10s.'

Isabelle nodded.

'He's sussed about the girls, too – a truckload of them, Ukrainian, coming into Dover on Wednesday.'

'With the Mac 10s?' Isabelle asked.

'Yes.'

'So where does the Astra Cadix hand-gun fit in?'

'He was bringing them in from Spain, before he got his contact for the Mac 10s.' Crowther looked at Alison then back to Isabelle. 'It's imperative we keep those Mac 10s off the streets of south London, hence the CO19 operation.'

Alison took a deep breath. This was about Sadie Morgan, not Eddie Chang. She had to keep them focused on the murder. They might cross paths with the CO19 operation – but they might not even be connected. 'I want you to concentrate on finding the husband and bringing him in,' she said to Isabelle and Crowther.

She issued a few more rapid instructions, then picked up her own bundle of paperwork and was about to declare the briefing at an end. Banham was there before her. 'OK, troops, let's get cracking,' he said decisively. 'I'm on my mobile if you need me.'

Alison stared at him. She could hardly remind him, in front of the whole team, that this was her case, but she really wished he would let her get on and run it.

The incident room door opened slowly, taking Alison's attention. Millie Payne crept in, looking round nervously.

Alison was dumbfounded. Didn't she know she couldn't just walk into a murder enquiry?

'Um, sorry to interrupt,' Millie said to her. 'I didn't know what to do. I'm very worried about my friend. She thinks she is being stalked.'

Alison was angry now. Millie Payne wasn't even a uniformed constable; she was a support officer, and a new one at that. She clearly didn't know the first thing about detective work, and she had just walked into the incident room without even knocking.

'You need to report that to the duty sergeant,' she snapped. 'You don't bring anything in here unless it's relevant to this murder enquiry.'

Millie was unchastened. 'I think it could be. My friend is playing Marilyn Monroe in a play.'

The room fell silent.

'Where does your friend live?' Banham asked.

'About four miles away. She said she keeps seeing the same man wherever she is. She used to work at Doubles with Sadie. She was a Marilyn impersonator too – a really good one.'

'Is she at home now? Banham asked her.

'Yes.'

'I'll go round and see her,' Crowther butted in.

'She doesn't know about Sadie,' Millie told them. 'I thought I'd better not tell her. I didn't want to frighten her.'

At last, she's managed to do the right thing, Alison thought.

Banham was talking to Crowther. 'You've got a lot on already, Colin. Your informant, and the husband.'

'It's OK,' Crowther said. 'I'll go after that. I'm pulling a double shift, working all night.' He turned back to Millie. 'Tell her to lock her door, and give her my mobile number.'

Isabelle gathered up her phone and other bits and pieces and looked across at Crowther to see if he was ready. Millie was still hovering by his desk.

'Do you think there might be a connection?' she heard the girl ask him.

'It's unlikely,' Crowther reassured her. 'But since she worked at Doubles it won't harm to take a statement from her.'

'I'm going round to her place now I'll wait for you there.'

Crowther squeezed Millie's arm and said something else, too quietly for Isabelle to hear. Isabelle stared at them, and slowly the penny dropped.

'Keep your phone on,' Crowther was saying. 'And ring me if you are concerned about anything.' He busied himself at his desk for a moment, and Millie perched on the side of it.

Isabelle was seething, but well aware there wasn't a thing she could do. Then his phone rang, and to her horror, Millie slid off the edge of the desk and walked towards her.

'I'm really worried for Lily's safety,' she said to Isabelle. 'She's a Marilyn Monroe impersonator, like Sadie – surely there must be a connection.'

'We think we have a lead Sadie Morgan's death,' Isabelle said tersely. 'It's nothing to do with Marilyn Monroe.'

Millie's eyes opened wide. 'What is it?'

'I can't discuss that with you. We'll go and take a statement from your friend, though.'

'I'll stay with her till you and Col get there.'

74

Col? Who did this little slag think she was?

Isabelle sat in silence as Crowther drove through the busy streets. Her pride had taken another battering, but she decided she couldn't afford to make an issue of it. Her best bet was to hang on to the little dignity she had left.

Not that that stopped her turning things over and over in her mind. Crowther had spent one night with her, then gone back to Penny – and now he was having it off with a new PCSO. How demoralising was that? Had she lost her touch? Normally she decided she wanted a man – never the other way round. She'd come up the hard way from a council estate, and learned to use what she had. And what she had was her looks, and whatever quality it was that made men fancy her. She chose carefully; each man had a purpose: usually a step up the promotion ladder. She and Crowther were both hell bent on getting that sergeant's post, and she had seduced him, thinking she could knock him off balance. But she had come unstuck; her plan had backfired. He got the promotion, and she had fallen hook, line and sinker for the tiny twerp. She still wanted him; it was like an addiction. Worst of all, the whole office knew what had happened. That was humiliating enough – but now to top everything he was bonking a bloody PCSO recruit. How bad could her day get?

His voice cut through her churning thoughts. 'Penny for them?'

'What?'

'What are you thinking about?'

'The case.' She paused pointedly. 'How about you?'

He flicked a glance at her, smiling his mischievous smile. 'Same as you. Let's hope Penny finds us some DNA from

75

that knife. Question is, why did Sadie have it? The drugs I can understand – they could have been Chang's, or she could have been dealing for someone else. She might even have been stupid enough to try to blackmail Chang.'

'That would be a motive,' Isabelle agreed. She fell silent again, but found she couldn't keep it in. 'That brainless PSCO was saying there may be a Marilyn stalker.'

'She's naïve, not brainless,' he said, too quickly.

'Alison and I think she watches too many TV cop shows.'

Now it was Crowther's turn to fall silent. It was a couple of minutes before he said, 'Chang told Alison and the guv that Sadie took drugs. It may just be as cut and dried as that. Drugs make you do stupid things.'

'So now we believe what Chang says?'

His phone rang. He flicked a glance at her as he pushed the button. 'Sergeant Crowther,' he said, with a slight emphasis on the first word.

Isabelle stared out of the window. He wasn't going to let her forget that he was the one who got the promotion.

'When will you go and see the kids?' Alison asked Banham. 'You really need to find out what's bothering Bobby.'

They had been sitting in her new office for almost an hour, drinking coffee and making lists and throwing ideas around. She flicked her wrist to check the time. 'If you go now you'll get to read Madeleine a bedtime story.'

'But…'

'If anything important comes up, I'll call you.'

Alison wavered between exasperation because he couldn't leave her to run the case, and sympathy for his

76

concern for the children. The missed trip to the zoo would have been playing on his mind all afternoon. 'Bobby will be delighted if you go and kick a football around with him for an hour, and I'll be glad to know you're getting some exercise.'

The memory of last night jumped into her mind again and her cheeks mottled with heat. Those soulful blue eyes that she had loved so long stared at her. She looked away.

'I was hoping to stay the whole night with you tonight,' he said quietly.

There was a knock on her door and one of the detectives peered round it. 'Something interesting on the CCTV from Doubles,' he said. 'Wanna take a look?

Banham nodded and stood up. Madeleine and Bobby were going to miss out again, Alison thought. She'd have to make sure he saw them tomorrow.

They followed the detective to his desk, and he jiggled the mouse to bring the picture up on the computer screen. 'Most of the images are in darkness,' he told them. 'But look, that's Sadie at the bar, and there she is coming out of the club. The time counter says three a m.' He rolled the film onwards. 'Now look at this. Isn't that the new PCSO by the bar? Fisher, isn't it?' He pointed to the time in the corner of the screen: 03:10.

'He said he didn't go in.' Alison banged the desk with her fist. 'He said he waited outside on the street for her. He's lying again.'

'Oh, he went in,' the detective told them. He stabbed a long finger at the membership book on the desk. 'Look, there. He signed in at 2.50 a m as a guest.'

'I think we need to talk to him again,' Banham said.

'Is that everything?' Alison asked the detective.

'Well, it's dark, but I think that's Sadie again, going out the door. And isn't that the doorman waiting for her? Johnny Gladman?' He ran the tape back. 'Then there's this.' There was a shot of the back of Terry King arguing with Sadie. 'Looks like she's having a bit of a go with that woman.'

'That's Terry King,' Banham said. 'He's a cross-dresser. Anything else?'

'A lot is quite grainy, but here earlier, we've got Sadie again. Looks like she's taking something from Gladman.'

'Drugs,' Banham said. 'Gladman has a record for dealing.'

'What about PCSO Payne? Is she in the club anywhere?'

'Haven't seen her yet.'

'She was there last night having a costume fitting, she admitted that.'

'Like I said,' he repeated. 'I can't see anything of her.'

'Never mind,' Alison said. 'You've done some good work. Even better if you've got the address handy for Andrew Fisher.'

The detective grinned and picked up the members' book. '54 Lupin Road.'

Johnny Gladman was on his hands and knees, using a dustpan and brush to pick up the pieces of broken beer glass. When Eddie Chang flew into one of rages, everyone kept their head down.

Eddie was holding Terry King by the throat against the wall outside his office. Terry coughed and gasped for breath. Eddie had thrown the glass at him, and it had

78

shattered against the wall. Johnny was busying himself cleaning up, trying to pretend he wasn't there.

'I didn't give her anything,' Terry wheezed. 'Those pills are mine, I swear, for when I can't cope.'

Eddie squeezed Terry's cheekbones and slammed the back of his head into the wall. 'Don't fucking lie to me. She was drugged up when she did her turn. Any of the customers will tell that to the police.' He hit Terry twice across the face, his signet ring grazing the already bleeding skin. 'You stupid fucking bitch.' He stepped back, straight on to Johnny's hand.

Johnny gritted his teeth to hold back the yell of pain. Eddie didn't even acknowledge him.

Terry covered his face with shaking hands. 'I'm sorry,' he shrieked. 'I just gave her water. She seemed dizzy. I thought she had taken something.'

As he took his hands from his face, Eddie head-butted Terry, and blood and snot spurted from his nose. Terry's scream was cut short as the doorbell shrilled.

Alison recognised the man who answered the door; she had been watching Terry King earlier, on the CCTV footage. Now his shaking hand held a tissue against his bleeding nose, and blood and mascara were smeared across his face.

She flashed her warrant card.

'It's about Sadie Morgan, is it?' Terry asked in a nervous, lispy voice. He stood back to let them into the club.

Alison exchanged glances with Banham before asking Terry, 'What happened to your face?'

'Oh, I er... I've just walked into the edge of the mirror. I wasn't looking.' He pretended to brush it aside, but he wasn't very convincing. 'I dress the wigs here, so I work with mirrors a lot.' He gave a false laugh. 'I caught my cheek, that's all.' His trembling hand patted the damage and he pulled it away quickly. 'It's not as bad as it looks.'

Banham walked away, leaving Alison alone with him. 'You must have known Sadie well if you dress the wigs?' she said.

'Yes. Yes, I did.' There was fear in Terry's eyes. 'I make the costumes and dress the wigs here, so I know all the girls.'

'Tell me about her.'

Terry dabbed a handkerchief over the congealing blood on his face. His voice went up in pitch. 'She was a very good Marilyn impersonator and a very nice girl.'

Alison raised her eyebrows. 'Did you know much about her personally? Did she confide in you, you know, girl to girl?'

She regretted the last remark the moment it left her lips, but it seemed to please him; the beginnings of a smile curved his dark lipsticked mouth. 'She told me she was going through a rough divorce.'

Alison noticed that one of his false nails was broken. 'Did she do drugs?'

Terry looked down. 'I… couldn't say.'

'Could you say if she sold drugs?'

The fear returned to his face, and he still didn't meet her eyes. 'I… wouldn't know.'

'We have reason to believe she did,' Alison told him. 'Perhaps Eddie Chang would know. Where is he?'

'He's in his office. I'll take you through.' He seemed keen to cut the conversation short.

'In a moment,' Alison said. 'Were you working here last night?'

'Yes.' Terry picked at his nail varnish and looked round to see if anyone was listening.

'How did she seem to you?'

He spoke quietly. 'OK. She was OK.'

Alison stared at him for a few moments. The more uncomfortable he was, the more he might say. 'OK? Just OK?'

'Yes.' He swallowed. 'OK.'

'What time did you leave the club?'

'When it closed. About five-thirty.'

'Where did you go?'

'Home.

'Can anyone verify that?'

Terry shrank back. 'What do you mean?'

Alison sighed. 'Do you live alone, Terry?'

'No.'

'So was your partner awake? Can she – or he – verify the time you got home?'

Terry's eyes opened wide. 'I... I live with Eddie.'

'Eddie Chang?'

'Yes.'

Alison closed her eyes. That was it, then; she wouldn't get any more out of Terry King. She thanked him brusquely and walked into the club.

Banham was studying the pictures on the wall. They were all of Marilyn Monroe, yet the board outside advertised a different lookalike show every night: Marilyn, Liza Minelli, Judy Garland, Sinatra, Elton John, Marilyn again, and Elvis. Tonight was obviously Liza Minelli; *New*

York, New York was playing in the background. It was early and the night had yet to get going; only a couple of customers were in there drinking. The barmaid was dressed as Marilyn Monroe, and she seemed ill at ease.

Johnny Gladman was still sweeping the floor with a dustpan and brush. 'Someone's a big Marilyn fan,' Banham said to him.

Johnny carried on sweeping.

Banham knocked sharply on Eddie Chang's office door. 'Come in,' Eddie's clipped voice shouted. 'To what do I owe this pleasure?' he added sarcastically as Banham and Alison walked in.

'We want the CCTV footage from the front of the building,' Banham said without preamble.

'I already told you, there's no camera there.'

Banham looked speculatively at Chang. 'I'm conducting a murder enquiry, and I need all your CCTV tapes. You know every person that arrives at the front of the club – it doesn't take much of a detective to work out there is CCTV out there. I want the last night's footage from outside that door.'

Chang said nothing.

'Co-operate with us, Eddie,' Alison said wearily. 'If we have to, we'll take this building apart.'

Chang fixed her with a cold gaze. 'You think I don't want this killer found? Sadie Morgan was my top Monroe impersonator. It's a race between you and me. I want to be the one to dish out the punishment.'

Alison held his stare. 'You lied to us. Earlier today you said you didn't know Andrew Fisher. He signed in last night, as a guest.'

82

He smiled, but not with his eyes. 'I have no idea who all my guests are. That's why they have to sign in. If this Andrew signed in, he must have been here. I gave you the CCTV from last night. I have nothing to hide.' He cupped his chin with his hand. 'Now, is there anything else? Only if you keep coming here I may start believing I'm being harassed.'

'You'd be right,' Banham retorted. 'We want last night's CCTV footage from the front of the club.'

Chang shrugged. 'OK. Since it's to help a murder enquiry, I'll admit I do have CCTV at the front entrance.' His mouth curved into a travesty of a smile. 'I keep it quiet. It helps me to keep the wrong sort out of my club.'

'I'll bet it does,' Banham said.

'Terry dear,' Chang called over Alison's shoulder. Terry King appeared silently in the doorway, still holding a tissue to his bleeding nose. 'The detective inspector and his little friend – ' Alison gritted her teeth – 'would like yesterday's CCTV tapes from the front of the club too.'

Alison wanted nothing more than to arrest him there and then for assault on Terry King. She dreaded to imagine how he treated the girls he imported for prostitution. But his days were numbered; within days CO19 would bust his sordid operation wide open and he would get his comeuppance.

When Terry King returned with the CCTV tapes she said, 'You should get your face properly seen to. It looks nasty.'

Terry opened his mouth to answer, but Chang cut in smoothly, 'I hope that's everything. We don't want to waste any more time, do we? We have a killer to catch.'

'Leave that to the police,' Alison said thinking how much like a snake he looked: slanting eyes, small flat nose, thin, wide mouth made even wider by the slanting scar.

Johnny Gladman followed them to the door. He raised his head, and Alison followed his glance to a tiny flashing red light on the roof. It was yet another CCTV camera, and it pointed to the courtyard behind the club. The cottage was back there, the place Crowther's snout had told them Chang used for the Ukrainian girls.

Was Johnny unconsciously checking the CCTV, Alison wondered. Or was he trying to drop them a hint that it existed?

CHAPTER SEVEN

It was hard to see the front of the house, let alone read the number. An overloaded washing line had been strung right across the front lawn.

Bruno Pelegino's mother lived at number forty-two; Isabelle walked up the path to check this was the right house. There was a large brass number 42 on the door, next to half a dozen stickers for the Red Cross, Salvation Army, wildlife rescue and a homeless African children charity.

Crowther dawdled behind, manoeuvring around the shirts, sheets, white chef's overalls and underwear hanging from the line.

Isabelle pulled her warrant card from her pocket and leaned on the doorbell. Crowther was surveying a pair of extra-large nylon knickers; she caught his eye. 'I don't think she'll be your type,' she said.

'You've got a one-track mind. That's what stopped you getting promotion.'

He had to bloody rub it in, didn't he? She was just about to give him a mouthful in return when the front door opened. The grey-haired woman behind it was short, tubby and middle-aged, and spoke in a thick Italian accent.

'He's not here,' she said sharply, staring at the identification in Isabelle's hand.

'Seems you were expecting us then,' Isabelle said. The woman's brown eyes were perceptive, but nervous.

The woman nodded resignedly. 'Sadie's parents told us.' She closed her eyes. 'My Bruno is devastated. She broke his heart, but he still loved her.'

'Where is he?' Crowther interrupted.

'He went out.'

Isabelle tried to inject some compassion into her tone. 'We do need to talk to him. Do you know where he is?'

'He hasn't done anything. He wouldn't hurt a hair on that girl's head. If she was murdered, it wasn't by my Bruno...'

'Where is he?' Crowther asked again.

'Getting drunk, I wouldn't wonder.' Mrs Pelegino bit her lip. 'She broke his heart. In this family marriage is sacred. I hated her for what she did to my son.'

'What did she do?' Isabelle asked.

'Broke the sixth commandment.'

'Which is?' Crowther sighed impatiently.

The woman seemed shocked that he didn't know. 'Adultery. Thou shalt not commit adultery.' She looked Isabelle in the eyes for the first time. 'But I'm still sorry she died like that.'

'You're very well informed, Mrs Pelegino,' Isabelle said.

'Where does he drink?' Crowther demanded.

'In the Crown, at the end of the road. When they close he'll go to the restaurant, but he'll probably get the sack, because he won't be fit to work.'

'Which restaurant?'

She hesitated. 'He works part-time in a few. I think today he is at Fernando's. Do you know it?'

'Yes, we do. Thank you.' Isabelle handed her a card. 'Will you ask him to call us when he comes home?'

'I'll ask him.'

'Don't ask him. Tell him,' Crowther said firmly. 'If we haven't caught up with him by the time he comes home, tell him to call us. And tell him if he doesn't, we'll be back to arrest him.'

'He didn't hurt her. He loved her.'

'We just need to eliminate him from our enquiries,' Isabelle said.

'I can do that. He didn't kill her. He was here at home.'

'When?' Crowther said flatly.

'When she was killed.'

'We didn't tell you she was killed,' Crowther said. 'You said that.'

'Her mother told me it's a murder enquiry.'

'Where was he last night?' Crowther didn't bother to hide his irritation.

'Here. He was here, in the house with me.'

'All night?' Crowther pushed.

'I have told you, he was here with me. He worked at Fernando's, and then came home.'

'What time?'

'Some time after I went to bed.'

'Which was?'

'Just after midnight.' She tried to close the door in their faces, but Crowther put his foot against it.

'Is there a Mr Pelegino?' he asked her.

'Beside Bruno? No, my husband is dead. We are Catholic. Catholics marry only once.'

'She's doing what any mother would,' Isabelle reasoned a few minutes later as Crowther slammed the car door and clicked his belt into place.

'Lying to save her son, and getting in the way of a murder

87

enquiry,' he snapped, firing up the engine.

Isabelle double-checked her safety belt. When Crowther was wound up it showed in his driving. He reversed too fast, swung the car round, and headed for the main road in a series of kangaroo jumps.

As he slowed for the junction he asked, 'Isn't there a commandment about lying?'

'We have no proof that she was.'

'He was violent with Sadie. We've got her diary, and witnesses.'

'Doesn't mean he killed her.'

'Quit winding me up. Let's just hope he's at Fernando's.'

Isabelle made no reply. There was no talking to Crowther when he was in this mood.

'Then we'll pay my snout a visit,' he went on. 'He doesn't know you, so you'll have to keep it buttoned, is that clear?'

'Yes.'

'Yes what?'

'Yes, sergeant.'

Crowther grinned and relaxed. 'I like it when you call me sergeant.'

Isabelle closed her eyes. Don't rise to it, she told herself.

Alison pulled down the visor to expose the mirror, and put a blue scrunchy between her teeth. Banham watched, fascinated, as her hands busied themselves twisting her long reddish-mousy hair back into a ponytail, and wriggled the scrunchy over the wild bushy mass to secure it at the nape of her neck.

She was beautiful. Her skin was pale and flawless, apart

from the dark circles under her eyes from the long hours she worked. He thought she was unusual and exquisite, rather like a rare specimen of squirrel. He watched her in silence, resisting the temptation to lean over and kiss her.

She rummaged in her bag and pulled out a floral cosmetic bag. 'When will you get to see the kids?' she asked.

'If there's nothing too much happening, I'll go tomorrow, after the morning briefing. I'll come in first thing, then I'll hand over to you and take them to lunch. Is that OK?'

'Absolutely fine. I think you should spend some time with them.'

She pulled out a little pot with *Homeopathic Lip Balm* on the lid, and was now spreading a little of the contents across her lips. He still wanted to kiss her.

'Will you talk to Bobby?' she asked, holding out the pot. 'Here. It's obviously intriguing you! Have a look for yourself!'

She started tugging a large rake-like comb through the ends of her ponytail. He took the pot from her and examined the writing on the lid.

'I'll try. I'll aim to be back sometime in the afternoon – but call me if you need me.'

She carried on pulling the wide-toothed wooden comb through her hair. Loose hair flew in all directions.

'You look great.'

'I look a sight. I should make more of an effort, especially if I'm going to play good cop on this one.'

He dropped the lip balm back in her floral bag, resisting the temptation to rifle through its contents, then reached over and pulled some fallen hair back off her face. 'You remind me of a squirrel more than ever with your hair

89

pulled back in that bushy tail piece.'

'It keeps it from falling over my face.'

He refrained from telling her that it was flying all over his car. 'That lip balm smells nice,' he said instead, immediately realising how corny it sounded.

'It's supposed to be strawberry.'

She pushed her comb back in her handbag, and this time he did lean over and kiss her. Their noses collided, and she jumped back. They both spoke at once.

'I'll have to put more on now.'

'It smells more like cherry actually.'

He suddenly felt like a sixth-former on his first date. The seven years they had worked together seemed to have vanished. It was a sort of new beginning.

She wiped something off his cheek with her fingers, and touched them to his lips. It definitely smelled more like cherry.

The words came out before he could stop them. 'Can I stay with you tonight?'

She looked into his eyes, and for a moment he thought she would agree. But she shook her head.

'I need to get my head around this case. I can't let myself be sidetracked.'

Was that her way of saying he wasn't up to standard? Well, it had been eleven years, and he had been very nervous.

He brushed her cheek gently. He wanted to tell her that he understood, and that last night meant all the world to him, that he loved her, that he was going to take care of her. But he didn't know how.

'There'll be time when we've wrapped this one up,' she

said, opening the car door. 'Come on. Let's go and give PCSO Andrew Fisher some more grief.'

His mind shifted into work mode as soon as Andrew Fisher opened his front door.

'Why didn't you tell us you were in Doubles last night?' he demanded, adopting his bad cop tone, the one which had gained him the reputation of being the detective no one argued with.

He didn't wait for the answer. He pushed past Andrew into the hallway of the small bungalow, closely followed by Alison.

'DC I Banham is asking you a question,' she said. Andrew stood pressed against the door, his acne-spotted face looking redder than ever.

He closed the front door. 'Come through,' he said nervously, and led the way into the lounge, which was occupied by three cats and a collection of DVDs that took up the whole of one wall.

'Why didn't you tell us you were inside the club last night?' Banham repeated.

'I wasn't.'

'So you've never been in the club?' Alison made no attempt to hide her disbelief.

'No.'

'So your name isn't in the guest book, and you haven't signed in twice in the last fortnight?'

Andrew Fisher tensed, then shrugged. 'Millie signed me in, while I was waiting for her. In case I wanted to go in. But I didn't. I waited outside for her.'

'When?'

'She had a rehearsal, or a fitting, something like that,

91

during our shift.'

'So you've never been inside Doubles?' Banham asked again.

'No, sir.'

'Andrew, we know that's a lie,' Alison said.

He turned away and stared at a wall covered in Clint Eastwood posters. Crowther would have been bowled over, Alison thought. He idolised Clint Eastwood, and had *The Good, the Bad and the Ugly* as a ring-tone on his phone. Judging by the signed poster that took pride of place on the opposite wall, Andrew was also a fan of James Bond. There were also autographed photos of the American astronauts who manned the first space shuttle. Boys will be boys, she thought.

'I think you are trying to protect Millie Payne,' she said gently.

Andrew shook his head.

'OK, if you weren't in the club, tell us where you were.'

He blushed like a beetroot again but said nothing.

Banham raised his voice. 'Fisher, you're a police officer and this is a murder enquiry. Now answer the question.'

'I didn't kill her,' Andrew said defensively.

'No one's saying you did. Yet. Where were you between two and five o'clock this morning?'

'Waiting for Millie.'

'For three hours?'

Andrew reddened again.

Banham closed his eyes and turned away.

'Where?' Alison asked more kindly.

He dropped his gaze to the floor now and shook his head.

'Look, we know you were in the club,' Alison said. 'We

have CCTV footage of you in there.' She sat on the sofa, and it dipped under her weight. 'Andrew, it's loyal of you to stand by Millie, but you're being extremely naïve. If we didn't have that footage of you at the time that Sadie was murdered, you might well be a suspect.'

She paused, momentarily distracted by a sound close by. One of the cats was licking itself, its body contorted in a strange yoga-like position as its tongue flicked back and forth over its tail end. She caught Banham's eye and struggled to keep a straight face.

'In some ways lying to save a colleague is a noble gesture, but in this case it's downright stupid,' she finished.

Andrew blushed again. 'I didn't want to get her into trouble. If I'd said I was in the club I'd have had to say why, and that would have meant dropping Millie in it.' He bowed his head. 'Yes, I was in Doubles last night.' He let out a large sigh. 'I went in while Millie had a costume fitting. She invited me in. She knows I like old films.' He waved at the posters. 'Given what happened it was unforgivable; I haven't stopped feeling guilty ever since. We went in around a quarter to two, and were back out on the beat by four. Both of us, together.'

Banham nodded. That was better. 'On the CCTV you're wearing a coat over your uniform.'

'It was the one I wore to work last night. Millie was prepared, she had her civvy clothes to change into. I went back to the station and got my coat. I wore it to hide my uniform.'

'I'll need the coat,' Alison said. 'To run past Forensics.'

'It's in the bedroom,' Andrew said. 'I'll get it.'

As he moved towards the door Alison made a decision.

She took a deep breath and launched in. 'Andrew Fisher, I'm arresting you for wasting police time. You have the right to remain silent, but anything you do say…'

He paled. 'What?'

'But anything you do say may be used is evidence. Do you understand?'

Andrew nodded, stunned into silence.

'Is this necessary?' Banham asked quietly as Andrew went to his bedroom to get the coat.

'Yes. He's a new officer, this is a murder enquiry and he's lied. He needs to learn a lesson. He and Millie Payne both need to learn that wearing a uniform isn't a game.'

Raymond Adams stank: a combination of stale perspiration, cigarette smoke, dirt and grease. He looked as if he hadn't washed for a month. His thin hands, gaunt face, and even his ears were grubby.

As he settled into the back of Crowther's car Isabelle breathed in a lungful of body odour and cracked open the passenger window.

Adams pinned nervous eyes on her. 'Who's she?' he asked Crowther in a smoke-steeped voice. 'I don't do no bloody talking in front of strangers'

His aggressive air fooled neither of them. The constant foot tapping and the tic at the side of his mouth told a completely different story.

'She's sound,' Crowther said.

'I don't know her.' Raymond voice rose. 'I'm risking life and limb here. Tell her to clear off.'

Crowther twitched a twenty pound note out of his pocket and held it just out of Adams's reach. 'You're risking nothing for me, my old son. I'd say it's all for the big fat fix this will buy you.'

Adams blinked a few times then focused on Isabelle. A grimy hand wiped the sweat from his top lip. 'All right. What d'you want to know?'

Crowther pulled the note back. 'What happened to that Marilyn lookalike, Sadie Morgan? You do know she ended up in the duck pond on the waste ground last night?'

'She played one off against the other.'

'Go on.'

'Johnny Gladman, the black doorman. She was his bit, and then there was the husband. Mr Chang don't like trouble.'

Crowther pulled his mouth into a tight smile. 'Mr Chang invented the word,' he snarled. 'He saw to it, did he?'

'No, he didn't. It weren't nothing to do with the club.' Adams pulled at his ear lobe. 'Chang's hopping mad about it.' He paused. 'The ex didn't like her seeing the doorman. The doorman didn't like her nosing into his business.' He reached over and grabbed at the money.

Crowther held it back. 'Not finished yet, old son. What's the news on the east European women? The shipment into Dover. Is that imminent?'

'They aren't here at the moment.' Adam's foot started tapping. 'I've heard its happening next week. Chang's put it on hold now because of all this business.'

'Keep me posted,' Crowther told him. 'There's a fat drink in it for you.'

'I'll make sure of it, Mr Crowther.' Adams looked around nervously and pleaded quietly, 'I've told you where to look for your killer. I'm risking my life for this. Give me the money'

Even in the dim light in the back of the car, Isabelle was aware Adams's hands were a little twitchier than when he had climbed in. He was getting desperate for his fix.

'Have you seen her ex-husband in the club?' she asked.

There was a silence. Crowther flicked angry eyes at her. Raymond looked at her, then back at Crowther.

'She's my girlfriend,' Crowther said. 'She's sound.'

Isabelle knew Crowther was furious with her. She said nothing more.

Adams tried to take the note but Crowther didn't let go. 'Answer the lady's question. The ex. He's Italian. His name is Bruno Pelegino.'

Adams shook his head. 'Have you talked to Johnny Gladman's brother?'

'Brother? Does he work at the club?'

'No, he's a kid. He's only fifteen. Name's Otis. He lives with Johnny. He's a right little tear-arse though, violent with it, takes after his brother.'

Crowther released the twenty pound note. Adams snatched it, leaned on the door handle and was on the street in an instant.

Isabelle waited for Crowther to give her an earful. He didn't. He gave her one of his winks instead.

'Well done,' he said. 'If you hadn't opened your mouth we wouldn't have found out about the brother. We got more out of him than I expected.'

Isabelle resisted the urge to smile, but maybe the day wasn't turning out so bad after all.

The smell of coffee permeated Alison's new office.

Banham had bought her a new machine as a promotion present.

He perched on the side of her desk talking on the phone.

'Penny had Millie's clothes from last night,' he said, clicking it off. 'A pair of jeans and a t-shirt and a coat. Still being tested.'

'I'm going to keep Fisher in overnight, teach him a lesson,' she said. 'He should know better than to lie on a murder enquiry.'

'Oh come on, it was to stop a work associate getting into trouble,' Banham protested. 'At least we know he's loyal.'

'Police work isn't a game. If they want to stay in the job they need to learn that.'

'I think you're being too harsh.'

She sniffed. 'Milk?'

'Please.'

She half-filled a mug from the coffee machine and topped it up with milk from a carton on the desk.

'Look,' Banham continued, 'we know Sadie was murdered between two and five in the morning. We have Andrew on CCTV during that time, and we know Millie was at the club as well. Our job is to find Sadie's killer, not train PCSOs in professionalism.'

'Sorry, no biscuits, Crowther's eaten them all.'

'It's not as if either of them is a suspect,' Banham persisted.

'We still haven't any CCTV of Millie in the club. Besides, it's not about being a suspect. If they want to be in the force, they have to learn to respect it.'

Banham flung his hands up. 'Have it your way. Are you hungry?'

'I want to go through the CCTV footage again. I'll send out for a takeaway later. You go home.'

'What about...?'

'I didn't get much sleep last night,' she cut in quickly. 'I'd like to grab all I can tonight.'

The skin at the side of his eyes crinkled. She loved that smile, but she read disappointment behind it now. She pushed the thought away; if she let it in, she wouldn't be spending the next few hours looking through CCTV footage.

'What are you looking for on the tapes?' Banham asked her, reaching for his coat. Good; he'd got the message.

'Chang said Sadie was doing drugs. He wouldn't dirty his own hands dealing. So I'm going to see if I can see anyone else dealing in there last night.'

'I'll stay with you,' he told her. 'Two can work quicker than one.'

She rubbed her forehead slowly. He was right. And it would be good to have his company. 'Thanks,' she smiled. 'But you've got to promise to go and see Bobby tomorrow.'

'If you promise to eat something.'

'Deal.'

'I'll go out and get the takeaway.' He picked up his sheepskin-lined black leather coat again. Lottie had given it to him as a late Christmas gift and a thank-you for supporting her through a bad time. Alison knew he still felt guilty that his twin had spent so much, but it was a great coat. She hadn't seen him wear it to work before, though.

She turned the tape machine on and CCTV images flicked across the screen at high speed. 'What's with the Astra Cadix?' she murmured. 'And where does the

98

bloodstained knife and crystal meth fit in?'

Banham could offer no answer. 'Col's meeting his informant tonight; that may turn up something. I'll get chicken and cashew nuts, shall I? Do you want prawn or egg fried rice?'

'Whichever.'

He left, and she gave the tape her full attention. After a few minutes she pressed Pause and looked more closely. Johnny Gladman and Sadie were outside the club; Johnny put something in her hand, then Terry King came out and snatched what looked like an earring from Sadie's ear. Johnny followed King back into the club, and Sadie set off up the street.

Alison ejected the tape and reached for another, which showed Sadie walking down the road, zigzagging and stumbling. She froze, and paused the tape. A car on the other side of the road had pulled out and moved off at a snail's pace.

'Who is it?' the voice said from the intercom.

'It's OK, Lily. It's me.'

The front door clicked, and Millie climbed the stairs. Lily was waiting at her own front door.

Millie was very edgy, but pulled herself together. She watched as Lily checked the stairs and landing before closing the door. Millie followed her into the living room. An empty wineglass stood on the table. If Lily had been drinking alone she must be scared.

'I can stay over if you'll feel safer,' she told her friend. 'But you do need to tell me about this stalker. Did you get a good look at him?'

99

'He's very odd looking,' Lily told her. 'He wears dark glasses and a raincoat, and I think he's got a toupée or a wig. He could be anybody.'

There was an awkward silence. 'You don't believe me, do you?' Lily said.

'Of course I do.' There was another silence, then Millie said, 'Look – you're playing Marilyn Monroe. She was a worldwide icon. There are lots of very strange people out there.'

'So you think he's harmless? I'm being stalked because I'm playing Marilyn Monroe?'

Millie chose her words carefully. 'Not necessarily. Tell me everything you remember about him, even if it seems silly.'

Lily shrugged. 'That's it. There's nothing else to tell.'

'You're not travelling to Birmingham alone?'

'No, the whole cast is travelling together. They're picking me up.'

'Here?'

'Yes.'

'Good. Do they know about the stalker?'

'They haven't seen him.'

The doorbell rang and both women jumped.

'I'll go.' Millie stood up.

It was Crowther.

'It's fine,' Millie said. 'He's a police sergeant, come to take your statement.' She smiled coyly, 'He's also my new boyfriend. He's gorgeous, and he'll look after you.'

Crowther's hair was standing on end like a cockatoo, and his rolled-up sleeves still looked like carpet samples. He smiled from ear to ear as he clocked Lily Palmer, five feet nine in bare feet and absolutely stunning.

Isabelle followed him, looking less than pleased.

'This is Colin. Sergeant Colin Crowther,' Millie said.

Lily looked unimpressed but shook his hand politely. 'Millie's told me all about you,' she said. 'I hear you're her new fella?'

Isabelle looked thunderous.

Lily poured them all a glass of wine. Crowther said, 'We found something in Sadie's flat that makes us think her murder may have been drug related.'

The colour drained from Lily's face.

'You haven't told her, have you?' Isabelle demanded.

CHAPTER EIGHT

Alison had left a message on Millie's mobile saying she wanted to speak to her. Crowther brought her into her office first thing Sunday morning. They both looked as if they'd dressed in a hurry. Millie's hair was greasy and sticking to her head as if she had just done a workout, and mascara was smudged around her eyes like a toy panda. Crowther's tie was knotted upside down, like a large orange and pink medallion against his chest. It didn't take a detective to work out why. Alison admired his energy, but still found Millie infuriating.

'There's no reason to believe Lily Palmer's stalker is connected to the murder,' she told her. 'We now have evidence that connects Sadie's death to something else.'

Millie looked at Alison with big innocent eyes.

'I'm still not taking any chances,' Alison went on. 'She knows and trusts you, so I'm assigning you to stay in close touch with her, like a family liaison officer. When she leaves for Birmingham tomorrow, I want you to keep in regular phone contact, and report back to me or Sergeant Crowther if there are any further sightings of this stalker, in London or Birmingham. Is that clear?'

Millie nodded obediently, then the blue eyes focused on Alison again. 'Look, you'll probably say I'm speaking out of turn, but Colin told me you've locked Andrew in a cell for lying to the police.'

Alison glared at Crowther. He was perched on the side of her desk, arms crossed over his chest, covering the tie. 'His name, while on duty, is Sergeant Crowther, and Andrew is PCSO Fisher. And you'll call me ma'am.'

'Ma'am, all this is my fault. PSCO Fisher was covering for me. I asked him to, while I had a dress fitting at the club.'

'Then consider yourself lucky that we haven't brought a charge against you too!' Alison was strung up, and surprised at how nervous she felt without Banham to back her up.

'I know I did wrong,' Millie said.

'At least you admitted you were in the club in your statement,' Alison said. 'Fisher denied it.'

'He did that for me,' Millie protested. 'I realise I was stupid, but I've learned my lesson and it will never happen again.'

Crowther was pleading her case with his puppy eyes; she clearly had him wrapped around her finger.

'Let me give you some advice,' Alison said, keeping a tight hold on her temper. 'If you want to do other work while you are PCSO, as an actress – ' she drew speech marks in the air – 'or anything else for that matter, you ask permission and tell your duty sergeant exactly what you're doing. Is that clear?'

'Crystal, ma'am.'

'That club is strictly out of bounds. You might want to think about what's important to you in career terms.'

Millie hung her head. Alison felt herself softening. It didn't last.

'Erm, ma'am, Colin and I were talking on the way in.

Don't get me wrong, I fully understand the club is out of bounds for me as a police officer – but I really would like to help find Sadie's killer. Could I carry on working there, with your knowledge, sort of undercover?'

Alison's eyes flared, and she turned them on Crowther. 'Whose idea was this?'

'It ain't a bad one,' Crowther shrugged.

'I'll be the judge of that.'

'Will you think about it?' Millie persisted.

Alison stared at her in disbelief. 'Go and report to DC Isabelle Walsh,' she told her. 'She is overseeing you. Lily has told her she'll be staying at home today, is that right?

'Yes, ma'am.'

'The patrol car in the area is keeping an eye on the block of flats, and you can go round after your shift. Stay with her tonight, and call in if you see or hear anything suspicious. If you notice a car nearby, make a note of the registration number.'

'Yes, ma'am. Erm, what about PCSO Fisher?'

You had to admire her, Alison thought; she stands up for her friends. 'He lied to stop you getting into trouble – I couldn't let that go. But he'll be released as soon as we have forensic clearance on his coat. He can go to Lily's with you after your shift.'

Alison paused, and gave Millie an appraising look. 'I won't mention this incident again, to you or your duty sergeant. I hope you've learned your lesson.'

Millie left, looking suitably shamefaced. Through the glass panel in her office door, Alison saw the squad gathering for the briefing. A few minutes later she was perched on the side of Isabelle's desk at the front of the room.

'OK, everyone,' she shouted. 'What's new?'

On the far side of the room was a large map of the area surrounding the park. The roads that had already received door-to-door visits from uniform were highlighted in fluorescent green; a pink highlight showed the next ones in line.

'The vehicle check you ran last night: the Volvo belongs to Bruno Pelegino's mother and is registered at her address.' This was Isabelle. 'The mother claims she was home on Friday night, so either she's lying or Bruno was driving it. He seems to have disappeared into thin air. Colin sat outside most of the night waiting for him to come home.'

'Is that right, Crowther?'

'Yeah. No sign of him, but I'll stay on it.'

Millie must have been with him, Alison thought; he wouldn't shirk his responsibility or lie to her. Good job Penny wasn't checking the car for DNA!

'Uniform are looking out for the car,' Isabelle went on.

'The car is on CCTV at 2.50 a m,' Alison said. 'The mother is lying.'

'She actually said she heard Bruno come in shortly after she went to bed, but couldn't confirm the time. Some time after midnight.' Isabelle read from her notes.

'Go back and ask her if Bruno has a car of his own. If he does, and he took it out Friday night, she's definitely lying – so bring her in for questioning.' Alison took a deep breath. 'But finding him is a priority, he's a key suspect.'

'On it, ma'am.'

She narrowed her eyes; was Crowther taking the piss? If

he was, it didn't show on his face.

'Anything come through on forensics yet?' she asked him. 'Or haven't you had time to talk to Penny yet?'

His grin told her the shot had hit its mark, but there wasn't a trace of shame in it. His response was businesslike. 'She has tests underway on the bloodstained knife and the hand-gun. It's just a matter of time.'

She moved on. 'The CCTV shows Johnny Gladman slipping something into Sadie's hand as she left the club on Friday – yet no drugs were found at the scene. Any thoughts?'

'Perhaps she handed them on to her killer,' a tall DC said from the back of the room. 'Perhaps there was an argument.'

'Perhaps the ex-husband found out she was taking drugs,' another DC suggested.

'She was getting divorced,' Isabelle put. 'Drugs are quick money.'

'Perhaps Eddie Chang's involved after all,' Alison mused. 'Maybe he got wind of her dealing and had her taken out?'

Crowther shook his head. 'Nah. There's more to it than that. Where does the bloodstained knife come in?'

Eric was leaning against the wall as usual, a cigarette behind his ear. He raised a hand. 'What about the other Monroe impersonator, the one who thinks someone is following her?'

Alison pursed her lips. 'PCSO Payne and her partner are going to stay with her after her shift. If there is a stalker we'll find him. Crowther and Walsh took a statement from her last night.'

106

'I think she's a frightened woman,' Crowther put in.

Alison nodded agreement. 'We've got a patrol car staying close all day, and the two PCSOs will stay with her this evening. Any sign of him and we'll pick him up. Eric, I want you to stay on liaison with Sadie's parents until tomorrow. They might tell you something.'

'Ma'am.'

'Col, you and I are going back to Doubles this morning to talk to Johnny Gladman and Terry King. I want to know what Gladman gave her outside the club. It could have been the handgun – it's a very small one.'

'We have to tread carefully at the club,' Crowther said. 'We can't afford to rock the CO19 operation. If he thinks we're watching the club, he'll cancel the pick-up at Dover. We can't afford for that to happen.'

'We can't afford for Chang to find this killer before we do either!'

A murmur of agreement ran round the incident room.

'I want everyone else carry on interviewing all the club members,' Alison continued. 'Statements from every staff member, all the impersonators, Elvises, Sinatras, Liza Minellis and most important every Marilyn lookalike. Isabelle, you need to concentrate on finding Bruno Pelegino. Try all the restaurants again, and try and get a search warrant; I know it's Sunday but use your charm. If he hasn't turned up by the end of the day, we can take his mother's house apart.'

They had been in the car for ten minutes en route for the club, and Crowther hadn't said a word.

'You're cross because I read Millie the riot act,' Alison

said.

'You were too harsh.'

Alison blew out a breath. 'We've just got promotion, Col. This is our first case; we want a speedy result. How will it look if Eddie Chang finds the killer before we do?' There was no response. 'Crowther, for God's sake, wake up. I am truly surprised at you. Have you fallen in love or something? She screwed up, big time. She needed to be told.'

Crowther gave her a quick glance. 'Sometimes you don't see further than your nose. Ma'am.'

Now he was taking the piss. 'Meaning?'

'Chang's a big fish to bring in. We've had an informant working at Doubles for months, and we still haven't netted the bastard. Think what a coup it would be if we nailed him alongside this murder enquiry.' He paused and glanced at her again. She didn't react. 'We've got a great opportunity – why not use it? Put Millie in there as an informant.'

'You are bloody joking.'

'My snout will keep an eye on her.' He gave her his schoolboy look that never failed to charm. 'Just of think it: your first case as DI, Sadie Morgan's killer and Eddie Chang both behind bars.'

He had a point. But it wouldn't work; the girl was too inexperienced, and didn't think things through. 'I thought you liked Millie? Aren't you concerned for her safety? Chang wouldn't hesitate to kill anyone who got in his way.'

'She wants to do it,' was all Crowther said.

She began to wonder how far he was prepared to go to get a result. Further than she was, obviously.

She shook her head slowly. 'She's not up to it.'

'She wants to make up for messing up last night. Why not let her? I'd say that's using your nous.'

'And I'd say that's using *her*. She's not had proper training, and she's not very bright either.'

'You're jumping to conclusions, because she's blonde and pretty.'

Alison didn't reply.

'Come on, Alison. If it goes wrong I'll take the rap. And you never know – it just might work.'

This was why he was one of the youngest sergeants in the force. He was a risk taker, and braver than she was.

'I'll run it past Banham,' she said.

She didn't tell him Banham had suggested it too.

They didn't expect the club to be occupied on a Sunday morning, but someone was always around, and they knew if they knocked for long enough the door would be opened.

Terry King greeted them, wearing a Marilyn Monroe wig and heavy make-up over the cut and bruising around his nose. He was dressed in an A-line black skirt covered in a floral apron, with middle-heeled black court shoes and a pink jumper with a roll neck right up to his masculine chin. Alison thought he looked like Dustin Hoffman in *Tootsie*. She had to fight to keep a straight face when she saw Crowther's reaction.

'Can we come in?' she asked.

Terry stepped back and pulled the door wider. 'Of course.'

They walked down the passageway, carpeted in stained floral green. The club smelt of stale beer and staler fried food, and was littered with dirty glasses, used paper plates

109

and the remnants of party streamers.

'Cleaner not turned up?' Crowther said, walking through into the club.

Terry smelt of cheap perfume, or more likely hairspray. He wiped his hands on his apron. 'I'm doing it today,' he said.

'How's your face?' Alison asked.

'Fine,' he said, covering the swollen cheek with his hand. His voice sounded cracked, like a teenage boy's.

'We're trying to piece together Sadie's last moments,' Crowther said. 'You're on CCTV with her, outside the club on Friday night. What was that about?'

He nibbled his thumbnail nervously. 'She was wearing one of our earrings when she left, and I chased after her to get it back. Those are genuine nineteen fifties replicas. They're difficult to get hold of and they cost a fortune.'

'Was she drunk?'

Terry paused. 'No. A little tired.' He rubbed his clammy fingers on his apron.

'Did she ever talk to you about her love life? Alison asked.

'It was complicated.'

'Meaning?' Crowther said flatly.

Terry's eyes flicked around the room. The CCTV was running. And his face was proof that Eddie knocked him about.

'Is Eddie Chang around? Crowther asked.

'He doesn't come in on Sunday.' Terry sounded apprehensive. 'It's just me and Johnny; we're doing the clearing up.'

'Where is he?' Alison asked.

'He's at home. I can give you the address…'

'We've got it,' Crowther said sharply.

'When you followed Sadie out, did you see anyone hanging around?' Alison asked.

'I wasn't looking,' he said quickly. 'I just ran out to get the earring. I was busy, fitting a couple of new Marilyn impersonators.'

Alison looked around the tawdry room. 'You said Johnny was here this morning. Where is he?'

Terry's Adam's apple moved as he swallowed. 'He's in the cottage at the back. I'll give him a call.'

'No worries,' Crowther said, heading towards the back exit to the courtyard. 'We know where it is. We'll give him a knock.'

A CCTV camera whirred as they walked through the courtyard. 'This is Chang's knocking shop,' Crowther said, careful to keep his voice low.

The cottage door was already open; Terry had warned Johnny Gladman they were there. Johnny's long Rastafarian plaits were twisted into an elastic band at the nape of his neck, and he needed a shave. He wore grubby, grey, baggy tracksuit bottoms and a vest, and his feet were bare. Crowther looked him up and down.

'You sleep late, Mr Gladman. It's nearly lunchtime.'

'Can we come in?' Alison asked evenly. 'We've got a few more questions about Sadie Morgan.'

Johnny hovered on the threshold.

'We can do it here, or down the station,' she pushed.

Johnny stepped back to allow them in.

Obviously no illegal immigrant girls there at the moment,

111

Alison thought. But maybe they could find a clue that they were expected.

Banham loved Sundays like this: days when he had time to buy his twin sister and nephew and niece lunch at a family pub.

They sat around the large wooden table; the plates crowded each other, and had one thing in common: large helpings of chips. Alison constantly nagged Banham about his unhealthy eating habits, and he often felt like a naughty schoolboy when she caught him chewing a chocolate bar. She never put enough sugar in his coffee either; he liked two heaped spoonfuls, and hers only added up to half a one. He tucked into a large cheese-burger and chips, relishing every mouthful.

Madeleine sat beside him, tomato ketchup all round her mouth, on her fingers and even in her long pale hair. Bobby had the situation under control. His chips were generously spread with brown sauce, which he sucked from the potato before he ate each one. Banham adored the children. He often looked at Madeleine and wondered what his own daughter would have been like, had she lived. She would have been like a big sister to Madeleine, and equally beautiful.

Now he was the only father figure Bobby and Madeleine had. And he needed to find out what was upsetting Bobby.

Lottie was drinking a very large glass of wine, and picking at fish and chips.

'Are you eating fish 'cause it gives you brains?' Madeleine asked her mother, her small mouth full of chips and tomato sauce.

112

Lottie laughed. 'Fish is good for lots of things. It makes you grow big and strong.' She held a forkful in front of the child's mouth. 'Here, it'll help you fight the bad fairies.'

Madeleine pushed the fork towards her brother. 'You have it, Bobby. It'll help you fight the bullies at school.'

'What bullies?' Banham and Lottie asked with one voice. They exchanged a glance; twin telepathy again.

What bullies?' Banham repeated, more urgently this time.

Bobby said nothing.

'OK,' Banham said cautiously. 'You can tell me after you've had a chocolate ice-cream sundae.' He took care not to catch Lottie's eye.

Bobby turned away.

'It's the big boys,' Madeleine said importantly. 'Not the ones in Bobby's class. Some big boys have got knives and guns. They hurt Felix Greene and they'll hurt Bobby too.'

Banham slipped his arm around her. 'Not on my watch, they won't.'

Lottie looked as surprised as Banham felt.

He knew all about Felix Greene. The lad had been stabbed in the road outside school; thanks to a speedy ambulance service, he had survived a deep knife wound an inch from his heart. No one had come forward with evidence, and he had claimed he didn't see his attacker.

Banham picked up a paper serviette and gently wiped the sauce from Maddie's face. 'Who's got knives and guns?' he asked, applying the serviette to her hands.

Bobby threw his fork on the table. 'I can look out for myself,' he said defiantly. 'I'm not scared of knives.' A beat passed, then he added quietly, 'But the guns are a bit scary.'

113

Banham breathed hard, pushing away the memory flash of the blood-splattered nursery. 'After we've had ice-cream,' he said quietly, 'why don't we kick a football about for a while, and you can tell me about it.'

Bobby's hands flew in the air. 'I ain't splitting on no one. I've talked more than enough already.'

Banham and Lottie exchanged a look. The boy was clearly terrified.

'Do you live alone?' Crowther asked Johnny Gladman.

Alison opened the door to another room and peered inside. She glanced over her shoulder; Johnny was watching her nervously.

'No.' He hesitated. 'My brother lives with me. He's out this morning.'

'You were one of the last people to see Sadie Morgan alive,' Alison said. 'You're on CCTV outside the club. You put something in her hand. Drugs, was it?

His 'Yes' was almost inaudible.

'So what did you do then? Follow her? Kill her?' Crowther said roughly.

Johhny looked anguished. 'No! I wouldn't hurt her.'

'In love with her, were you?' Alison asked.

'It wasn't like that.'

'So what was it like?'

'She was a sweet girl. But I am not allowed to talk to the Marilyn girls.'

'You're on CCTV talking to her.'

'I only asked her if she was OK.'

'What drugs did you give her?' Crowther asked.

'Just… just a little grass.'

He was lying.

'You could have followed her,' Crowther goaded. 'The tape shows you going back into the club, but who's to say you didn't go straight out the back door, into the courtyard and through the gate into the alley? You'd have been at the end of the road before she was.'

Johnny looked terrified. How on earth did he hold down the job of club doorman, Alison wondered. He was the least menacing bouncer she'd ever seen.

'This is all my fault,' Millie said. Andrew was signing for his possessions at the custody desk.

'Tell that to DI Grainger and Sergeant Crowther.'

'I already have. But I didn't know you were in the club. I thought you were waiting for me outside.'

'You said you wouldn't be long, but you were ages. I got cold and went inside.'

'Just as well, as it happens, or you would have been a suspect. I'm really sorry about all this – I feel awful. You've been a really good friend.'

Andrew made no reply, and they set off for the car park in silence.

'Where's your car?' Andrew asked.

'Colin drove me in this morning.'

'Stay out with him last night, did you?'

'You know I'm seeing him.'

Andrew shrugged. 'I haven't got my car either. I was arrested last night, remember. Looks like it's the bus.'

'We have to go to Lily's. We're on liaison there.'

'I really need a shower after that cell. Look, let's get a bus to my place and I'll drive us to Lily's.'

Millie shook her head. 'Better not. We have to be there by six. You go, and I'll fetch my car and pick you up. Be ready – I don't want to get into any more trouble for being late.'

Lily was staying home, where she felt safe. Hyacinth, her Siamese cat, was playing up; she hadn't eaten her breakfast, and hadn't come back since Lily let her out into the communal gardens earlier that day. The day was drawing in and she decided to go and call her. It was safe out there; there was CCTV.

She pulled her cardigan around her and left the door on the latch. 'Hyacinth,' she called.

But there was no sign. Siamese cats were notoriously clever; this one knew Lily was leaving her with a neighbour, and clearly wasn't pleased. It was a game Lily knew well.

After about ten minutes she gave up. The cat would reappear when she was hungry. She closed the front door behind her and made her way up the stairs to her own flat.

She heard a light rustling noise as she walked into the kitchen.

The cat was on the window sill. Lily picked up the saucer of prawns and pulled the curtain back to tempt her to come in.

But the sill was deserted.

She stood still and listened. The noise was coming from the other room. Clever cat, she'd sneaked in through the front door while Lily was out in the garden.

She rattled the tray of prawns and called again. In the hallway she stopped in her tracks; the front door was wide open, and she was positive she had released the latch when she came in. She closed it quickly and hurried back into the kitchen.

The shadow came from nowhere. Then the pillow was over her face and she was fighting for breath. At first there was no pain, just a desperate need for air. She tried to fight to free herself, but the arms holding hers were stronger. She kicked back, but her garden wellingtons made no impression. She panicked as the pain entered her head like a screwdriver. She went wild; someone was yelling, and she couldn't tell if it was her own voice or her imagination. Her arms and legs flailed out as she realised she was fighting for her life. Her brain screamed for oxygen, and the pillow pressed tighter; her nose was being sucked into her face, and she tasted vomit in her throat. Even when her legs buckled and her body slumped, she willed herself to keep fighting.

Then everything went into slow motion. The knife-like pain seemed to retreat and the vomit began to choke her. She heard a laugh in the distance, and she felt as if she was floating; white stars danced in the blackness. They grew smaller and smaller and smaller, until there was nothing but black.

CHAPTER NINE

Mrs Turnbull wore a flowery dress, a flowerier apron and thick grey tights with sheepskin slippers. She was stout and timid, and wiped the corners of her eyes with the edge of her apron as she told Alison how she came to find Lily's body.

She had come out of her flat when she heard Hyacinth mewing to be let in. Lily's door was shut; she knocked for several minutes, and when Lily didn't answer she used the spare keys Lily left with her to allow the desperate cat into the house. She followed it in to check if Lily had left food – and that was when she saw the body, with a note lying by her side.

Mrs Turnbull didn't think she had touched anything. She had staggered back and leaned against the wall, taking some deep breaths before dialling 999. Then the two PCSOs had turned up.

Alison felt dreadful. A question buzzed around her head: should she have sent a liaison officer around sooner, and not relied on a patrol car to keep regular checks?

She went over everything in her mind. Lily had assured Millie that she was staying home with the doors locked, that she had a friendly neighbour, and if she heard or saw anybody strange she would dial 999 immediately. According to Isabelle she had only seen the stalker outside the rehearsal room – never near her home.

Alison simply hadn't believed the stalker had any

connection to Sadie Morgan's murder. The knife and drugs found in her flat and the hand-gun in her bag led them straight to Eddie Chang. And Lily had only told Millie that she *thought* someone was following her. But now, looking down at this woman, a Marilyn Monroe impersonator like Sadie, she had to ask herself if she could have stopped another murder.

Banham was standing at the top of the stairway as Alison came out of the flat.

'Millie Payne and Andrew Fisher turned up about five minutes after the 999 call,' she told him. 'Trouble seems to follow them around.'

Banham put a steadying hand on Alison's arm. 'You couldn't have predicted this,' he assured her. 'You did what was right, followed up on what we had.'

'I should have taken what she said more seriously, had someone round here earlier.'

He squeezed her arm, then turned to study the surroundings. 'Are there any other exits from here?'

'There's only the front door. The killer had to come in that way. There's no CCTV camera inside the building either, but there is one in the grounds, and another in the underground car park.'

Forensic officers were everywhere, in the flat, up the stairway, on all fours at the main entrance to the block, all dressed head to foot in blue plastic suits.

'This note was left with the body.' Alison handed Banham a sheet of paper in a transparent evidence bag. The words *Your Turn Now* were handwritten in blue biro. 'Millie Payne took it from Mrs Turnbull. So both their prints will be on it. Penny has a handwriting expert she can

119

call on – we may have a lead there.'

Banham hovered uncertainly.

'You don't have to go in,' Alison said quietly. 'But it's all right – she was suffocated.' She paused. 'And the poker from the fireplace has been pushed up her anus.'

His eyes closed and he clenched his teeth, swallowing hard as Max Pettifer walked out through Lily's front door.

'I thought I saw your car pull up,' he said, grinning at Banham's obvious discomfort. 'Are you going to stay out there all day, or are you coming in to do your job? Not too much in the way of gore, so hopefully you'll keep your dinner down.'

'Dinner? What dinner? I should be so lucky. I expect you had plenty of time to finish yours.'

Alison closed her eyes. Why did he have to rise to the bait? They were like children. She looked at Max with ice in her gaze. 'We've got work to do.' She walked doggedly into the flat. Banham followed.

Lily lay face down, arms straight and body heaped on the rug by the fire. Her rear was angled upward, and a thin poker from an ornamental set by the gas fire protruded from her back passage.

Banham stood rooted to the spot. 'Was she alive or dead when that happened?' he asked Max.

'Dead, I'd say. There's little blood.'

Alison moved in closer. 'What are those marks on her wrist?'

'Where she was held,' Max told her. 'There's a boot mark on the back of her leg. We might be able to find a match for that.'

'Do you think it's the same killer?'

'Hard to say.' Max's head bobbed from side to side. 'There are similarities. He pointed with a gloved hand to a faint bluish-black tinge around her mouth. 'Your pond victim had that colour too. It's bruising from pressure on the area. I'd say it's likely they were both suffocated, with a pillow, perhaps.'

'Same size hand?' Banham asked.

Max shook his head. 'Couldn't say at the moment.'

'How soon can we get your report?' Banham asked him.

'Same as usual. When it's done.'

The two PCSOs were sitting on stools in the neighbour's kitchen. 'Trouble seems to follow you around,' Alison repeated.

Millie was dry-eyed but shaking. Andrew held her hand.

'What time did you get here?' Banham asked them.

'Mrs Turnbull said she'd just called 999.' Millie looked at Alison. 'Do you think someone is... targeting Monroe impersonators?'

'What makes you say that?' Banham asked her.

'Well, two of them... I just thought...'

'Don't,' Alison said crisply. 'Leave the thinking to us. Where did you find the note?'

'Mrs Turnbull found it. I told her not to touch anything, that the police would want her not to go on to the crime scene. She said she'd found the note next to Lily, and she handed it to me.'

Alison sighed. 'And you took it.'

Millie nodded. 'I had to.'

Alison decided not to ask why.

Andrew was silent and white-faced; his pink pimples

121

stood out. Millie on the other hand had calmed down, and spoke fluently: quite different from the previous murder scene.

'You both know the procedure,' Alison said briskly. 'We need your clothes. Get into forensic suits, then straight back to the station to give full written statements.'

'Are we suspects?' Millie asked, her nerves showing again.

Alison's voice was flat. 'We need to eliminate you.'

'Can you get me the details of a knife attack, Isabelle?' Banham stopped at her desk on the way to the front of the incident room for the briefing. 'St Abbot's school. Felix Greene, stabbed inside the school gate.'

Crowther stopped what he was doing. 'Fifteen-year-old black kid, ten months ago,' he said. 'Nearly fatal, but he survived. Hey, guv, cool coat.'

Banham ignored the comment. 'You remember it?'

'I was on the case. Knife just missed the heart; kid was unconscious for ten days. It was touch and go. He said he remembered nothing. No evidence, case dropped.'

'Any suspects?' Banham tensed.

'One of his gang.'

'So someone he goes to school with?'

'It's happening all over the place,' Crowther reminded him. 'It's only the fatalities that make the papers. It's gang culture. They think their gangs will protect them, but that's what's killing them.'

'The kids are scared,' Alison said, aware of what was going through Banham's mind. 'Especially of the weapon carriers.'

122

'How do we protect him? Them?' Banham hastily corrected himself.

'There's another gun and knife amnesty coming up,' Alison said. 'Let's hope people take notice. But more than that – we have to try to educate the younger kids.'

'So how do I protect Bobby?'

Her heart went out to him; he looked so sad and helpless. 'All we can do is teach him to protect himself, and avoid trouble.'

'Felix Greene is fifteen,' Isabelle said. 'Bobby is years younger than that.'

'But if we don't do something, by the time Bobby gets to fifteen, everyone will be carrying guns.'

There was a silence, and Alison wished she'd kept her mouth shut. The colour had drained from Banham's face.

'We can start by putting Eddie Chang away,' Crowther said decisively. 'Imagine if those Mac 10s got into teenage hands.'

'I'd rather not,' Banham said. 'Get me the paperwork on Felix Greene's case, will you, Isabelle?'

He walked away, and it took all Alison's resolve to wrench her attention back to the murder case. 'Anything back from Forensics yet?' she asked Crowther.

'I've just spoken to Penny. Looks like she's pulling another all-nighter after today.'

'So you'll be working too.' It wasn't a question.

'I'm going to meet Ray Adams, our informant at Doubles. Then I'll be chasing up Bruno Pelegino with Isabelle.'

'So that's why you're wearing a flashy tie?' Isabelle teased. 'Because you're coming out with me?'

123

The room was filling up for the meeting and the start of a new golden time, the first twenty-four hours after another murder case. Fresh pictures had appeared on the board next to the ones of Sadie Morgan: Lily Palmer, face down, similar bruising to Sadie, but her rear end in full view and a poker protruding from her rectum. There were also photos of both girls dressed as Marilyn Monroe, and it was hard to tell the difference between them.

Alison addressed the room. 'As you see, we aren't ruling out the possibility that these two murders are connected. Until an hour ago, our chief suspect was victim number one's ex-husband, who we're still trying to trace. But Lily Palmer worked at Doubles with Sadie Morgan, so that's our main focus now. We need to interview everyone connected to that club, all the staff and the other Marilyn lookalikes.'

Crowther chipped in. 'PCSO Payne knew her well, and was first on the scene again.'

Alison flicked an irritated glance at Crowther. 'I'll interview both the PCSOs. You concentrate on finding Bruno Pelegino.'

Ray Adams opened the door of the car and slid into the back seat of Crowther's car. The tic under his eye was working overtime and his fingers tapped the back of Crowther's seat, irritating him intensely.

'Had your fix, mate?' Crowther asked dryly.

He studied Adams in the mirror. Ray Adams's eyes flicked and blinked, his pale, dry tongue wriggled around his mouth, his knees twitched from side to side. Even from the driver's seat Crowther could smell the man's rancid breath. And this junkie was his main source of information which would put away one of the biggest villains in the criminal world.

Adams scratched his ear, then his head, then his ear again. 'Mr Chang's on the warpath. He's got men waiting for Pelegino, and he's gonna have his balls cut off and drive him out of town.'

'Is that right?' Crowther left a short pause. 'So why would Pelegino want to kill Lily Palmer?'

'Chang reckons she knew Pelegino threatened to kill Sadie.'

'If Chang is gonna take his balls off, he must know where to find him.'

'I know where to find him,' Adams said.

'You'd better tell me, then, hadn't you?'

'It'll cost a bit.' His eyelids flapped wildly.

Crowther sharpened his tone. 'You're already on the payroll; you need to start earning your keep. Else I might have to bring you in and have you searched.'

Adams didn't answer.

Crowther took a roll of money from his pocket and peeled off a twenty. 'Don't you fuck me about. Where's Pelegino?'

'He's at Angelino's.'

'Are you sure?'

'Yes, I followed him there, bit more than half an hour ago. For Mr Chang. He's there now, eating supper.'

Crowther grabbed his radio and called it in, keeping his eyes on Adams. The man certainly needed his fix; he was getting more jittery by the second. 'What about the girls?' he asked, switching the radio off. 'The Ukrainians. When are they coming?'

125

Adams scratched at the back of his neck. 'They're here.'

'What?'

'They're in the country, but I don't know where. Mr Chang won't bring them up here yet. He says it's too dangerous with you lot crawling all over him.'

'So what's he gonna do?'

'He is sending me and Gladman down to Dover in a van to get them. Wednesday, he said. They'll be in the cottage at the back with Gladman till he sells them on. The Mac 10s are coming in from Serbia the same day, and there's a delivery of crystal meth as well.'

'Is that all definite?'

'Depends if the pressure is off from you lot. He's going after Pelegino – he thinks that'll get you lot off his back.'

'So if we arrest Pelegino, and back off from the club, it'll all go down on Wednesday? '

Ray Adams nodded. 'That's the plan. I'll let you know for definite.'

Crowther handed him the twenty. 'I want to know the second they are on Chang's property.' Adams's cheek began to twitch again. 'Don't worry, I'll keep you well out of it.'

Ray took the note. 'Can I go now?'

'No.' Crowther examined his fingernails. 'Who killed Lily Palmer?'

'I told you. Pelegino.'

'No way. Have you been at the club all day?'

'Since lunchtime.'

'Who was missing this afternoon?'

Ray became still. 'All of them on and off. Terry went out with Mr Chang, and Gladman went off for a while. Then

126

Terry and Mr Chang came back and Terry went off on its own.'

'My money's not on Pelegino killing Lily.'

'Mr Chang thinks he did.'

Banham had spent half his career talking Alison's way out of fines for motoring offences. Today she was driving as erratically ever.

'I was going to pay for you to have some more advanced driving lessons,' he said, 'but since you didn't do too well with the last lot, I thought you'd rather go to Venice.'

'You're such a romantic,' Alison replied flippantly.

She wished he'd shut up about Venice; she was still blaming herself for not doing enough to prevent Lily Palmer's murder. She still wasn't sure that she should have started the affair with Banham at all, but right now all her own problems were on hold.

'It's nothing to do with romance. It's because they haven't got roads in Venice.'

That made her smile. He was her best friend and she didn't want to lose that; she just didn't think he was ready for a relationship. She wondered if he ever would be, after what happened to his wife and baby.

'Have I offended you? I was only teasing.'

'No, of course not. It's just – the case. These two women. Do you think it's the same killer?'

He rubbed a hand across his mouth thoughtfully. 'Let's reserve judgement until after the post-mortem tomorrow.'

'I'll report back to you.'

'No need. I'm coming.'

'You don't have to.'

127

'Yes, I do. I said I'd support you through this case. I'm coming to the post-mortem. End of.'

His eyes were burning into her.

'Your squirrelly eyes have got those black flecks in them,' he said.

'I'm edgy, that's all. I want this killer.'

'We all do.'

She spotted a parking space just too late and reversed back down the road, narrowly missing a passing chauffeur-driven six-row limousine. The driver wound down the window and gave her the finger.

She to-ed and fro-ed into the space, tapping bumpers in front and behind. Banham's eyes never left her. 'What?'

'I think I love you,' he said quietly.

Before she had properly registered the words his phone chirped.

'Crowther, yes, what have you got?' He listened for a moment. 'Crowther's brought Pelegino in,' he said to Alison. 'He's ballistic, ranting and raving.'

'Lock him in a cell,' Alison retorted.

'Better let Isabelle in on the interview,' Banham told Crowther. 'Italians respond to pretty women.'

Alison nodded agreement. 'Has Isabelle got the details I asked for? The knife attack at St Abbot's?' His eyebrows moved towards each other as he listened to Crowther's response. 'The kid said he remembered nothing, but his best friend was suspected,' he repeated. 'But no evidence, so no case.'

Alison gave him her full attention.

'The friend's name is Otis Gladman!' He turned to Alison as he repeated Crowther's words. 'His brother, and

128

next of kin, is Johnny Gladman.'

Bruno Pelegino's body language spoke volumes. He strutted into the interview room in a pair of jeans a size too small and tastelessly snug around the crotch. He was no taller than Crowther, but the black t-shirt clinging to his well toned pectoral muscles made him look more like a smaller version of John Travolta in *Saturday Night Fever*.

Isabelle told him to sit down and turned on the recording machine.

She opened her mouth to cue up the recording, but Bruno slapped his hands down hard on the table and stood up to face her.

'You have no right to do this,' he shouted. 'You have bullied and frightened my mama, and now you are accusing me of killing my wife.'

His breath had a pungent reek of garlic and onions. His eyes and hair were dark, and his olive-toned skin less than perfect. Isabelle found him laughably sexless.

'Not accusing,' Crowther corrected. 'Asking. Did you? Did you kill your wife?'

'No, I did not kill my wife. Is that it? Can I leave now? This place makes me claustrophobic.'

'If you stop shouting,' Isabelle told him unsympathetically, 'I'll explain why we need to eliminate you from our enquiries.'

She began to cue up the recording again, but before she had finished the sentence Bruno started shouting again. 'You think I would kill my own wife? She left me, but I always want her back. I done nothing. Why you accuse me?'

129

'Shut up,' Crowther snapped. 'We ask the questions.'

'I have rights!'

'So do we. If you don't shut up, I'll stick you in a cell until tomorrow.'

Bruno sat down, leaned back and folded his arms. His dark fringe fell over his eyes, and he stared belligerently at Isabelle.

'You refused a solicitor,' she pointed out calmly.

'I don't need solicitor, I done nothing.'

Crowther was bored with his theatricals. 'How long since you last saw your wife?' he asked.

'I don't know.'

'It's not a difficult question.'

'She threw me out. I had to go back to live with my mama.' His voice dropped. 'But I still loved her and wanted her back.'

'You thought knocking her about would help, did you?' Crowther stabbed at him. Crowther loved women and abhorred wife beaters. Isabelle knew he would be on a short fuse, and it was up to her to keep the interview moving in case he lost it. It wouldn't be the first time he had hit a wife-beater.

Bruno thumped the desk. 'I slapped her, yes, but I didn't kill her. Don't you dare say I killed her. I will kill anyone that says I did.'

Crowther leaned across the desk. 'I will dare. And I'll dare lock you up and throw away the key if you don't keep it together.' He moved back. 'We found your wife's diary. There are entries describing how you hit her – not slapped her, hit her hard – and tried to smother her. Did you know she kept a diary?'

130

Bruno crossed his arms but said nothing.

'I bet you bloody didn't.' Crowther was a rough diamond himself; he'd witnessed a few domestics when he was growing up. 'There are lots of references to your brutality in your wife's diary. It says you tried to smother her.'

'She has exaggerated.' Bruno kept his arms folded – to stop himself lashing out at Crowther, Isabelle thought.

'I slapped her.' He shrugged. 'What man wouldn't slap his wife when she steps out of line?' He glared at Isabelle as if she was dirt.

'Where were you on Friday night?' Isabelle asked quickly, in case Crowther was about to show him what a slapping felt like.

'At work. Then I went home to my mama.'

Crowther blew out a breath. 'Did you go anywhere, after work, before you went home?'

'No.'

'Funny that,' Isabelle said. 'We've got your mother's car on CCTV, near Doubles club. She says you were driving it on Friday evening.'

There was a pause. 'Yes,' he said slowly. 'I worked near there on Friday. I might have parked it near the club.'

'What time do you finish work?' Crowther asked.

'About eleven, maybe a bit later. It was Friday.'

'It was there at three o'clock on Saturday morning.'

Bruno flung his hands in the air. 'I did not kill her. Why you keep asking me?'

Isabelle and Crowther waited.

'OK. I waited for Sadie on Friday. I was in the car near the club. I saw her come out.' His voice cracked with emotion. 'I love her. I wanted to see her. I had to know if

131

she left the club alone. She did, so I drove off. That was it.'

Crowther sniffed. 'Do you know a Lily Palmer?'

'No, I don't.'

'She worked at Doubles. She was your ex-wife's friend.' Isabelle leaned on the *ex*.

Bruno tapped his fingers on the table. 'Wife. Not ex. Catholics marry for life.'

'She was divorcing you.'

'It takes two,' Bruno said. 'If I no sign papers, she can't get fucking divorce.'

'Are Catholics allowed to swear?'

Crowther was clearly trying to wind him up. Isabelle changed the subject. 'Where have you been all day today?'

'At Angelino's, my cousin's restaurant. I drank too much last night and fell asleep there. When I woke up it was nearly time to start work, so I had a shower there and started at five o'clock.'

'Who else was there?' Crowther asked.

'Nobody. I have a key to the restaurant. My cousin was there last night, but he left me to sleep. He has a family.'

'So you were alone today?'

'I slept all day.' He became aggressive again. 'My cousin will tell you I drank a lot last night.'

'I bet he will,' Crowther said. 'Question is, will we believe him?'

132

CHAPTER TEN

Beside the life-size cardboard Marilyn Monroe in front of Doubles' front door, a small board advertised an Elvis Presley lookalike evening. Banham and Alison flashed their warrant cards at the Marilyn lookalike on reception; she picked up the phone to warn Eddie Chang.

Banham recognised the song playing in the background as the major Elvis hit *Are you Lonesome Tonight?*. It was only ten o'clock, too early for a club to get lively. A few customers, all dressed as Elvis, propped up the bar. One was rehearsing on stage, alongside a pianist whose playing struggled to match the impersonator's tuneless singing. Banham caught the pained expression on Alison's face and they both stifled a giggle.

Cocktail waitresses wandered around, dressed in long red skirts split higher than the prices of the cocktails they served. Banham's mother had worked at the famous Park Lane Bunny Club as a cocktail bunny girl when he and Lottie were babies; he suspected this was nothing like that.

Eddie Chang walked out of his office, narrowing his snakelike eyes and twisting his thin mouth into a sneer when he saw Alison. He was as impeccably dressed as ever, in a dark blue Italian silk suit over a pink shirt, with a tie and matching handkerchief in a brighter shade of the pink. Heavy gold cuff-links peeped through the edge of the sleeve, and a Rolex diamond watch adorned one wrist.

133

'I didn't have you down as Elvis fans.' He clicked his fingers to attract a waitress, the oversized diamond ring on his perfectly manicured little finger glinting in the lights. 'First drink's on the house.'

'It's not a social call,' Alison answered.

His eyes moved north. He stepped back towards the office and opened the door.

'What can I do for you?' He spoke to Banham, ignoring Alison.

Alison answered. 'Lily Palmer was found dead this afternoon.'

Chang looked surprised.

'Where were you between four and seven p m?' she asked.

He sighed. 'You think I killed her too?'

'Just answer the question,' Banham said dryly.

'I was here, doing my books. And before you ask, I have at least four witnesses. My doorman, Johnny Gladman, was here.' He paused. 'Some of the time. Terry King too, sewing sequins, his favourite pastime.' He leaned back against his desk, looking Alison up and down with distaste. 'I think he went out to buy some bits from the market, but he was here most of the day.' He touched his index finger to his cheek. 'Let's see, who else can speak for my innocence?' The finger traced his hairline. 'Oh yes, my pot collector and cleaner, Ray Adams. He was working today.' He looked straight into Banham's eyes. 'Let me find this killer,' he said softly. 'No one messes with my girls.'

'She wasn't one of your girls,' Alison said. 'She had left.'

His cold eyes burned into her. 'Temporarily.' He picked up a pencil and tapped the palm of his hand. 'She went to do a theatre job. Most of my Marilyns are models and actors; they all come and go.' He laid the pencil down with great care. 'Two of my best Marilyns.' He shook his head slowly and repeated, 'No one messes with my girls.'

'Have you any idea who might want them dead?' Banham asked.

Chang tidied the papers on his desk into a pile. He looked up. 'When I find this killer, he'll wish you'd found him first.'

'Did Sadie Morgan have any boyfriends?' Alison asked.

'She was having it off with my doorman,' he said, his tone edged with scorn. 'Johnny Gladman.'

'You don't approve?' Banham questioned.

'She deserved better.'

'You, for instance?' Alison pushed. Chang just smiled.

'Have you found the husband?' he asked. 'He bruised her beautiful face, in here. There are witnesses. Ask me nicely, I could find it on CCTV.'

'We'll wait,' Banham rapped.

Chang opened the door and stood waiting for them to leave. 'It may take a while. Why don't you have that drink?'

'I'd rather talk to Johnny Gladman,' Alison replied.

Chang made a little mocking bow and led the way out into the club. The same Elvis impersonator was now crucifying *Crying in the Chapel.* Alison spotted Ray Adams washing down tables, a roll-up cigarette in the corner of his mouth and eyes nearly out on stalks.

Gladman wore old jeans and a black t-shirt; the suit jacket on top obviously belonged to someone else – it was far too tight. His hair was still in plaits, held at the nape of his neck by an elastic band. His entwined hands lay on the

135

table, but he struggled to keep his dirty fingers still.

'You were very friendly with Sadie Morgan, weren't you?' Alison asked after a few uncomfortable silent moments.

There was something about him that didn't add up. He had been done for drug dealing, yet his face was careworn rather than the rough gauntness she would have expected in a small time estate dealer. He spoke softly.

'She was my friend, yes.'

'More than a friend.'

'No.'

'Rumour has it you were,' Banham pushed.

'Rumour has it wrong.'

'Did you know Lily Palmer?' Alison asked him.

'Yes, she worked here until a few weeks ago.'

'She's dead.'

He looked stunned.

'Did you know her well?'

'No.' The colour had left his face and his eyes were half-closed.

'Where were you between four and seven today?' Banham asked him.

There was a pause. 'Home. I live in the cottage at the back. I'm the caretaker here.'

'Anyone live with you?'

'My brother Otis.' He paused. 'Some of the time.'

'Was he with you today?'

'No, today I was alone.'

'Otis was involved in a stabbing at St Abbot's school last year,' Banham said. 'What do you know about that?'

Johnny looked puzzled. 'His friend Felix was stabbed.'

136

'Felix Greene.' Banham's tone hardened. 'And he won't say who did it.'

'It wasn't Otis,' Johnny said quickly. 'He was his friend, man.'

'Where is Otis now?' Banham asked.

He became noticeably nervous. 'He's out. I don't know where. I never know where.' His eyes reminded Alison of an animal caught in a car's headlights.

'You should know,' Alison pushed. 'He's only fifteen.' Johnny shrugged. 'He goes out with his friends. That's all I know.'

'I need to talk to him,' Banham said.

'What about?'

'Felix Greene.'

'I'll tell him.'

'Do that.' He handed Johnny a card. 'Tell him to call me, and tell him if he doesn't, I'll come looking for him. All right?'

'That stabbing was nothing to do with Otis,' Johnny said, suddenly sounding stronger. 'He wasn't even there when it happened. You've got that all wrong.'

'Just pass the message on,' Banham told him.

'Meanwhile,' Alison said firmly, 'we're investigating another murder. Can anyone else vouch for your whereabouts this afternoon? As your brother isn't here.'

Johnny looked nervous. 'Someone here might have seen me. I don't know.'

'The side entrance from your cottage leads to the road,' Banham said. 'If you'd gone out that way no one here would have seen you.'

Johnny didn't answer. Eddie Chang was approaching

137

with Terry King.

'I've found some CCTV footage going back a month or so,' Terry said, handing Alison a pile of DVDs. 'Bruno and Sadie are on there a lot.'

Eddie sneered at Johnny. 'You and the husband having a few ugly rows too.' He began to walk away.

Johnny's face took on a greyish tinge.

'Mind if we take a look around your cottage?' Banham asked casually.

Eddie stopped. Johnny looked at his back. 'Unless you've got a search warrant you'll have to ask Mr Chang.'

'No problem,' Eddie turned and smiled his rattlesnake smile. 'But you will need a warrant. That might be difficult on a Sunday night. See you tomorrow, perhaps.' He looked at Alison and added, 'If you can persuade a magistrate to let you harass an innocent citizen.'

Terry was instructed to see them out, or more likely to make sure they left the premises. He was dressed in a purple floral corduroy skirt that finished just below his knees, a light- coloured blouse under a pink cardigan, low-heeled shoes and dark glasses.

'How is your face? Alison asked him as they headed for the door. His nose was still swollen and shiny purple bruising showed around the glasses.

'Getting better thank you,' he answered curtly.

'How did you get on with Lily Palmer?' Alison asked him as they reached the end of the dingy passageway.

It was hard to make out his eyes, but he was clearly uncomfortable with the question.

'To be honest I didn't like her much. I thought she was a bitch. She was unkind to me.' His heavily pencilled eyebrows moved. 'But that doesn't mean I'm glad she was killed. Eddie just told me,' he added quickly. 'Lily was a good Marilyn, but she wasn't popular. Sadie had that extra vulnerable quality. People liked her.' His voice dropped. 'I cared for Sadie. I'm so sorry she's dead. But Lily...' He sighed and shook his head.

'They talk to you, don't they?' Alison pushed. 'All girls pour their hearts out to their hairdresser.'

Terry was about to answer, but Eddie Chang suddenly appeared at the end of the passageway. Terry opened the door and ushered them into the street. Chang disappeared.

'You were saying?' Alison stood on the threshold, a hand holding the door open.

'Sadie had husband trouble,' Terry said softly. 'Check out the tapes I gave you. I wouldn't be surprised at anything he did. He was from Sicily.'

'You think Bruno could be responsible for both the murders?' Banham asked.

Terry looked uneasy. 'Lily knew a lot about him and Sadie. He has connections in Sicily, that's all I can say.'

'You've got my number from last time,' Alison reminded him quietly. 'Call me if you think of anything else. Or just if you need to talk.'

As they walked back to Alison's badly parked car, Banham called Crowther. 'Still nothing back from Forensics,' he said, clicking his phone shut.

'The post-mortem should turn something up,' Alison said. 'The same bruising pattern to both their faces suggests the same killer.' She looked at Banham. 'But you're right – something doesn't add up.'

'Why would Bruno kill Lily?' Banham said. He stroked

139

his cheek. 'I need to shave.'

'I like the unshaven look.'

He slipped an arm around her waist. 'Let me take you home and cook you dinner.'

'Not yet. We need to think. What had Lily got over Bruno? Besides knowing he hit his wife? And the poker in her anus – what was that about?'

'Someone who can't perform sexually? Banham suggested.

'Eddie Chang got very shirty when I asked if he was in love with Sadie.'

'Or Terry King?'

'There's Gladman too.'

'One of them killed the women, and the others are his alibi.'

'Question is which one?' Alison pointed her key at the car. 'Then again, maybe there's a killer out there who we haven't thought about. Maybe Millie Payne is right, and we should be widening our search. There could be people who are so obsessed with Marilyn Monroe that they hate anyone trying to imitate her.'

'That's why I think we should let Millie go undercover. She already has a job there – we should make use of it.'

'I'm worried for her safety. She's keen and gullible. That's not a good mix.'

'We could send Andrew Fisher in with her; he's besotted. They've already been seen in the club together, and he can take care of himself and her. If our killer's in that club we have to dig them out – we've only got three days to the CO19 raid. Time isn't on our side.'

'I'll think about it.'

'Whoever it is may be planning to kill again.' He opened the driver's door for her. 'I have to talk to Bobby's headmaster. I need to see what he has to say about Otis Gladman and the knife attack on Felix Greene. I'll do that in the morning, then join you later.'

'No problem,' she said gently. The post-mortem was in the morning; he had obviously changed his mind about attending. 'I'll fill you in when you get back.'

He slid into the passenger seat beside her, pushed her hair off her face and kissed her tenderly on the forehead. 'Venice,' he said. 'Something to work towards.' He kissed one of her eyes and then the other. 'I'd like to cook you dinner, then give you a bath and put you to bed.'

For a moment there was nothing she wanted more. But she pulled away. 'I have to go back to the office for a bit. I need to get my head around a few things.'

At the station she went straight to the incident room and tuned into the CRO files. First she looked up Terry King. Terry was registered as a man. He was a transvestite – possibly even a trans-sexual, a man who wanted to be a woman. That was a motive in itself. Marilyn was an icon of femininity, enough to make anyone jealous, especially as Eddie Chang, Terry's lover, was obsessed with her. Terry had been in and out of youth offenders institutions during his teenage years, for drug pushing, aggravated burglary and car stealing. His last offence was in 1995, when he was fifteen. He hadn't served time in an adult prison.

Johnny Gladman had been done for small time drug dealing last year; he was given a suspended sentence, but hadn't been in front of the courts since.

Eddie Chang's list of youth convictions was as long as his arm, and he had been in Feltham YOI at the same time as Terry King. But he hadn't been charged with anything since 1989.

It was hard to believe. The man was the biggest drug baron in South London, a known arms dealer, a smuggler of immigrant minors who he abused and sold into prostitution – and no one had managed to prove it. Well, he was in for a big surprise. She couldn't wait to see his face after the raid, when they charged him with so many offences that he'd be lucky to get out before he was pushing up daisies. Maybe a double murder as well if she had anything to do with it.

But he was clearly besotted with Marilyn Monroe; why would he kill his own impersonators? He had been running Doubles for five years and no one who worked there had died; why now?

She needed coffee. She walked into her office, the small space behind a partition in the incident room. If she was going to sit up half the night reading criminal records and watching CCTV of Bruno abusing Sadie Morgan, she needed a strong pot of the Arabica Banham had supplied when he bought her the machine.

The next thing she remembered was the smell and sound of coffee beans being ground. The records were all over the floor, and the red On light of the office DVD player was flashing. Banham was spooning coffee into the machine.

She sat up, trying not to yawn. 'I thought you weren't coming in till later.' She pushed her knuckles into her eyes. 'I must have dropped off.'

'I rang your flat. I was going to come and pick you up. When I didn't get an answer I figured you'd probably stayed here, but I thought I'd better check. Milk?'

'Oh, er, no.' She took the cup he held out. The coffee was hot and strong, just as she liked it. But she wished he would stop trying to look after her.

Bobby wasn't keen, but when Banham arrived he was ready with his school bag and a brave smile.

'You won't let the big bullies hurt Bobby, will you?' Madeleine said when he picked her up for a hello kiss.

'There are no bullies,' Banham said stroking his adored niece's long golden hair. 'No one's going to hurt anyone.'

'Yes, there are, Uncle Paul.' Madeleine was quite insistent. 'They pick on him because you're our uncle and you're a policeman. Naughty boys don't like policemen, do they?'

Banham was lost for words. He hugged Madeleine close and set her down on the doorstep. 'Come on, champ,' he said, holding out a hand to Bobby and trying to sound upbeat. But it wasn't easy.

Bobby said nothing in the car. When they reached the school gate, he got out, shook Banham's hand in place of a hug, and ran off with his school bag and jacket hanging untidily from his shoulder. Banham watched him join a group of boys of his own age. Within seconds he was kicking a ball and running around.

A large poster at the edge of the playground drew Banham's eyes: the forthcoming knife and gun amnesty, appealing to everyone to hand in their weapons. Someone had slashed a huge X across it, and scrawled in large red letters NO CHANCE.

It was eight-twenty. The assembly bell would go in

twenty minutes. Wasting no more time, he headed for the headmaster's office.

Mr Lyons, the head, seemed as concerned about the problem as Banham was.

'This gang culture,' he said, rubbing his glasses with a handkerchief. 'I wish we knew how to tackle it. Remember that Muslim boy last year? Beaten and hospitalised, and we never found out who did it.'

'The Felix Greene incident was similar,' Banham 'No one saw – or no one's telling.'

'The lad says he remembers nothing.' Mr Lyons shook his head in disbelief. 'The word is Otis Gladman did it, but we all find that hard to believe. The two boys were inseparable. They even live in the same block of flats.'

'Flats?' Banham frowned. 'Are you sure? I thought Otis Gladman lived with his brother in the cottage behind Doubles club?'

Mr Lyons pulled a register from a drawer in his desk and flipped it open. 'No, he lives on the Bay Estate. He and Felix used to go to and fro together on the school bus.'

'Who does he live with?'

'His brother Johnny is down as his next of kin. I believe he's Otis's only relative. The mother died a year ago, and there was no father.'

'How did the mother die?' Banham asked.

Mr Lyons stared at him. 'Don't you know? She was shot, gunned down in the street, outside the shopping parade on the estate.'

Banham did remember; it was on his patch. He just hadn't associated it with the Gladmans. A forty-two year old Grenadian woman was gunned down in broad daylight in a busy shopping centre; no witnesses came forward and no one was ever charged.

'A street shooting like that would have made national headlines a few years ago,' Mr Lyons said sadly.

'I'd like to talk to Otis Gladman,' Banham said after a few moments' silence. 'Can you pull him out of assembly?'

'I doubt he's here,' Mr Lyons told him. 'He hardly ever turns up. I've sent notes and texts to his brother, let the LEA know, even informed Social Services, but nothing has been done. There's a backlog, they say; other maters take priority.'

'My interest in this is personal as well as professional,' Banham said. 'My nephew Bobby Banham attends this school. I think he's being threatened. I'd like you to keep an eye on him, and get back to me, let me know who is frightening him.'

'It's common, I'm afraid. Since the stabbing a lot of the younger boys are nervous. We do our best, try to make sure they always leave with someone, and keep telling them to come to us if anything is bothering them. What more can we do?'

The man slipped his cuff back and checked the time. But Banham wasn't done. 'You can keep your ear to the ground. I'm not prepared to take any chances with Bobby's safety.'

Mr Lyons sighed. 'If Felix Greene won't tell us anything, I can't exclude anyone. It's your job to find out what happened, not mine.'

'Oh, I intend to. But I'll get nowhere without your full cooperation.'

'You'll have it.' Mr Lyons was on his feet and walking to the door 'We can only do our best. If it's not knives it's screwdrivers.'

The man offered his hand and Banham reluctantly shook it. It wasn't his fault; he was doing what he could.

The assembly rang as Banham passed the playground. Bobby ran with a few others to get into his class line. He seemed happy enough. Then Banham noticed an older boy staring at Bobby; he realised that Banham was watching him and averted his gaze.

Banham walked to the far side of the playing field before looking back. The older boy had joined his own line, and was joshing with some boys his own age. Banham told himself he had to let Bobby stand on his own two feet.

He still waited until the class lines had filed into the building before heading off to the car.

Isabelle Walsh was wading through the mounds of reports on her desk. Crowther sat at the desk in front of her, getting an update on the forensic situation from Penny for the morning meeting, and taking the opportunity to sweet-talk his girlfriend. It was really getting to Isabelle.

What was it about Crowther that women found so bloody irresistible? His mass of untidy dark brown curls reminded her of Denis the Menace, and his home-knitted striped child's jumper had probably shrunk in the wash. His clothes never fitted properly, he didn't own a comb, yet all she could think about was getting back into bed with him.

This wasn't supposed to happen. Men fell for her, not the other way round. She was gorgeous, with large blue eyes and shiny shoulder length hair that was a natural dark brown. Today it was pinned up in a French plait with the sides curling down over her face. She was dressed simply, in body-hugging jeans and a clingy, lemon roll-neck jumper. Heads turned wherever she went – yet this tiny toerag at the desk in front of her had ditched her, and she had to sit here rifling through reports on what time people in the houses around the park went to bed while he sat in front of her muttering sweet nothings to his current woman, who he was now two-timing with PCSO Millie Payne.

The only good thing about the day was that Alison had made a large pot of really good coffee and told them all to help themselves. As she poured herself a cup she glanced at Crowther. His hand was in the air, waving at her. This was unbelievable: he actually expected her to bring a cup for him too. And while he was on the phone to Penny!

Rise above it, she told herself. She poured another cup and carried it carefully to his desk. If only he knew how she had to fight the urge to pour it over his head. He put his hand over the mouthpiece and winked at her. 'Thanks, babe,' he said.

Did he have a nerve or what?

It was a couple more minutes before he put the phone down. 'Are you going to tell me the news before the meeting?' she asked.

'Ballistics have confirmed the bullet found in Sadie's bag matches the gun found in the park, the Astra Cadix.'

'Question is what was Sadie doing with it?' Isabelle said.

'There are prints on it, but it hadn't been fired recently.'

Alison came out of her office and stood in front of the pictures of the dead girls. The room fell quiet.

'OK, what's new?'

'Penny just rang,' Crowther said. 'The only DNA they picked up at the Sadie Morgan crime scene belongs to the

PCSOs,'

'No particles of Sadie's skin on the footpath?'

He shook his head. 'There's a footprint which matches Millie Payne's shoes.' 'Payne by name, pain by nature,' Isabelle scoffed.

'So we're no further forward,' Alison said.

'Perhaps she had a stalker too,' Isabelle suggested. 'She might have borrowed the gun for protection.'

Alison nodded. 'I think we have to assume the two murders are linked. I suppose that's progress of a kind.'

Monday was always a busy day for Stars and Types, the celebrity lookalikes agency, but today they were especially stretched. Marilyn Monroe lookalikes seemed to be in big demand. Marilyns always made money, in films or television commercials. Girls who could sound like her too, and imitate the famous childlike, breathy American twang, were popular for voice-overs. The local Doubles club provided no end of work for them, as waitresses and sing-alikes. Marilyn was more popular now than in her lifetime.

Today Doubles was auditioning new Marilyns, and the agency had sent everyone they had. The queue of hopefuls stretched right along the street and around the corner, and it wasn't getting any shorter. As fast as they left, more wannabe Marilyns arrived.

Mouth was watching, unnoticed behind the broad trunk of a huge, ancient fir tree on the other side of the road. Now, which Marilyn to go for? It made a person giddy, all these women pretending to be Marilyn Monroe.

How did some of them have the nerve? One was fifty if

148

she was a day; her thighs were uglier than the trunk of the fir tree.

Mouth hadn't found the right one yet. No one out of this lot deserved to die like Monroe. A grubby shirt sleeve wiped away the sweat brought on by a combination of nerves and excitement. The costume stank, and the wig still felt like a dead rat. Mouth leaned back against the tree until the sweating subsided. Then she was there. She had just walked up and joined the queue.

She was perfect.

The first things Mouth noticed were the red stilettos. Then the legs: seamed stockings, exactly right. She wore a flared dress, not unlike the one in *The Seven Year Itch*, the film in which the goddess herself stood over a fan which blew her white pleated skirt up in the air.

This would-be Marilyn had a tiny waist and a perfect cleavage, and a face that at the right angle could *be* her; she even had the black beauty spot just above her mouth. She was the one. All Mouth had to do was set it all in motion.

The girl couldn't be allowed to move out of sight, yet it was vital not to be seen, at least not yet. Mouth went back behind the tree, watching as the queue moved; how clever to think of the newspaper to hide behind; it was easy to peer over the top and watch her as she drew nearer to the audition. Mouth knew she'd be chosen.

She entered the building and Mouth waited patiently. When she came out she clutched a piece of paper. She had got through; she would be a Marilyn.

Or would she?

She walked away, and Mouth followed her into the next street. Now it was time to make a move.

149

'Excuse me.'

She looked up, startled. Her eyes were huge and blue, just like Marilyn's.

'I saw you go into the audition. How did you do?'

'Who are you?'

Stuck up little cow. Why didn't she just answer the bloody question? Mouth knew the answer anyway. 'I work for an advertising company, and I wondered...'

But before the sentence was properly finished she turned and walked away.

Bitch.

She was going nowhere, though she didn't know it yet.

A bus came along as she walked to the corner of the road. Mouth panicked for a moment. If she boarded, it would be gone too quickly and the chance would be lost.

The bus was a 47. Her delicate hand with the bright red nail polish reached out and hailed it. Mouth watched as her crisp, cotton dress disappeared inside and the door closed behind her.

Mouth ran, panting with exertion and frustration; that awful sweat was breaking again. The chance was gone, and she had been perfect.

Mouth wanted to be sick, then almost cried with relief. A taxi was coming down the road and the For Hire sign was flashing.

CHAPTER ELEVEN

Alison tried not to breathe in the sickening smell of putrid flesh overlaid with disinfectant. She turned her head away, and only heard the sound of the saw ripping into the greying flesh, spilling blood that pooled into the sluice below the gurney. She turned back to see Michael, the assistant, remove Sadie's heart and put it aside to be weighed and dissected.

Another assistant arrived with a bag of sandwiches for every-one's lunch. Alison had a strong constitution, had seen over a hundred murder victims and attended countless post-mortems; now for the first time she felt queasy and swallowed down the bitter taste of bile. She was suddenly aware of the embarrassment poor Banham suffered, and how powerful guilt was. It clung to her now, creeping and embracing her like a weed choking the life out of healthy plant, making her doubt her own judgement. Could she have stopped the second murder?

Michael was sawing into the top of the head as if it was a boiled egg. Alison concentrated on the label around the ivory toe, identifying the corpse as Sadie Morgan. When the brain had been removed, Alison allowed herself to study the remains of the bloated face. A lot of skin was missing from the nose and cheeks; she had been dragged a fair way along the ground. Chances were high then, Alison thought, that she was killed quite near the alleyway where they found the bag; she was probably targeted and followed. It could well be the same stalker, whatever Banham thought.

Heather Draper, the pathologist, was gowned in green overalls and blue gloves. She spoke softly into her dictaphone as Michael finished weighing the brain.

One of the CID detectives took the opportunity to move in and photograph the face close up.

The sawing, peeling back of the skin and removal of more organs seemed to go on longer than usual today – or perhaps it just felt that way to Alison. Finally Heather turned to her, holding a hair between a pair of tweezers in her blue-gloved hands. She carefully put it in an evidence bag and handed it to the exhibits officer.

'Suffocation and asphyxiation,' she told Alison. 'That was in the windpipe. The killer could have had a fur coat, or it may have come from a glove, or maybe an animal. I hope that helps.'

'There were ducks in the pond where she was dumped,' Alison commented.

Heather shook her head. 'That's Penny's territory, not mine. I'll let you know the contents of her stomach later. There's the edge of a footprint on her face too. I can't say whether that came before or after the suffocation.'

'Anything about the shoe it came from?' Alison asked.

'We've sent the outline over to Penny.'

Michael moved back in and began to sew the opened body up with black thread. Alison closed her eyes; no need to watch this part.

Her thoughts drifted back to Banham, and the situation they had made for themselves. She had long accepted that he would never get over Diane and Elizabeth; would she be able to go on living with that? Did she even want to? She had always seen herself as a career girl, not the type to settle down. Perhaps letting him get too close was a mistake for both of them. She wanted to progress in the force, and he needed someone who could devote more time to him.

Lily Palmer's body was wheeled out and unzipped. Alison gave herself a little shake. Back to the job in hand.

Once again a smell of stale meat rose from the sluices as the electric saw opened the cranium and Michael removed her brain. As he cut into Lily's young, flawless body and removed her stomach and heart, Alison kept swallowing back bile. It scalded her throat like a finger jabbing into her, asking the question, could she have prevented this?

'She hadn't been dead long when she was found; rigor hadn't set in,' Heather said. 'The poker up her anus caused some bleeding.'

'So it was done before she died?' Alison asked.

'Or within moments. The sphincter muscle is torn – normally there would have been more blood from that. I'd say it happened just after death.'

'The killer was angry, then,' Alison said, half to herself. 'Why? What had she done?'

She thanked Heather and was about to unzip her forensic overall when the pathologist turned, holding up her tweezers again. 'Another hair, caught between the front teeth. Give it to Penny.' She carefully placed it inside another evidence bag.

'The same as the first victim?' Alison asked.

'Looks identical,' Heather said. 'And Lily Palmer wasn't found in a duck pond.'

The bus stopped right in front of the taxi and the girl stepped off.

'Pull over!' Mouth screamed, flinging a twenty pound note at the driver for the fare and waving the change aside. What was money?

She walked away past a parade of shops, stiletto heels tapping on the pavement. Luckily Mouth knew this area. Imagine if the chosen girl had lived the other side of beyond? She could hardly walk in those high shoes. That amused Mouth; little did any of them know they might need to run!

Mouth wore boots, easy to run in. They hurt like hell, too, when pressed into a face.

An alleyway between the shops led to a small side street that joined the one the girl was heading for. Mouth made use of the short cut, legging it quietly and quickly, until only a few yards separated them. Mustn't be seen, but mustn't lose her. She had that sexy Marilyn walk; her curvy figure wiggled sexily in the figure-hugging blue and white dress. Mouth could almost hear the fabric rustling. Just thinking about that pillow brought a rush; oh, the sense of power when they surrendered to it and fell with a thud as the life was squeezed out of them.

A man was coming towards her. He obviously knew her; he waved and called, 'Amy!' Then big arms slipped around her shoulders, and they walked on together up the hill and down the side of a house.

Mouth seethed as the man put his key in the front door. They were walking in, together, a happy couple.

Not for long! This was the chosen one; she wasn't going to get away. All Mouth needed was an opportunity.

Alison stood in front of the whiteboard. She had trouble telling which girl was which as she relayed on the findings of the postmortem, until she concentrated on the pictures taken at the murder scenes.

'There was a common denominator: two identical hairs, one on each victim. Sadie's was her windpipe, Lily's caught in her teeth. Perhaps the killer wore a fur coat or gloves.'

'A marabou boa?' Crowther suggested. 'All the Marilyns at the club wear red marabou boas.'

A spatter of applause went round the room at that, and a few jeers of *Know-All Col*, Crowther's nickname.

Twenty-four detectives were now on the case, some seconded in. All were aware that they needed a quick result. The long-planned raid on Doubles was only two days away; a lot hung on catching this killer quickly. Alison was already feeling the mounting pressure.

'No sign of sexual intercourse with either victim,' Alison said. 'And yet the poker in the anus has something phallic about it, doesn't it?'

'Perhaps our killer's impotent,' Isabelle suggested.

Banham had hung back, letting Alison take the lead. Now he took a step forward. 'I think there may be a copycat killer,' he said. 'The second murder was more frenzied, the first suggests a calculated killer. I'm not at all sure it's the same person.'

'The second one could have been in more of a hurry, guv.' This was Crowther.

'What about the hair?' Alison said.

'Like I said, the feather boas,' Crowther pointed out. 'Both girls wore them.'

'Or…' Banham picked up a marker pen and pointed to a picture of Eddie Chang.

'Wears a toupée!' Crowther said triumphantly. 'He's a known killer, and would stop at nothing. He's got to be top of the list.'

'How do you know he wears a toupée?' Isabelle said derisively.

'Millie told me.'

'Oh, that's gospel then.'

'She's sure.' 'She's slept with him,' Isabelle goaded him. 'How else could she be *sure*?'

'Enough, you two,' Alison said. 'OK, we need hair samples from everyone at the club.' She pointed at two detectives standing close to the door. 'You go with Crowther. Make sure you include Chang and Terry King and Gladman.'

'Ma'am.'

Banham tapped the board. 'We can't discount Bruno Pelegino, husband of the first victim,' he said. 'We've got motive and opportunity: Sadie was trying to divorce him, and he's on CCTV watching her as she left the club.'

'He has an alibi for both murders,' Isabelle said sadly. 'We had to let him go.'

'His alibi is as weak as dishwater. He's still a strong suspect for Sadie.'

'But not Lily Palmer.'

'That's my point,' Banham persisted. 'Two killers.' He pointed to the picture of Johnny Gladman. 'Small time dealer, done last year. Seen on CCTV giving Sadie something; he says it was a small amount of grass, but we found none in her bag.'

'Motive there is jealousy,' Isabelle said. 'Perhaps she turned him down.'

'Terry King.' Alison pointed to the strange-looking man dressed as a woman. 'Lives with Eddie Chang in a homosexual relationship. Maybe resents all the Marilyns, because of Chang's obsession with them.'

'The poker would fit with that,' Isabelle agreed. 'But has an alibi. He was at the market buying sequins, and has receipts to prove it.'

'Oh, come on, who gets receipts from a market trader?' Banham scoffed. 'That's Chang's doing – he could provide receipts for buying immigrant women.'

'Terry King's a wig dresser,' Isabelle pointed out. 'Around hair all the time.'

Alison nodded. 'We need to find out more about that hair.' She looked across at Crowther. 'We're waiting on Penny again.'

Crowther gave a quick nod, took out his phone and left the room. Alison gave the rest of the squad a swift recap, and had just finished when he returned.

'Penny's got a positive ID on the fingerprints on the knife, and the gun found in the first victim's bag. Wait for this: the prints belong to Otis Gladman.'

The silence was electric. Every eye was on Banham.

'Guv, it gets better.' Crowther paused until he was sure he had everyone's attention. 'The blood on the knife. It's Felix Greene's. This is the knife that stabbed him.'

Banham closed his eyes and steadied himself on the edge of the nearest desk. 'We'll bring him in,' he said to Alison. 'I've got an address from the school.' He looked across at the two detectives by the door. 'And when you go back to the club to get hair samples, you can arrest Johnny Gladman for withholding evidence. He told us his brother lived with him, and he doesn't. And make sure he's got his mobile on him – if we have trouble finding Otis we'll use it to trace him.'

Crowther grimaced. 'Ma'am, Chang is getting nervous. If we go in with our size twelve boots this morning, we could blow the CO19 operation.'

A couple of detectives sniggered. 'Size twelve! Size six, more like,' Alison caught. She glared around the room and everyone fell quiet again.

'This is a double murder enquiry,' Banham said. 'That has to take precedence.'

'There are other lives at risk if we rattle Chang's cage,' Crowther disputed. 'The girls he's bringing in may be illegal immigrants, but they're only kids. I wouldn't want their deaths on my conscience.'

Banham gave him a long look. Crowther continued, 'There is a solution, guvnor.'

'I'm listening.'

'Millie Payne. She's already got her feet under Chang's table. I think we should let her stay there, undercover.'

Alison shook her head. 'She's made enough mistakes already. She doesn't have the experience.'

There was a pause. Then, 'I'm with Crowther,' Banham said. 'I think we should run with it.'

Alison closed her eyes. Dammit, why did he have to keep questioning her decisions? It was her case; she needed to get on with the job without interference.

But she had seen that steely glint in his eyes too many times. He wasn't going to let this go. 'OK, 'she said reluctantly. 'But I want someone in there with her.'

'Andrew Fisher can go – he can make out he's her boyfriend,' Crowther said. 'He'll look out for her – he's dots about her.'

'I've got a better idea.' Alison looked at Isabelle. 'You'd make a fabulous Marilyn. They're auditioning today.'

Whistles of approval came from every corner of the room, but Isabelle looked horrified.

Crowther put his two penn'orth in. 'She's got no tits, and a voice like a foghorn.'

'She doesn't have to sing,' Alison snapped back.

Isabelle shook her head firmly. 'I wouldn't get the job. And even if I did, I couldn't do it.'

'Oh, come on, Isabelle,' Alison coaxed. 'You're beautiful, you could dress as Marilyn any day. And you're a damn good detective; you'd be such an asset to the case.'

Isabelle still looked dubious.

'How about applying to be a Marilyn lookalike waitress?' Banham suggested. 'Then you wouldn't have to perform. You'd have more freedom too, walking around the club serving drinks.'

'Colin's right,' Isabelle said. 'I don't have the boobs for it. They'd turn me down.'

Alison threw a look at Crowther, willing him to say something encouraging.

'You could always wear a padded bra,' he said sarcastically.

'It's not about size – it's quality that counts,' Alison said. 'Isn't that what you're always boasting about Crowther?'

More guffaws ran round the room.

'Those PCSOs may be brave, but they're completely unqualified for the job,' Alison went on. 'We need an experienced officer in there.' She looked Isabelle in the eye. 'You're the best, and you'd make a great Monroe. Tell me you're up for it? Please?'

Isabelle hesitated, but gave a little nod. She turned to face Crowther, and said in a voice that carried right round the room, 'I wouldn't jest about *little* if I was you. And I don't mean your height.'

There was more laughter, and Crowther came right back at her. 'Well, you've certainly got the mouth to play Monroe!'

'Oh, give it up, Crowther,' Alison said wearily. Just when she needed Isabelle to be on top form, he had to go and stick the knife in. He could be such a shit; he'd used Isabelle, and the entire squad knew how much he'd hurt her. Why couldn't he just leave it alone?

Isabelle was glaring at him furiously, hurling things into her shoulder bag.

'You'll do great,' Alison said to her. 'You've got all afternoon to practise. Get Millie to help you – she knows all the moves.' The girl had her uses after all, she reflected. 'The auditions go on till about seven tonight,' she finished.

Crowther was looking serious for a change. 'Just a thought, ma'am,' he said, carefully avoiding Isabelle's irate glare. 'She'll have to change into costume with all the other girls, so she won't be able to wear a wire. She could put my number in her phone, and tag it Mother. The she can call her mum when there's something to report.'

'Isabelle?' Alison queried.

'I suppose so.'

'Fisher can wear a wire,' Banham pointed out.

160

Isabelle nodded. 'He has to do as I tell him, OK?'

Alison smiled. 'OK,' she said.

The opportunity Mouth had been waiting for came sooner than he expected.

The happy couple walked together up the path to the house; the man went ahead and put his key in the front door. She went inside, but he didn't follow. Instead he headed for the path at the side of the house, leading to the garden. Mouth watched him go into the shed at the end of the small lawn and reappear with a large shovel.

A smile spread across Mouth's face as the man propped the shovel against the garden table and returned to the shed. This kind of opportunity didn't happen every day. It was risky, but Mouth thrived on risks.

The man emerged from the shed backwards, struggling with a heavy lawn mower. Mouth sprinted across the road and leapt over the six-inch wall into the garden, grabbed the spade in gloved hands, raised it in the air and smashed it down hard across the man's skull. He staggered, but didn't go down; he turned round and got a good look. That brought a rush of adrenalin; Mouth lifted the shovel again and smashed the bastard's face. He staggered, and blood shot out of his nose and landed on Mouth's sleeve. Another hard blow and his face looked like a watering can that had sprung a leak; blood spilled out in all directions. He flung his hands up, trying desperately to defend himself and crying like a miserable fox under attack from a pack of savage hounds. Then he fell to the ground.

A second later his hand shot out, grabbing at Mouth's ankle. Mouth leapt back and jumped on the hand, and gave him another whack across the head in case the bastard thought of trying to get up. The man didn't move. Luckily Mouth was wearing those boots: handy for giving a good kicking. Shame not to use the opportunity. The eyes first, blinded already from the blood pouring from the head. The head started jerking, and a phlegm-like substance flew out from somewhere, landing on Mouth's jeans. Then the head lolled to one side, and the man lay still. Mouth thought that was it, but planted first one boot then the other on his face just to make sure. The cranium crunched and the jaw disintegrated. A final kick in the ear guaranteed that the interfering bastard would never get up. Things were suddenly going well.

But what happened next threw everything out of kilter.

She was wearing nothing but a lacy pink thong and a tiny pink tank top that finished delicately just above her tummy. She stood in the doorway looking as scared as hell; she had obviously heard the rumpus and come down to see what was happening.

She looked terrified, and started to retreat inside the house. As Mouth advanced, she tried to push the door closed. The thought that she might dial 999 started the adrenalin rush again. Mouth dropped the spade and shoved a blood-spattered boot against the door before she could shut it. She started to yell, and pushed the door against the boot. Mouth pushed back, the door gave way, and both feet were in the hall. She stood frozen to the spot as the door slammed shut.

Now perhaps she'd show some proper respect.

Then the bitch started to run. Mouth grabbed her bare ankle and pulled her back down the stairs one by one. God, she could scream! A good belt across the side of the head soon shut her up.

Another clout made sure; her head banged hard against the wall, and she fell still. Mouth peered at her; her neck hung awkwardly, and she appeared to be unconscious.

Good, Mouth thought, now she wouldn't do all that resisting stuff. This one had to look like a proper sex attack. That would really throw the stupid coppers.

Mouth tugged clumsily at her lacy vest. The woollen gloves were full of the bastard's blood and bits of stone and stuff from the garden spade. But after a few moments the vest covered her pale, shiny, ringletted hair and revealed her pink nipples. They weren't pert and sticking up like earlier; they looked squashy and swollen against her breasts. Mouth reached into a pocket for a flick-knife, and slit her at the side of one nipple. The blood spurted straight away. That did the trick; the nipple no longer looked offensive.

She deserved a lesson for all that howling and screaming; the knife touched her upper lip for a second, dug into the faded red pout and drew a cross from one side of the mouth to the other. The blood was quite funny; it shot up like a small leak in a perished shower hose.

That was when the stupid cow woke up, opened her eyes wide, then rolled them back. Now she was ugly. Bloody hideous, in fact.

Mouth left her slumped on the stairs and went in search of a pillow. Disappointingly there was no resistance when it pressed down across her face. That was almost the best part: the kick to the back of the knees to subdue them, the bluish tinge that spread as they fought to stay alive; that was fun. But this one was over in an instant. Blood had stopped

163

pumping from the nipple and the lips. She was well and truly dead – the main point of the exercise even if it hadn't exactly gone to plan.

Mouth was anxious that some nosy passer by might snoop round the side of the house and see the bastard lying in a lump on the back lawn. He was dead too; his own fault, stupid fucker shouldn't have got in the way. Mouth had to get out of here now, and hope for the best.

Banham noticed the used condom left rotting along with a few old dog turds – at least, he hoped they were from dogs. It was enough to put anyone off having sex, he thought.

Alison was attaching a crook lock to her car then double-checking she had locked it. He stood at the entrance to the run-down Bay Estate waiting for her to catch up with him.

Banham wanted Otis Gladman in the interview room. His prints on that gun had opened up a whole new line of enquiry, and he was concerned that it could put Bobby at risk. The truth of the Felix Greene stabbing had yet to be discovered, and it was far from impossible that it was connected to the murder of the two women.

Cigarette packets, fast food containers and scraps of paper blew around in the wind as they walked into the estate. They had decided to park some distance away; it wasn't often that a car left around here was intact when its driver returned, even after a short visit. The residents of the estate recognised the police a mile off, and would delight in removing the wheels of Alison's Golf.

'It's the tenth floor, I'm afraid,' Banham told her. 'You can bet the lift isn't working.'

'No problem for me,' she said. 'It's you that doesn't use your gym membership.'

Banham sped off and started running up the graffiti-clad, urine-smelling concrete stairwell, avoiding the rubbish that littered the steps. But Alison was waiting on the tenth floor with a smile on her face when he breathlessly caught her up.

'I'm nearly ten years older than you,' he said by way of an excuse.

'Six years, and you take too much sugar in your coffee.'

She was in great shape, mainly because she had the self-discipline to go to the gym after a long day on a case. It only served to make him feel overweight and inadequate.

A couple of black youths in hooded sweatshirt tops and sagging jeans sauntered toward them. 'Who you looking for?' one asked. Banham spotted a shiny handle sticking out of the boy's waistband. He was carrying.

'I'm looking for Otis Gladman. His brother sent me.'

The youth shrugged. 'Never heard of him. He don't live round here.'

The second youth folded his arms and leaned back against the brick wall. Within a few seconds three more youths had appeared out of nowhere, and stood beside the first two.

'He lives at 102, I think,' Alison said. There was menace in the air, and she knew there might be even more boys close by. Her police radio was in her pocket, but the sight of it could start a riot on an estate like this.

She set off for the landing, but the first youth took a step and blocked her way.

'I said he ain't here.'

Banham backed towards the stairs. This wasn't safe for

165

either of them. But Alison decided to front it out. 'He told me I could get something if I came to his flat.'

A taller, brown-skinned boy stepped toward her. 'You're not listenin', lady. He don't live here.'

He glanced down at his belt. The handle sticking out looked as if it belonged to a meat cleaver.

'OK. We made a mistake.' Banham put a hand on Alison's shoulder. As he turned to leave, he came face to face with another half-dozen teenagers, all in baggy jeans and hoodies, with dark bandanas over their faces. Shiny blade handles were evident in every belt.

Banham stood for a second, his heart thumping hard against his ribs. He wasn't concerned for himself; his fear was that Alison would come off badly if something kicked off and there was no time to call for back-up. He tried to walk past the boys, but they blocked him. He deliberately avoided their eyes, slowly walked around them and started to walk down the stairs, with Alison close behind.

They hadn't reached the bottom of the first flight when all hell broke loose. A hail of bricks and bottles flew after them, and shouts of 'Pigs!' and 'Fucking feds!' followed. Banham ducked to avoid a couple of bottles, and as he turned to check if Alison was OK, he saw a small table hit the back of her head and bounce off her shoulder. It smashed to the ground, and all his instincts dragged him towards the stairs.

'Leave it!' Alison shouted. 'Do you want to get yourself stabbed?'

He opened his mouth to protest, but she cut him off. 'We'll sort it later. I'm fine.' She clearly wasn't. 'Let's get out of here. We'll call for back-up when we get to the car.'

166

They ran.

As soon as they reached the safety of the road, Alison called for uniform back-up. She knew only too well that the youths would have scattered by the time they got there, but they had to try.

'I bet one of them was Otis Gladman,' Banham said, clicking his seatbelt as Alison started the engine.

'We need Crowther and a fleet of uniforms with dogs,' Alison said. 'If anyone can sort that little lot out, it's Col.'

'I'm not risking Crowther,' Banham said. 'He's too hot-headed. We'll get Johnny Gladman to bring the lad in. Otis is under sixteen; he should be under parental control.'

His phone rang and he stabbed the Speak button. It was Crowther.

'Guv, there's been another murder. This one's a double.'

CHAPTER TWELVE

The news of the double murder had reached Crowther through his mate DI Charlie Sandford, who was based a couple of miles from the scene. Charlie had spoken to a neighbour; it seemed the female victim, Amy Bailey, had been to audition at Doubles; Charlie had called Crowther right away. It was only a matter of minutes before the news was confirmed by HOLMES, the police computer system which connects similar murder cases in different parts of the country.

'That's it, then,' Alison said as Banham clicked his phone off. 'The Doubles undercover job is off.'

Banham's phone rang again. This time it was Isabelle. He listened in silence for a few moments, then said, 'Are you sure? You can pull out – no one will think the worse of you.' He listened again, said 'OK, then,' and switched off.

'She's determined to go in now,' he told Alison. 'Crowther tried to talk her out of it, but now there are three lookalikes dead she's not having it. The PCSOs too. They want this joker as much as we do.'

'I know. But I'm not happy about it. I still don't think Payne and Fisher are up to the job.' Alison stepped on the accelerator and lurched over a succession of speed bumps.

'Isabelle is sharp as a razor,' Banham assured her. 'If she has the slightest doubt about their safety she'll pull out.'

'I wish I felt so confident.'

'Christ, Alison, stop, the lights are red!'

She slammed her foot on the brake and the car juddered to a halt. 'Can you please stop behaving like my father?' she said through gritted teeth. 'They were amber.'

'Sorry. I'll let you kill us next time. How's your shoulder?'

'It's fine,' she said curtly. 'What about the raid on the Bay Estate?'

'It's in hand. They're taking a dog patrol; the lads are bound to leg it. Wait till I get my hands on the bastard that threw that table at you.'

Isabelle had dressed herself up in a clingy black skirt with a slit at the side, seamed stockings and stiletto-heeled shoes she could barely stand in. She stood in a long queue of hopefuls, all auditioning for a chance to be Marilyn Monroe. And she hadn't the faintest idea what to do.

All the same, another woman had been killed, and if stopping the killer meant getting a job as a sodding Marilyn Monroe impersonator, that was what she'd do. Millie had tried to coach her in the sexy pout and provocative wiggle, but she had to rush off so she wouldn't be late for her own rehearsal at Doubles.

If they pulled this off and it led to a result, when the next sergeant's post became available perhaps she wouldn't be overlooked. A Marilyn cocktail waitress was her best bet, as Banham had suggested; that would allow her to walk freely about the club under the pretence of serving drinks.

Her normal dress code was jeans and trainers, and she felt ridiculous, not to mention uncomfortable, standing here in a skirt with a side-split as high as her thigh. She had borrowed it from one of the public relations secretaries at the station. Millie had lent her the stockings and suspender belt and the high-heeled red shoes, and she wore her own cropped red bodice top, the one that emphasised her tiny waist. Crowther had paid her a back-handed compliment; he liked the cropped top, he said – it would draw attention away from her tiny bust. She wanted to hit him, until he smiled that smile.

The only thing that kept her here was the knowledge that there was a third lookalike victim. She agreed a hundred percent with Alison that Millie Payne was too inexperienced and too keen: not a good combination for working undercover. Isabelle knew all the dangers of the snake-pit she was going into, but feared Millie hadn't a clue how ruthless Eddie Chang was. Millie was besotted with Crowther and wanted to impress him. Crowther, of course, was taking advantage.

Andrew Fisher was less of a worry. He lacked experience too, but he was obviously sweet on Millie Payne, so he'd watch out for her. That was all Isabelle wanted; it left her free to move about the club and find out exactly what was going on.

But she had to get the bloody job first. She was a small-bosomed brunette with about as much idea how to wiggle her arse as her pet tortoise Lettuce; yet she if she was turned down Andrew and Millie would have to pull out too.

She stared at the other girls in the queue. Any one of them could be the next victim. Now there were three, it was clear that the common denominator was this club. But she needed to be very, very careful not to screw things up for CO19. Gang crime involving knives and guns was increasing, and if those Mac 10s made it out there, there would be carnage in no time. Eddie Chang had no respect for human pain or life, and he stood to make a packet; if he got a sniff of the fact that she was CID, the whole operation was blown.

But she wanted him behind bars. Besides, she had passed her sergeant's exams, and getting promotion meant getting noticed. This was her chance and she was going to grab it.

The queue was moving quite quickly, and she was now inside the club. She glimpsed Millie sitting in the far corner, having her wig checked by Terry King. Terry was top of her own list of suspects, alibis or no alibis. He so wanted to be a woman. His lover Eddie Chang was obsessed with the sexy, feminine Marilyns; that must really make him jealous.

Chang looked the prospective Marilyns up and down as they paraded past him. Some he dismissed like sides of meat. Others were asked to get up on the stage and do the Marilyn walk. Perverted bastard, Isabelle thought; he was really enjoying the legs and suspender belts and bum-wiggling. Was he gay, or was he bi? Or was the Marilyn Monroe thing just a fetish? The club was a shrine to the star; there were even photos pinned up by the door of the real Marilyn's grave, with one solitary red rose on it. So would his Marilyn worship make him more likely to kill the girls that pretended to be her, or protect them?

The queue moved again. Now she could see what she was in for. Terry King had finished combing Millie's wig, and was handing each girl a numbered card. Then the girls walked past Chang, and if they weren't dismissed, they had to get up on the stage and do the wiggle and a short impersonation. Eddie Chang was like a child in a sweetshop.

171

Only a handful of girls remained before her in the queue, and she still hadn't a clue what to do. She suddenly realised what stage-fright was. Her only hope was to flirt and be charming; she was good at that. That, she decided, was what she would do, no matter how his narrow slanted eyes and ugly twisted mouth revolted her. Terry King's reaction would be interesting too.

Terry handed the girl in front of her a card. The girl wiggled past Chang on to the stage and started singing *I Wanna Be Loved By You.*

Isabelle noticed the mobile in Eddie Chang's hand start to flash as the girl sang. He hardly took his eyes off the girl as he checked the screen and put the phone to his ear.

'To what do I owe this privilege?' Isabelle heard him say. What was wrong with a simple hello? He seemed to be interested in what the caller had to say, although his eyes never left the girl. After a few seconds he burst out laughing. 'My ship has come in once again,' he said, clicking his phone shut.

The Marilyn on stage ended her audition with a thrust of her hip, a turn of her shoulder and the famous '*Ooh Boopy Doo*' in a breathy American whisper.

Eddie clapped his hands. 'Yes, yes, yes,' he said. 'You've got a job.'

Terry King gazed at her with loathing. He pushed a card in Isabelle's direction without even a glance. The girl stepped carefully off the stage, and Isabelle closed her eyes. Showtime.

Make or break time, more like.

She glanced at the card. There was no number on it after all: just handwritten words.

172

There were police blockades at both ends of the road, and Forensics had already arrived. Hordes of blue-overalled officers were inside the sealed-off area that was now the scene of a double murder. Some took photographs; one held a camcorder; others crawled on all fours, looking for any tiny particle of evidence around the garden where the young man lay with his skull broken open.

Two officers were erecting a white scene-of-crime tent which stretched across the garden, up the path to the house and as far as the blood-splattered front door. The door was open; the tiny hallway which was also splashed with blood, as was the staircase where the female victim lay.

DCI Charlie Sandford was talking to Banham. He turned to greet Alison as she approached. 'Congratulations are in order, I hear,' he said. 'DI Grainger now.'

'Thanks, Charlie.'

'Her name was Amy Bailey,' Sandford told her. 'I called you because there was this note saying *Your Turn Now* with her body. Col Crowther had filled me in on your current case, so I put it on HOLMES and rang your nick.'

'Much appreciated,' Alison said.

'I've already talked to a neighbour Amy spoke to this morning. Apparently she was going for an audition at that club, Doubles. Fancied herself as a Marilyn Monroe lookalike.'

'Did you find out anything about the boyfriend?'

'He moved in quite recently. Love's young dream, according to Mrs Thing.'

'Looks like the boyfriend got in the way,' Banham

suggested. 'It all looks very messy,' Alison said. 'There could be DNA – we got some from the last murder, so we may even get a match.'

'Don't rule out a copycat,' Charlie Sandford warned.

'I'm not ruling anything out. I'm going to cross all my Ts and dot all my Is. Looks like I've got a serial killer for my first case.'

Charlie was looking at her appraisingly. 'Did I mention you're looking great?'

'Thank you.' Alison hid a smile and avoided Banham's eyes.

'Not a lot more we can do here,' Banham said brusquely. 'We'll have to wait for the forensic report.'

He hadn't ventured into the house, she thought. Crowther had told them what to expect: the female victim was upside down at the bottom of the stairs, her face covered in blood and mucus and bone splinters. Her bleached blonde hair was rust-coloured with dried blood, and the stairs and walls were pretty foul as well.

Charlie Sandford was still looking at her. 'Let me know when you're going to the gym again,' he said. 'Perhaps we can work off our excess energy together and talk over the case.'

Alison opened her mouth to reply, but Banham was there before her. 'All her free evenings are taken,' he told Sandford curtly. 'We are off to Venice together as soon as we catch this killer.' He flicked a glance at Alison. 'You'd be better using your excess energy in finding out who killed these poor people.'

Johnny Gladman hadn't spoken a word since Crowther had

brought him in. Crowther wasn't a bit surprised. He had obeyed Banham's order to go to the club to take hair samples from the staff including Chang and Terry King, and against his better judgement he had arrested Gladman for lying about his brother. Chang had flown into a rage and told Johnny not to say a word until his solicitor arrived.

Johnny knew how to obey orders too.

Crowther got the message loud and clear: Johnny Gladman was one of Chang's people. The chances were high that his brother Otis was too. The team Crowther had sent to scour the Bay Estate for Otis were having no luck. Crowther was not a happy bunny.

He decided to leave Johnny Gladman to cool off in a cell, and called his snout Ray Adams for a meet.

Adams sounded terrified. 'Gimme a break. Eddie Chang's going spare now you lot have taken Gladman,' he said. 'He knows someone is feeding information to the cops. As soon as he finds out it's me, I'll be singing soprano.'

'Be there!' Crowther barked. 'You know the score. I need some answers.'

This case was getting to him. Talk about a baptism of fire. He'd been in on this CO19 operation from the start six months ago, and now they were so close; the raid was only two days away now, and they were up for a major result. Getting Eddie Chang off the streets would mean big brownie points for everyone involved.

But now these murders were complicating matters no end; Crowther didn't doubt Chang was behind them, but they left the whole operation a lot more fragile.

That was why he had pushed Alison to let Millie go

under-cover in the club and he was quite sure she was capable. All the same, it was bloody dangerous; he knew why Alison was reluctant. The forensic results told them Otis Gladman was involved; now they needed to find out how.

More important, they needed to find him.

The back door of Crowther's car opened and Ray Adams crawled in. The tic above his mouth was working overtime. The pressure was obviously getting to him too.

Good. Two of the officers in that club were Crowther's friends. He needed to know what they were facing.

'There's been another murder of a Monroe girl,' Adams told him, wiping a shaking hand across his mouth.

'So it's got back to Chang, has it?' Interesting. 'Or did he have something to do with it?'

Ray Adams shook his head. 'He didn't even know this one. She didn't work at the club. She went for an audition today.'

'So how did he find out?'

'He got a call, about an hour ago.'

'Who from?'

'I don't know, Mr Crowther. I heard him telling Terry King, that's all. He still reckons Pelegino is behind it. He says he only left him walking because you lot knew he was after him. When everything's gone down on Wednesday, he's having Pelegino taken out.'

'So the pick-up of the Ukrainians is still going ahead?'

Adams sniffed. 'You've pulled Johnny in,' he said licking his mouth. 'That's made Mr Chang nervous. It's on for Wednesday night at the moment, but he'll pull the plug if you're still holding Gladman.'

'Said that, did he?'

'Said it to Terry King.'

'Did he indeed?' Crowther paused. 'Terry King lives with Chang, doesn't he?'

'Yeah. So what?'

'Bet he, or fucking *she*, doesn't like those Monroe girls.'

'He liked Sadie.' Ray looked at him. 'I dunno what you're thinking, but Terry wouldn't upset Mr Chang. He wouldn't dare, specially now. He's feeling the heat from you lot. Those girls from Ukraine are supposed to get picked up by me and Gladman. If you keep Gladman locked up, it ain't gonna happen, and Mr Chang won't be happy.'

'We're not happy either,' Crowther said. 'Another woman has been killed.'

'Chang says it's Pelegino,' Adams insisted. 'He says he's gonna find him and hang his balls on the door of the club.'

'When did he say that?'

'After Lily Palmer.'

Crowther fell silent. Eddie Chang was a clever bastard and liked to play the police; but he regarded those girls as his personal property, and if he knew for sure that Pelegino had killed them, his balls would already be hanging out to dry.

Either Chang didn't know for certain – or he killed them himself, or at least arranged it. But why? And the gun in Sadie's handbag – what was that about? Otis Gladman was another unknown quantity; Sadie had the bloodstained knife with his prints on it; where did come into the whole mess? Was he working for Chang?

Trouble was, Ray Adams wasn't the brightest coin in the collection; a lifetime of drugs had seen to that. Crowther decided to lead him.

'Who did Lily Palmer not get on with?'

Ray wiped his runny nose with the back of his hand. 'The other Marilyns. She weren't popular. Sadie and her were rivals. Johnny was going out with Sadie.' He sniffed and blinked. 'And Lily knew about Sadie's trouble with her old man.'

'And Terry King, how was he with Lily?

Ray turned out his bottom lip. 'Didn't like her. He liked Sadie though.' He shook his head. 'I get confused sometimes which one's which.'

Now there was a thought to ponder. 'Is there anyone else who might do that?' he asked slowly.

'What?'

'Muddle up the girls.'

Ray shrugged. 'Anybody might. All the bleedin' same, aren't they?'

'What about Otis Gladman.'

Ray shrugged again. 'Maybe. He's a bit loop-the-loop anyway. They say he stabbed a kid at his school.'

'Who's *they*?'

Ray's cheek twitched again. 'Your lot! Who else?' He tugged at his earlobe. 'He nicked a gun from Mr Chang's cellar.'

'The cellar? The club cellar, you mean? I thought the firearms were kept in the cottage.'

'Some. He keeps some stacked in the cellar too.'

'Are there any there now?'

'Some, yeah.'

'What sort?'

'Not sure.'

178

'Well, find out. I need to know. Has he still got Astra Cadix hand-guns?'

'Yeah, I think he's got them.'

'In the cellar or the cottage?'

'Dunno. I'm not allowed in the cottage.'

'So you don't know if Otis Gladman lives there?'

Ray rubbed his face. 'He did. But not any more. Mr Chang banned him when he stole the gun. He had to go back to the Bay Estate. But he has to live with Johnny officially, like, cos he's only a kid.'

'So he fends for himself?'

'I suppose so. Mr Chang doesn't like him hanging around, says he's trouble.'

'I need to know where to find him.' Crowther was losing patience. 'That's what I pay you for. Find out. Call me, later tonight.'

Ray nodded and put his hand out for the note.

Crowther ignored it. 'And keep your fucking ears pricked. Three women are dead and I need some answers. Tonight.' He watched Adams in the mirror, scrubbing his face with the back of his hand. He needed his fix.

'I have to go back before they miss me,' he said pathetically.

'OK.' Crowther handed him the twenty. 'Ring me later, yeah?'

'Are you still on for Wednesday, then?'

'Probably.'

'Will you let me know when you're going in, so I can make sure I've no gear on me?'

'Yes,' Crowther said after a beat. 'Might even be a bonus in it for you if we catch Chang red-handed.'

179

Adams opened the car door quietly and let himself out. Crowther drove off, but pulled over when his mobile began to flash Penny's number.

'Babe?'

'Got an interesting development on the hair in the windpipe of the victims,' she said. 'It's animal hair, not human. Some kind of feather; I tested for duck. I'm waiting for the green light on that.' There was a pause. 'But Lily Palmer wasn't anywhere near any ducks.'

'Could it be marabou?' Crowther asked quickly.

'Could be, yes.'

'All the Marilyn Monroe girls wear marabou feathers,' Crowther told her. 'Interesting to see if the third victim has a feather particle. She had only auditioned.'

'We won't know for a day or so. But just in case we draw a blank on that – did Sadie Morgan have any pets?'

'Lily had a cat. I don't know about Sadie. I'll get Eric to ask the mother.'

'Something else interesting – the handwriting on the two notes. Each note was written by two different people.'

'So there could be two killers, like the guv said?'

'No – two people on each note. Whoever wrote the word *Now* didn't write *Your Turn*. The Os are different. The person who wrote the second O is probably left-handed. The handwriting expert reckons the second O starts from the left and the first one starts from the right. Definitely two people.'

Back at the car, Banham's phone bleeped to tell him he had a message. It was Crowther; Banham called back, and the young sergeant rapidly ran through the new information he'd squeezed out of Ray Adams. Banham cut him short. He wanted to call the station for an update on the uniform team sent to the Bay Estate to find Otis Gladman.

'They legged it, sir,' the desk sergeant told him, 'but the report says one of the youths called another one Gladdy.'

Banham thanked the sergeant and clicked the phone shut. 'Looks like he is living on the estate,' he said to Alison. 'He's probably in a squat somewhere. The gangs look out for each other.'

'So the stabbing of his friend might have been down to gang rivalry?'

'Gangs. No wonder Bobby's scared out of his wits. He hates school now, and he used to enjoy it.' He closed his eyes. 'Crowther's going to get Gladman to write something, to see if he's left-handed,' he went on after a few moments. 'His clothes have already gone to Forensics, although if he's Chang's poodle he'll have changed them. We won't have any problem getting a warrant now, though – he'll have dumped his other clothes in the cottage.'

'If it is his writing, it will still only prove he wrote the notes, not that he killed them. And no note was found with Sadie.'

Alison braked sharply and leaned on the horn as a car pulled out from a side road. Banham swallowed hard. 'I still think there are two killers,' he said.

'Maybe Chang ordered the murders, and different people carried them out.'

'Let's hope Isabelle got the job.'

'I'm still not sure about those PCSOs,' Alison said.

'Isabelle's very experienced,' Banham said. 'She came a very close second to Crowther for the sergeant's post. But it's not my case; it's your call. If you're not happy, pull them out.'

'Eddie Chang knew about Amy Bailey's murder this afternoon. How long before he susses there are three undercover police in his club?'

'Your call,' Banham said again. 'But we only have two days. After Wednesday night the club will be shut down, and Eddie Chang will be behind bars for a very long time.'

'Only if CO19 find something.' She slowed for a traffic light. Banham squeezed her arm. 'It's dangerous and complicated, but keep your nerve. This time next week, we could be in Venice.'

Alison rubbed her eyes. There was a long way to go before that.

'You need something to eat,' he said, stroking her knuckles with his thumb.

She pulled away from the lights. 'After the evening meeting.' He checked the time. 'We've got half an hour. Let's drop in on Lottie, then I can check on Bobby. It's on the way.'

Lottie was cooking chips. The smell wafted through the hallway and out through open window beside the front door. It made Alison hungry.

'You skip too many meals,' Banham said. 'I'll have to get Lottie to feed you up.'

Alison bit back the sharp retort. She'd have to nip this in the bud. She would never cope with being mothered, especially where food was involved.

'I'm sure Lottie has enough on feeding her children,' she said, trying not to sound snappy.

The door opened to reveal Madeleine, who shrieked with joy. 'Uncle Paul! Mummy, it's Uncle Paul! And Alison!'

Banham scooped her up in his arms. 'Where's Bobby?' he asked, digging in his pocket for the box of Heroes he'd bought at a petrol station shop. 'Half of these are for him.'

Lottie appeared at the end of the hall. 'Have you come for tea? It's only chips and sausages. There's plenty. Not very glamorous, but it's Bobby's favourite.'

'I think Alison would like some chips,' Banham said.

Alison was embarrassed. 'I really don't want to put you to any trouble.'

Lottie winked. 'My pleasure. Um, Bobby's in the lounge watching a film. He's been crying again. Bad day at school.'

'I'll help with the tea,' Alison said tactfully, following Lottie into the kitchen.

'Uncle Paul's got us Heroes,' Madeleine squealed as Banham carried her into the lounge.

'For after your tea,' Banham reminded her, depositing her gently on the carpet. Maddie poured the sweets all over the floor and opened two, popping them both in her mouth at once.

Bobby was lying on the floor on his tummy watching *Shrek*. He showed no interest in the Heroes, usually his favourite sweets.

Banham touched his shoulder and felt his back arch with tension. For a few moments they all watched the green monster romancing the princess.

'Did you see Otis Gladman today?' Banham asked casually.

'He doesn't go to school any more.'

183

Banham frowned. After a few seconds Bobby went on, 'One of the big boys said he'd left, but… but…' His eyes filled up and he swallowed hard. 'But he's watching me…'

'He got a letter,' Madeleine butted in through a mouthful of chocolate.

Bobby scrambled to his feet and ran out of the room. Banham heard his footsteps in the room above. Madeleine's hand crept into his and he pulled her close to him.

After a long few moments Bobby returned, and handed Banham a screwed-up piece of paper. It had been folded in four, and on one quarter in block capitals was printed PIG'S BOY. On the other side Banham read *If you squeal*, then underneath in different handwriting, *Your Turn Next*.

Banham's heart slid into his stomach.

CHAPTER THIRTEEN

Two minutes later, twenty-four hour surveillance was in place for Lottie and the kids.

'Stay in the house,' he told the children. 'I'll be back tomorrow with a bucketload of DVDs.' His face was grave as he said to Lottie, 'I'm the other end of the phone, twenty-four-seven.'

She looked horrified. 'You don't think...?'

'No,' Alison cut in. 'Paul is being careful, that's all. You need to do the same.'

'Where to now?' she asked him as they left the forensic lab. He had put the note into Penny Starr's hands himself.

'To find Otis Gladman.'

She opened her mouth to point that that this really wasn't a good idea in his present frame of mind, but the chirp of her phone forestalled her. It was Crowther.

'Isabelle's in,' he told her. 'She's a cocktail waitress.'

'Good. Is she there now?'

'Ask him if there's any sign of Otis Gladman,' Banham said, holding out a hand for Alison's car keys. She tossed them to him; he opened the door and slipped into the driving seat.

'That's why I rang,' Crowther said. 'Penny just told me about Bobby's note. Terry King gave Isabelle a piece of paper just before her audition. It said *Your Turn Now*.'

Alison froze. 'Hang on a tick,' she said, and passed the phone to Banham. He listened for a few seconds as Crowther repeated his news, then turned the ignition key. 'We're on our way to the club. I'm going to find that little toerag.'

'Hold your horses, guvnor,' Crowther said. 'We've got Johnny Gladman here. Otis's number is in his mobile; we can find out exactly where he is from here. Best you don't go to the club and rock any more boats. According to Millie, it's usually Johnny who helps with the auditions, not Terry King. I've got Johnny to write *Your Turn Next* on a piece of paper and sent it over to Penny. Isabelle's going to try to get hold of the note she was given and bring it back to the station with her. Penny can't get the handwriting analyst in before tomorrow anyway.'

'I want to question Otis Gladman,' Banham yelled into the phone, swinging the car round in a u-turn. Alison took a deep breath as he pulled out into the main road without looking and received a tirade of car hoots. Talk about the pot calling the kettle black, she thought.

'His phone is switched off at the moment,' Crowther answered warily.

'That's it, then,' Banham said. 'He could be hiding in the cottage. That's where we're going.'

He clicked the phone shut and threw it into her lap. Why would Otis be at the cottage, Alison thought; it wasn't even logical. But there was no talking to him in this mood. They drove in silence apart from the horn blasts and shouts as his driving grew more and more erratic. Alison was relieved when they arrived outside the club.

As he drew into a parking spot, she tried again. 'Paul, let

186

Crowther trace him. We can get him picked up properly.'

'His fingerprints are on the knife that nearly killed Felix Greene, and on a gun found in a dead woman's bag. And now he's threatened my nephew. I want him brought in.'

'You're letting your emotions blur your judgement. Nothing will happen to Bobby.' His rage was infectious, though; she took a deep breath to calm herself. 'No one will let it. The house is already under surveillance.' She put a hand on his arm. 'Please, Paul. Be guided by me, just this once. If he's in there, he'll run, and it'll be harder than ever to track him. And the last thing we want is to cock up the CO19 operation.'

His tone was icy. 'You were right, Alison. Business and pleasure don't mix. A week ago you wouldn't have dared speak to your senior officer like that.'

'Oh, wouldn't I?' How dare he pull rank on her now!

'We're going in. We have evidence connecting Otis Gladman to the attempted murder of Felix Greene, as well as to Sadie Morgan's death.'

And if he hadn't threatened your nephew, we'd be back at the station doing the job properly, she thought. But she said nothing. She couldn't let him go in there alone in this mood. She stepped out on to the pavement, resisted the urge to slam the car door and followed him into the club.

Banham ignored the bouncer on the door and carried on walking. Alison flashed her warrant card as she went past; if the bloke had come the heavy, Banham would have knocked him to the ground without a second thought.

Eddie Chang rolled his eyes as they walked into the dimly lit club. Millie was standing by the bar talking to Andrew Fisher; she looked away quickly. Alison could have kicked herself; she should have found some way to let them know there was no need to worry – not that Banham had given her much of a chance to think about anything very much. She had to just hope they wouldn't panic and blow their cover.

She caught sight of Isabelle in a corner of the club; it was dark and she could just about make her out under the glamorous blonde wig and long, clingy dress covered in red sequins. She was serving drinks, and gave no indication that she'd noticed them. Thank goodness for a professional, Alison thought, feeling relieved Isabelle got the job, as well as taken aback at how glamorous she looked.

'To what do I owe this privilege?' Eddie Chang asked, his arms folded across his body and the enormous diamond ring glistening in the club lights.

'Where's Otis Gladman?' Banham barked.

Chang shook his head and smiled. 'Tut tut. Not a good day for the Gladman family. Your pint-sized colleague was in earlier. He arrested Johnny.'

'Where's Otis?' Banham asked again.

'Why on earth would I know? Am I his keeper?'

Alison stepped forward, trying to give the impression that at least one of them had a cool head. 'He lives in the cottage with Johnny,' she said. 'Can we have a quick look, just in case he sneaked in without you knowing?'

'Be my guest.' Chang waved a flamboyant hand at the back door. 'I presume you've got that warrant?'

'We can get one.'

'Then I suggest you do exactly that.' He stepped in front of them, blocking their path. His tiny eyes reminded Alison of Lily Palmer's Siamese cat.

188

'Something to hide?' Banham asked.

'You know me. Clean as a whistle.'

'If you see Otis tonight, please ask him to call us,' Alison said patiently. 'It's important we talk to him.'

'Why would I see him? Surely you know I've barred him from the club. Why don't you ask his broth...?'

Banham grabbed him by his silk lapels. 'Just tell him.'

It was getting late when they got back to the station. Crowther was in the incident room, waiting for them.

'Johnny Gladman's solicitor insisted I charge him or let him go,' he said. 'I had to return his possessions including his phone. Didn't matter, though – we've got a trace on Otis's phone and we'll be able to pinpoint the kid when he switches it back on. Meanwhile all spare units are out looking for him.'

'I'll stay here,' Banham said. 'I want to be here to interview him. You two go home.'

Alison and Crowther exchanged glances.

'They may not find him tonight,' Alison said carefully. 'Why don't you go and be with Lottie and the kids?'

'I'll stay,' Crowther offered. 'I'm waiting for Penny. She's working on the double murder and might even have some results soon. And I've put a call out to my informant, Ray Adams. He's not answering his phone.'

'We've just come from Doubles,' Alison said. 'Adams wasn't there.'

'Get a warrant arranged for first thing in the morning,' Banham said to Crowther. 'I'm going to tear that cottage apart if Otis Gladman doesn't show up tonight.'

'CO19 won't like that,' Crowther said flatly.

Banham stared at him in disbelief.

189

Thanks, Col, Alison said silently. 'We won't find anything, guv. Otis knows we're on to him. If he was there he'll have moved on now.'

Banham face was a deep purplish-red. 'He's a murder suspect,' he said through clenched teeth. 'It's our job to solve that murder. Get a warrant.'

That was it, Alison decided. Enough was enough. 'I'm sorry, Paul, but you have to back off,' she said with authority. 'This is my case, and I think your emotions are clouding your judgement. I'm asking you to go home and leave it to us. We'll keep you up to speed.'

He stared at her. She held her ground and stared back. They had clashed before, but never like this.

It was Crowther who broke the electric silence. 'She's right, guvnor – you are emotionally involved. You don't want to put our officers at risk.'

Banham closed his eyes.

'It feels like sitting on the edge of a knife,' Crowther continued. 'But all we can do is sit out.'

The angry colour had drained from Banham's face, but his expression was still impassive.

Alison knew she was on thin ice, but she held her own. 'We've already got four murders,' she said. 'We can't afford any more mistakes.'

She was putting her neck on the line. Whatever their personal feelings, he was her senior officer. But he was out of order, his emotions were getting the better of him. 'If Otis is involved in this case,' she said firmly, 'or responsible for the stabbing at Bobby's school, or the note, we'll prove it. That's a promise.'

Banham's shoulders slumped, and Alison felt the tension

give way with an almost audible twang. 'I'll come home with you, if you want,' she heard herself say.

Crowther frowned and shook his head.

'No,' Banham said. 'You're right. We can't afford to make any more mistakes.' He walked heavily to the door and closed it behind him.

Alison blew out a long breath. 'That took a lot of guts,' Crowther said. 'But it was the right thing to do.'

It was nearly midnight and Isabelle's feet were killing her. She had just given a cocktail order to the Marilyn barmaid, and was waiting with her tray.

Eddie Chang had been watching her all evening. When she auditioned for him, he hadn't seemed very interested in her; she had given him a real sob story to get the job – she told him she was desperate, needed money, and any job at all would do. Somehow it had worked; he hired her, but only to wait tables and clean the loos. That suited her just fine; it meant she could move around the club without arousing suspicion.

Terry King fitted her out with a wig and dress, and she had been working for the last six hours with only a twenty-minute break, in crippling high heels. Fortunately it was Monday, Marilyn Monroe tribute night; she had the opportunity to chat to the other Marilyns. She'd watched Millie Payne's Marilyn impersonation too, and she had to admit the girl was sensational.

She was booked to work until two o'clock, and Crowther had given her two tasks.

She had to get down into the cellar and check it out for firearms; and she needed to get back the note Terry King

191

had given to her just before her audition. He had taken it from her as she was introduced to Eddie Chang, and given it to the girl behind her in the line.

Everyone's attention, including Eddie Chang's, seemed to be on the stage. The impersonator was about to appear for her next Marilyn Monroe set. The cellar door was ajar. Perfect. She nipped through it and down the steep stairs as quickly and quietly as the bloody shoes would let her.

She moved swiftly round, opening and shutting boxes and crates and feeling the wall for concealed hiding places. The floor was concrete so there was nothing under that. She found nothing. She made her way stealthily back up the stairs, and nearly jumped out of her skin as a shadow appeared at the top by the door. She pressed herself against the wall and waited for it to pass. It moved closer. Then a head appeared around the cellar door.

Millie Payne.

She continued up the stairs and walked past her into the club with a quick smile. Millie was learning.

Her drinks order was lined up on the bar. Millie came up to her as she put the glasses on her tray. 'Everything OK?' she asked quietly.

Isabelle nodded and rearranged the drinks. 'I need the find the note Terry gave me in the audition line.

'Note?' Millie looked blank.

'It says *Your Turn*. He gave it to each girl just before she auditioned. Any idea where it might be?'

'In the changing room, I should think,' Millie answered doubtfully. 'That's where Terry spends most of his time. I'm in there a lot at the moment. Shall I see if I can find it?'

'Do you think you can do it without getting caught?'

'If you can keep Terry occupied out here for a bit, I can try.' A note of excitement crept into Millie's voice. 'What were you looking for in the cellar?'

The barmaid came back with the rest of the drinks for Isabelle's order, so she didn't have to answer. She filled her tray and headed back to the waiting customers. Flirting and joshing as she served them was the easy part of the job.

Next time she looked up Eddie Chang was staring at her. He beckoned her over. Her heart hit her stilettos. Please God she hadn't been seen going down to the cellar.

'Something's not quite right about you,' Chang said looking her up and down.

Isabelle pasted a defiant look on her face, but her heart was racing.

'It's your make-up. You need to work on it. Your eyebrows are wrong, and you should have a beauty spot on your top lip to the right of your mouth.'

She was exhausted. Her feet ached, the rough sequinned material was rubbing into her legs, sweat dripped down the back of her neck from the disgusting wig. But she realised this was the best chance she would get. She batted her eyelids and turned on the pathetic act which had got her the job.

'I don't want to let you down,' she said. 'I really need this job, Mr Chang. I'm saving to get some private hospital treatment for my mother. My second break is due; I'm happy to forfeit that if Terry would give me a little time to help me get the make-up right.'

The snake-like face broke into a smile.

She'd done it. She'd fooled him. Terry King would be out of the changing room for twenty minutes: plenty of time

193

for Millie that to find the note, ready for the handwriting expert in the morning.

For the second morning in a row Alison woke to the smell of fresh coffee. Today, though, it was Crowther holding the pot. Banham was nowhere to be seen.

It had been a strange few days. She'd been promoted to DI; her first case was shaping up to be one of the nastiest the squad had ever investigated; she had started and ended a love affair with the man she'd wanted for seven years. And on top of everything, she'd only had about two hours' sleep in the last forty-eight. No wonder her head was spinning.

'Best thing he ever did,' Crowther said, annoyingly cheerful considering it was six o'clock in the morning.

'What?'

'Buying you a coffee machine instead of a plant for your new office.'

'I probably shouldn't have spoken to him like that. He is our boss after all.'

'And you feel guilty because you slept with him.'

As usual Crowther knew exactly what was running through her head.

'Right. I shouldn't have done that either.' She let out a deep sigh. 'I seem to have made a lot of mistakes in my first few days as a DI.'

'He's using that to make you feel guilty,' Crowther told her, wrapping her hand around the coffee cup and patting it affectionately. 'The truth is you were right and he was wrong. He'll realise that eventually, and respect you for it.'

'I'm not so sure.' She sipped the coffee.

'I am,' he said. 'If you hadn't sent him home he would

194

have blown the CO19 operation. What you did took guts.'

'Perhaps.' She took another sip and set the cup down on the desk. 'Otis Gladman can't have gone far.' She combed her fingers through her tangled ponytail. 'I reckon he's still on the estate. He's only a kid. Where else would he go?'

'The place is swarming with uniform. They'll pick him up sooner or later.' He pulled a chair up beside her. 'Isabelle brought the note in last night after she finished at the club. Millie found it in the dressing room. You were asleep. It's gone to the handwriting expert now. If it matches the note Bobby got, chances are high Otis is our killer.'

'He's only fifteen, Colin. Just a kid. What's the world coming to?'

Crowther scratched his neck. 'We had to let Johnny go. The solicitor was giving us grief. We only had obstructing a murder enquiry to charge him with, and it wasn't worth the hassle.'

'If we have him followed, he'll probably lead us to Otis.'

Crowther picked up a felt tip pen and started writing Os on the whiteboard. Alison noticed he was using his left hand.

'You know what I think?' he said, standing back to study his work. 'I think whoever wrote those notes is likely right-handed. They wrote with their left hand to disguise their writing.' He scrubbed out the row of Os. 'Isabelle said Terry King did her make-up tonight. He's right-handed.'

Crowther's phone rang. 'Brilliant!' he exclaimed after a brief conversation.' Otis Gladman has turned his phone off again, but they managed to trace it. He is in the vicinity of the Bay Estate.'

Alison frowned. 'Why turn it off again? Someone must

have warned him there was a trace on it.'

'Ray Adams lives on that estate,' Crowther said thoughtfully.

'What? Ring him, find out where he is.'

'I've been trying,' Crowther said. 'He hasn't answered his phone since I saw him yesterday.'

By six-thirty the incident room was packed. Crowther as he put his head around the office door to tell Alison they were waiting for her.

'Isabelle is like your worst nightmare this morning,' he grinned. 'Her feet are blistered and her legs scratched from the spandex, and she's got a sore arse from being pinched. She's ready to kill someone and says she's putting in for danger money.'

'I won't mention my shoulder, then,' Alison said. Crowther raised his eyebrows, and she remembered she hadn't mentioned it to him. 'The bloody Bay Estate. Flying bricks and a coffee table in the back of the neck. All in a day's work, isn't it?'

His grin grew wider, and he swung out of the office leaving the door open. He always cheered her up. He'd slept even less than she had, in a corner of the office on the grubby floor, but he looked no different from usual this morning. His jeans hung low, revealing his Simpsons boxers, and the elbow of his brown jumper was darned with something that strongly resembled the yarn used in post-mortems to sew corpses back together. Alison smiled. His girlfriend was a forensic officer; maybe it was one of the perks of the job.

Two more pictures were pinned to the board: the

196

savagely beaten faces of Amy Bailey and Joshua Timpkin. The perfect couple, according to friends and neighbours, just starting a life together.

'The killer walked around the side of the house and took a garden shovel to his head in broad daylight,' Alison told the squad. 'Someone must have seen or heard something. This killer is either a professional or a headcase.'

'It looks like the killer was after Amy, and Joshua was just in the wrong place at the wrong time,' Crowther suggested. 'Which implies we're looking for someone who panicked. Probably not a professional in that case.'

Alison stood by the whiteboard studying the pictures of all three women. In life they looked so similar. 'We have a serial killer,' she said solemnly. 'That was the third. The key factor is Doubles. They all worked, or wanted to work, as Marilyn Monroe look-alikes. But why these particular girls? Were they targeted, or unlucky?'

'Could the Marilyn Monroe thing be a coincidence?' one of the detectives asked. 'Maybe they all found out what Chang was up to and he had them killed.'

'Amy Bailey had only auditioned half an hour earlier,' Alison told him. 'It's unlikely she found out anything Chang didn't want her to know just standing in a queue.'

Millie Payne and Andrew Fisher were sitting just inside the door.

'Maybe the killer followed her from the club,' Andrew suggested.

Alison was still looking at the pictures. It wasn't much more than forty-eight hours since they'd pulled Sadie Morgan out of the pond. She gazed at Sadie's water-sodden face, and the sense of failure almost overwhelmed her. It wasn't just the three murdered women; just when she thought she was getting close to Paul Banham, he had gone off on a quest of his own. She felt as if she was drowning too.

Crowther must have noticed. He took over.

'Two of the women had notes left with their bodies, saying *Your Turn Now*.' He held up clear plastic evidence bags containing the notes. 'There's another one which says *Your Turn*, which came from Doubles. Good work, Millie.'

There was a spatter of applause. Alison turned to face the squad and saw that Millie Payne had the grace to look embarrassed.

'Did you get a note when you auditioned at the club?' she asked the young support officer.

Millie was dressed in jeans and yeti boots, with a brown leather jacket zipped up to her neck. She looked from Crowther to Andrew Fisher and back again, then shook her head. 'I didn't audition. Lily introduced me to Eddie Chang. He seemed to like me –asked me to do an impersonation of Marilyn on the stage. I'm a trained actress, so I didn't find it difficult. He seemed to like it, and offered to train me as an impersonator, so I could take over from Lily when she went on tour.'

Alison nodded at Millie and moved on. 'We had to release Johnny Gladman and bail him. According to our informant he is doing the pick-up for Chang, and we don't want to throw any more spanners in the works.'

'I don't know why we brought him in,' muttered Eric, in his usual place at the back of the room.

Alison ignored him. 'We're having him followed, and hopefully he'll lead us to his brother. The blood on the knife

Crowther found in Sadie Morgan's the flat is a match for Felix Greene's, and Otis's fingerprints are on it. The gun as well. Finding him is our priority at the moment.'

'Any chance you might be able to get into the cottage tonight and have a nose around?' Crowther asked Isabelle.

'I'll try.'

Millie suddenly put in her two penn'orth. 'It's a big risk. There's CCTV in the courtyard.'

'I'll make that decision,' Isabelle told her sharply.

Alison sighed. 'Are you all back in the club tonight?'

'If I don't get sacked for kicking some arse-pincher's balls,' Isabelle answered.

Alison smiled. 'Rather you than me.'

'If you do manage a recce on the cottage,' Crowther said, 'I'll need to keep in touch with you.'

'Phone,' Alison said. 'Absolutely no wires; far too dangerous with costume changes.'

'DCI Banham suggested I might wear a wire,' Andrew Fisher said. 'I don't wear a costume.'

'No way,' Alison said. 'You're not halfway experienced enough. Isabelle, did you put Crowther's number in your phone under Mother?' Isabelle nodded. 'Good. You can ring each other as often as you like without arousing suspicion.'

The phone on Crowther's desk started to ring. He picked it up and listened for a few moments. 'We've got a DNA match on Lily Palmer and Amy Bailey,' he said. He listened again, paling visibly. He put the phone down and took several breaths before speaking.

'It's Ray Adams,' he said. 'His DNA is all over the second, third and fourth victims.'

CHAPTER FOURTEEN

Ray Adams lived on the sixteenth floor of the high rise block. Crowther had decided to leave the back-up cars around the corner and try to get to Ray's door before he called them in. That way he reckoned there was less chance of Adams legging it.

Besides, the relationship between police and residents was delicate. A mere sighting of a uniform would start the chants of *Feds* or *Filth*, and that would give Adams a head's start. If he got out of his flat, they were talking needle-in-haystack chances of pulling him in.

Crowther was taking no chances. He was furious with Adams, and with himself as well; it was he who had put the informant into Doubles, and though he knew a junkie like Ray would sell his own mother for a fix, he certainly hadn't had him down as a cold-blooded killer.

'Watch yourself here,' he said to Isabelle as they turned into the estate. 'Some bastard hurled a table at Alison yesterday. We don't want bruises on that perfect body of yours.' Just in case she read anything into the compliment, he added, 'You need to flaunt it at the club tonight. I'm relying on you to find out if Ray Adams has put a spanner in the CO19 operation.'

He pulled the car into a space and turned the engine off. 'Quick and quiet,' he told her. 'And no shouting 'Police' outside his door. If he doesn't answer, we call for back-up then kick the door down.'

He'd obviously been spending too much time with in-experienced PCSOs, she thought, banging his car door shut.

'Hey, don't abuse my car. That door doesn't need slamming.'

'I wish your dick was in it.'

They stared at each other for a long moment. Then his mouth curved into that little boy grin and he said, 'No, you don't. You wish it was in you.'

He was right, but she wasn't going to give him the satisfaction. He looked at her speculatively for another moment, then shook his head and turned away. 'Let's go and get this bastard,' he said.

Two black youths on bicycles rode up to them as they walked towards the flats.

'Want us to look after your car, mister?'

Crowther knew this breed. He had been one himself. His own father had been a renowned villain; when he was killed, young Colin had fended for himself. At nine years old he had wheeled and dealed, washed cars, begged pennies for the guy, bought and resold, staying just on the right side of the law. His mother had breakdown after breakdown and couldn't cope with anything much at all. He had been a tiny kid, and it had been hard; but he got by, and managed to stay out of care, all the time waiting for the day when he could take his school exams and get out and join the police. When the time came, his childhood on the streets made him wise and astute. He understood these kids.

But he didn't like being cornered.

He shook his head.

The kid nearest to him leaned over his handlebars. He

was no more than thirteen. 'I could make your life very difficult, mister. 'My mate's got a gun, see.'

Crowther looked the boy in the eye and put his hand in his pocket. He slowly pulled out a five pound note. 'I'd better be nice to you, then,' he said.

Isabelle wondered if the kid could hear the note of menace in his voice.

'OK,' Crowther went on. 'You can look after my car. If it's well looked after there'll be another of these when I get back.' He dropped the fiver on the ground in front of the bike. 'If it's not...'

He left the vague threat hanging in the air. The boy slipped off his bike and stopped to pick up the note. Crowther put his foot on the edge of it and grabbed the boy by the collar. 'What kind of gun has your mate got?' he asked quietly.

'Little pop-gun. Astra something. Like the car. But he's getting a Mac 10.'

Crowther moved his foot and the boy snatched up the five pound note. Crowther stepped back. 'My car's in good hands then.'

Both boys cycled away at speed. Crowther watched them, arms folded. 'That's Otis Gladman,' he said.

Isabelle's head spun round and she put a hand on her radio.

'Don't.'

'But...'

'Just... don't.'

She dropped her hand. Whatever her personal feelings about Crowther, this was his territory. 'OK. But why didn't you pull him? It won't take him long to work out who we

202

are, and he won't hang around.'

'Oh, he'll hang around. I've told him he'll get more money when we get back. If we arrest him now, we'll alert the whole estate and lose Ray Adams.'

'Banham won't be happy if we lose him.'

'He won't be happy if we lose Adams either,' Crowther said. 'Trust me.'

Crowther lifted his radio and quietly gave the back-up team a description of Otis Gladman's clothes. 'Let's make it snappy,' he said to Isabelle. 'It's sixteen floors. We'll take the stairs.'

They made their way up the filthy stairway, carefully avoiding the bin liners of rubbish which lay rotting at every corner. Isabelle covered her nose with her hand as the stench of urine, shit and putrid food threatened to overpower her.

'The dustmen refuse to come here,' Crowther told her. 'They're afraid of getting stabbed.'

'Wasn't one was thrown over a balcony because he thought some woman had left a manky old chair out for collection? She said he tried to steal it – she liked to sit on it to watch the world go by.'

'Oh, yes, I remember that. Got off, didn't she? Pleaded insanity.'

As they approached Ray Adams's flat, a small crowd of youths blocked their way. Isabelle recognised the two black youths.

'I thought you were looking after my car,' Crowther said to them.

'For a fiver? You're kidding me. We'd rather have the car.'

Crowther showed no sign of fear, but he jerked his head towards a passageway just behind them. Isabelle quietly backed into it and whispered into her radio.

Crowther opened his wallet and took out a twenty pound note. He handed it to the boy. 'Will that do?'

'Take his wallet,' the youth said to the boy Crowther had spotted as Otis. 'And his phone. Gladdy, take his fuckin' phone.'

Otis stretched out his hand. 'You heard, mister.'

At that moment more than a dozen police cars sped into the estate, sirens shrieking. One of the older youths pulled a knife from his boot. 'He's Fed,' he said.

Crowther stood his ground. Behind him twenty or thirty uniformed police were heading for the stairs. Crowther looked straight at the boy holding the knife. He almost felt sorry for him; it was plain that he would rather run than fight, but he couldn't lose face in front of his mates.

A white van followed the cars into the estate and another team of uniformed police jumped out and headed for the stairs.

The boy lunged with the knife but Crowther was quick. He grabbed the boy's wrist and twisted the knife to the ground. The others hesitated as he stepped on the knife and forced the boy's arm up his back, but then they all jumped in aiming kicks and yelling at Crowther. Isabelle ran to his aid just as the first uniforms arrived.

It was all over in a few minutes. Truncheons and knives flashed through the air, some youths legged it and others were rounded up. Crowther emerged with one hand dripping blood and the other gripped around Otis Gladman's ankle. Isabelle jumped in and handcuffed the boy.

'Otis Gladman?'

'Yes.' He wasn't as cocky now. She read him his rights and handed him over to two burly uniforms.

Crowther ignored the small audience on the balcony above and ordered two of the remaining uniforms to break down Ray Adams's door.

The flat was empty.

Isabelle stepped over used needles, dirty laundry and old fast food containers to get to the kitchen. Two bottles of soured milk stood in the fridge, and a wilting cannabis plant stood in the corner.

'He's not been around for a few days,' she said, pulling on forensic gloves and flicking through the debris on the floor. 'Looks like he rents it out as a drug den, to make money to feed his habit.'

'That and snitching lies to us.'

'And killing innocent people.'

They walked back down the sixteen flights guarded by a pair of uniforms. 'Not been a good morning,' she said.

Remarkably, Crowther's car was still intact. 'How's your hand?' she asked. The handkerchief he had tied round his fingers was stained red. 'Will it need stitches?'

'Doubt it. Bit of TLC wouldn't go amiss though,' he said, with one of his little-boy-lost looks.

She took his hand and kissed it gently.

'There, it's better already,' he said with a grin.

'Do you want me to drive?'

'OK.' He pulled his keys from his pocket with his good hand.

'I was worried back there,' she said. 'For your safety.'

Crowther slid into the passenger seat. 'Don't know why. You're next in line for sergeant.'

A flying brick landed on the ground next to the car.

'Leave it,' she told the angry uniformed officer. 'We still need to find Ray Adams. Try to avoid confrontations.'

She fired up the car and looked at Crowther. 'I promise not to tell it was a kid who stabbed you,' she said.

'What happened to your hand?' Alison asked Crowther.

He took Banham's china mug off the shelf and helped himself to her coffee. 'It's nothing. A run-in with Otis's mate.'

'Banham wants in on the interview,' she told him.

Crowther spooned three sugars into the mug and poured a coffee for her.

'He is our senior officer,' she reminded him.

He sipped his coffee and shrugged. 'He's still too emotionally involved. There's a lot resting on this. If he threatens the CO19 op once more, I'm going over his head to get him taken off the case.'

'It's your career you're risking.'

But in all conscience she couldn't disagree with him.

Time to build some bridges, though. She headed out of the squad room and down the corridor to Banham's office.

She knocked; there was no reply. She waited a few seconds, then opened the door. He was sitting at his desk, elbows propped and chin resting on his hands.

She stood in the open doorway, unsure of her welcome. 'I came to say I'm sorry,' she said. 'About the way things are between us.'

'No need. Come on in.'

206

She closed the door behind her. 'But I'm not sorry about what I said last night.'

He fixed his blue eyes on her, as if he was trying to work her out. She took a deep breath. 'Nor am I sorry that I slept with you. I care for you very much.' She swallowed hard. 'I'm in an impossible position. I understand exactly how you feel about Otis Gladman – in your position we'd all react the same way. But it is my case, after all. So I'd like you to leave the interview to me and Crowther.'

His unblinking blue gaze seemed to penetrate her soul. He was angry, but she was determined to stand her ground.

'Yes, *DI Grainger*, it's your case. But I'm your superior officer.' He laid his forearms on the table and linked his fingers without taking his eyes off her. 'And as your superior officer, I would remind you that your priority is finding Ray Adams. His DNA is on three of the murder victims. I want him found and brought in.'

'We've got uniform out all over that estate looking for him.'

'Good. Keep me informed. I visited Mrs Pelegino this morning and took some hair from her cat for comparison with the fibres found on Lily Palmer and Sadie Morgan. It's with Forensics. Would you let me know when those results come through?'

'Sir.' She stood up straight. If he wanted to play this by the book, that was fine by her. As long as…

'I'll be in the interview room with Crowther and Otis Gladman.'

The note was on the table in front of Otis.

Johnny Gladman was there as an appropriate adult, but he

looked almost as scared as his brother.

'This was sent to my nine-year-old nephew,' Banham said.

Even Crowther felt edgy when he spoke in that tone. This was a copper you didn't want to get nicked by.

'Did you send it?' Banham asked, jabbing the air in front of the teenager.

Otis looked at Johnny as if he had the answer.

'He's talking to you,' Crowther snapped at Otis. 'Answer the question. 'Did you send that note?'

Otis was a tall, well-built boy with long dreadlocks like his brother, but right now his brown eyes were wide and bulging with terror.

'Not quite so cocky without your mates to back you up, are you?' Crowther pushed.

'It's my writing,' Johnny said. 'Not his.'

Banham swung round to look at Johnny. 'Go on.'

The beads at the ends of Johnny's dreadlocks scraped on the metal table. The clatter almost drowned out his voice. 'Mr Chang doesn't like his staff talking to the girls when they audition, so I write a note. It says *You're Next*, or *Your Turn Now*.'

'This one says *If you squeal* as well,' Banham said. 'Who wrote that?'

Johnny and Otis spoke in unison. 'I did.' Johnny added quietly, 'Eddie Chang frightened him into doing it.'

Banham stared at Otis. 'Well, you need to be a lot more frightened of me than of Eddie Chang,' he said.

Otis's eyes widened even further.

'Where do you live?' Crowther asked him.

Otis looked at his brother, who was wiping perspiration

208

from his upper lip.

'He asked you a question,' Banham snapped.

'He lives with me,' Johnny said. 'We have a flat on the Bay Estate. I work as caretaker the club, and sometimes I have to stay over in the cottage. Mr Chang won't let Otis stay there with me.' His forehead furrowed and he seemed to be having trouble getting the words out. 'Our mother was killed last year, so I'm responsible for Otis.'

'You leave him on his own on the Bay Estate?' Crowther exclaimed. 'For godsake, he's only fifteen. I'm amazed no one's told Social Services.'

'I n… need my job,' Johnny stammered.

'I do fine on my own,' Otis said defiantly.

'Hanging out with youths with knives? That's your way of doing fine, is it?' Crowther held up his hand, still wrapped in his handkerchief. 'You're lucky I haven't nicked you for this. Yet.'

Otis's eyes opened like saucers.

'Why won't Chang let you live with him?' Banham asked Johnny.

'There are women there sometimes.'

'Women – or girls?' Banham pushed.

Johnny shrugged.

'For the disc,' Banham said.

Johnny raised his hands.

'OK, if you like. Girls.'

'If I like?' Banham snarled. 'If I like illegal immigrant girls, not much older than children, being used for prostitution?' He slapped the table. 'Is that what you meant?'

Johnny nodded reluctantly.

209

'For the disc,' Crowther said. 'Johnny Gladman is nodding.'

'He'll kill me,' Johnny said quietly.

Banham ignored the comment. 'Where is the next batch of these women – girls – coming in?'

'They're here.' He drew a sharp breath, realising he had told them something they didn't know. He shrugged. 'We picked them up from Dover last week.'

Crowther and Banham exchanged looks.

'OK, moving on.' Crowther leaned across the table, pushing his face into Otis's. 'The gun that we found in Sadie Morgan's bag, with your fingerprints on. Where did you get it?'

Otis looked at his brother. Johnny nodded. 'I stole it,' Otis said. 'From the cottage.'

'The cottage?' Crowther questioned urgently. Adams had said it came from the club cellar. 'So there are the guns in the cottage? Where?'

'There's a secret panel,' Otis said.

'Which room?' Crowther barked.

'The back bedroom. Where the fireplace used to be.'

'It's a big space,' Johnny told them. 'You can climb in there, and there's a way out, up on to the roof. That's where the girls hide when there's a raid.'

'And there are guns there now?'

Johnny nodded. 'A consignment of Mac 10 sub-machine guns. Mr Chang's shipping them out tomorrow. He's got a buyer.'

'Who?'

'I don't know. Mr Banham, you got to promise you'll protect Otis.'

A fat tear rolled down Otis's cheek. Banham ignored it. 'Who is Chang's buyer?'

'Mr Chang told me if I tell the police anything, he'll kill Otis.' Silence pulled taut between them. 'How would you feel if someone threatened to kill one of yours?'

Banham stared at him in disbelief. Johnny's gaze dropped.

'I'm sorry, man,' he said. 'You got to believe I would never have hurt your Bobby. Chang was going to hurt my kid brother. What was I supposed to do?'

'Help us to put Chang away,' Banham said quietly. 'Do that and all your problems are over.'

'He's cleverer than you.'

'He told you that, did he?' Crowther crossed his arms and leaned back in his chair. 'Your brother is in a lot of trouble, Johnny. He needs a guiding hand. Help us to put Chang away, then you can do your duty and keep him out of trouble.'

After a few seconds Johnny nodded. 'It started when our mother was shot.'

'Shot?' Banham asked.

'In the High Street last year. She was gunned down in broad daylight.'

'I remember,' Banham said. 'What was that all about?'

'She owed Mr Chang a lot of money for drugs. He'd had given her a job as a Tina Turner lookalike, then he fed her drugs. He does it to all the girls who aren't strong enough to say no to him. As soon as Mum had a habit, he made her turn tricks. Then when she got out of control, he had her shot.'

Tears were pouring down Otis's face.

'How did you come to work for him?' Banham asked Johnny.

'He came to see me, told me how sorry he was, how much Mum meant to him. He said he'd look after me and Otis, and offered me a job at the club. I was stacking shelves in the local supermarket and he told me he would pay me double so I could take care of Otis. I told him I didn't want to get into anything to do with guns or drugs.' He wiped his nose with the back of his hand.

He's not much more than a lad himself, Banham thought.

'He agreed, and I started at the club. Within a week there was a raid, and I got taken in. He'd planted the drugs on me. Mr Banham, that's God's own truth. But I got done for it, and now I've got a record.'

Banham was still and listening.

Johnny was in his stride now. 'The Social could have taken my brother into care. I told him that was it, I was having no more to do with him. Next thing, Otis's mate Felix gets stabbed. Otis found the knife in his schoolbag, still covered in blood. I was pretty sure Mr Chang put it there, so I tackled him, showed it to him. He put on a pair of gloves, took the knife from me, and said if I tried to leave him, he'd have Otis done for attempted murder. Otis's prints were on the knife, see.'

Otis sat up a little straighter. 'Like the gun I nicked out of the back of the fireplace. Mr Chang took that too.'

Johnny was fighting back tears. 'I told Sadie what had happened,' he said thickly. 'She knew Mr Chang kept all kinds of stuff in the cellar, so she went down there to look. She found the knife and hid it at her place, and I stole the gun back and gave it to her as well. I gave her a key too, to

212

the lock-up where he keeps the crystal meth. That's what you saw me giving her last Friday. It wasn't grass at all. She was going to bring everything to you, tell you the truth and ask for help. But he had her killed.' He shook his head violently. 'And it's all my fault.'

Banham flicked a glance at Crowther.

'Who else could have known that Sadie had taken the gun and the knife from Otis?' Crowther asked.

'Dunno. Must have been someone she thought she could trust.'

'Why won't Felix Greene talk about his attack?' Banham asked Otis. But he knew the answer before the lad spoke.

'Mr Chang said he'd finish the job if he says anything.'

'So why did you write that note to my nephew?'

'He said if I did that for him, I could come back and live in the cottage.'

'He's been fending for himself and hanging around with the estate gangs. He was heading for trouble,' Johnny said. 'I'm sorry, man. We wouldn't have hurt the kid, it was only meant to scare him.'

'You did that all right!'

'OK, it was stupid. I was just looking out for my brother.'

'What about the other two Marilyns?' Crowther asked. 'Lily Palmer and Amy Bailey? Why did he have them killed?'

'I don't know.'

'Who killed Sadie Morgan?'

'Honest, man, I don't know.'

'Ray Adams?'

'I don't know much about him, except he works at the club.'

'He lives in the same block of flats as you, on the Bay Estate.'

'I run errands for him sometimes?' Otis said sheepishly.

'What?' Johnny grabbed his brother's arm. 'Tell me you weren't delivering drugs.'

Otis shrugged. 'Guy's got to eat.'

Johnny slapped the side of his head. 'This is all my fault. I have been trying to take care of him.'

Banham and Crowther looked at each other.

'You said you gave Sadie Morgan a key,' Banham said, pushing an evidence bag across the table. 'Is this it?'

Otis nodded. 'It's for Ray Adams's lock-up garage next to our flats,' said Otis. 'H14 – number fourteen, Heather block.'

'OK.' Banham tilted his chair back. 'You've both been very helpful – at last. We'll call that a wrap for today.' He switched the recording machine off. 'Just wait here a minute.'

He stood up and Crowther followed him out of the room. Alison had been watching the interview through a two-way screen. She joined them in the corridor.

'Do you think they are telling the truth?' she asked.

'Yes, I do,' Banham said. 'You'd better get over to that lockup, but don't go on your own. Take Crowther with you. The estate is surrounded by police and the residents are spoiling for a fight.'

'I think we should keep them both here,' Crowther said. 'For their own safety.'

'Isabelle is at Doubles tonight, isn't she?' Banham asked.

'With Millie and Andrew,' Alison agreed.

'She really needs to try to get into the cottage and

214

confirm if the girls and guns are there,' Crowther said. 'If Gladman is telling the truth, the raid's a bust – they'll have been shipped out by Wednesday. I'll get on to CO19, suggest we bring the raid forward to tonight. We could have Chang banged up this time tomorrow.'

'I'll get the FME to take a sample of their hair,' said Alison. 'We can use that as a way to keep them here.'

Banham nodded his agreement. 'I'm still not a hundred percent about Johnny Gladman. If he's so afraid of what Eddie Chang might do to Otis, it's not impossible he killed Sadie Morgan himself, to protect the lad.' He looked at Alison. 'I don't think Ray Adams killed Sadie. It was too calculated a killing. I still think we are looking for two killers.'

'I agree.'

Banham looked at her. 'Do you?' was all he said.

Crowther suggested that Alison park around the corner. He didn't want to come back and find a brick through the window, and he didn't fancy getting into another scrap. She didn't argue. She was very fond of her green Volkswagen Golf.

The police presence was strong and the atmosphere tense. As they walked towards the block of garages past the rusting swings in the deserted playground, shouts of 'Fascist bastards' and 'Sausage meat' echoed off the walls. Missiles fell from the balconies: half-bricks, chunks of wood, even a bucket full of urine.

'It's OK telling the uniforms to avoid confrontation,' Crowther said wryly. 'The council won't even send a plumber out here. They call it the outlaw village. The fifteen-year-old with the biggest gun becomes the leader.'

'All the more reason to keep those Mac 10s from hitting the streets,' Alison said. They arrived at the dilapidated, graffiti-smeared garages and searched for H14.

'It's down here,' Crowther said. He took out the key and pushed it into the lock. 'Bastard doesn't fit!' he exclaimed.

'So Otis Gladman was leading us a song and dance after all.'

'No. Hang on.' Crowther wiggled the key around. 'It is the right key, but I think the lock is blocked up.'

Alison radioed for help. A couple of well built uniformed constables arrived with a battering ram.

The lock gave way under the weight, but the door only moved a few inches. A dozen or so flies buzzed out, shining blue in the cold air. Alison swatted at them with her shoulder bag, and Crowther slipped a hand around the door to find the problem. Suddenly he gagged and stepped back, looking down at the ground. Blood had pooled around the door.

'Break it down,' Alison ordered the uniforms. They pushed until the door opened far enough to see inside.

Ray Adams was lying on the concrete floor with a small, round bullet hole in his chest and tiny burns all over his naked body. His lower half lay in a pool of congealing blood. More blood had bubbled and dried on his face and neck, the area smelt like an abattoir. On the floor lay two lumps of flesh; Alison slipped her hands into plastic forensic gloves and pushed them with a fingertip, disturbing a swarm of hungry bluebottles.

'They cut off his penis and tongue,' she said through clenched teeth.

216

As Crowther called it in, and Alison walked to the back of the lock-up, where a dozen or so crates stood covered in sacks.

'No prizes for guessing what's in here.' She sliced through the sacking with a penknife; white powder ran out on to the floor.

'There's enough crystal meth here to kill half of England,' she said.

'What's the betting this place is registered in Ray Adams's name?' Crowther said. 'Chang will deny all knowledge.'

At the lunchtime briefing a fifth victim was added to the white-board. The photo of Ray Adams, trussed up like a turkey, missing his sexual organs and tongue and his body covered in cigarette burns.

'There's no doubt whatever that Eddie Chang is behind this killing,' Alison told the assembled squad. 'The fact that Adams was tortured means he did something to upset Chang.'

'I reckon he took his penis off because he interfered with the victims sexually,' Crowther said. 'I'd bet his orders were just to kill them, but he lost control. Question is, why did Chang want them killed?'

'DNA proves he murdered Lily Palmer, Amy Bailey and Joshua Timpkin,' Banham said. 'But not Sadie Morgan; all traces of DNA were washed away in the duck-pond. We do know she wasn't sexually assaulted.'

'Perhaps he did kill Sadie, and wasn't high on drugs when he did it. Then next time he was, so the attack was more vicious.' This was PCSO Andrew Fisher.

'Good point,' Banham said. 'It's possible.'

Crowther shook his head. 'No, mate. I knew him pretty well. He couldn't cross the road without a fix. He'd never have had the bottle to kill Sadie Morgan unless he was out of his skull. That was a calculated killing. Someone followed her, smothered her, then dumped her in a way that removed all traces of DNA. Ray Adams didn't have the brain for that.'

'Lily knew she was being followed,' Millie piped up. 'She said she thought it was one of those weirdos that follow celebrities. He wore a raincoat and dark glasses, and an obvious wig – as if he was deliberately in disguise. That could be Ray Adams.'

'It could be anybody,' Alison snapped. Millie was still annoying her. 'All we do know for sure,' she went on, 'is that Ray Adams killed Lily Palmer, Amy Bailey and Josh Timpkin.' She counted off the points on her fingers. 'All the women worked as Monroe lookalikes. They were all smothered. Sadie and Lily had identical animal hair on them; Amy didn't. Lily and Amy were killed in similar ways; Sadie's murder was different. Are we missing something here?'

'We need to identify that hair,' Banham said.

Crowther chipped in. 'The FME has taken a hair sample from both the Gladman boys, just to eliminate them really.'

The fax on Crowther's desk started whirring. He leaned over and pulled the paper free.

'It's from Forensics,' he said. 'The hair found in the women's windpipe contained some kind of perfume.'

There was a moment's silence, then Isabelle said, 'Hairspray. In the Monroe wigs. They're made out of

218

animal hair, aren't they?'

'Eddie Chang wears a toupée,' Millie said uncertainly.

Banham shook his head. 'He doesn't do his own dirty work.'

Crowther was still reading the fax. 'It looks as if the hair came from a bird,' he said.

'There were ducks in the pond with Sadie Morgan,' one of the detectives said. 'But why in the second victim's throat?'

'Bruno Pelegino's mother runs a sanctuary for wounded wild animals,' Banham said.

Alison nodded.

'Birds too?'

'I think so. And Bruno is living with her. I think it's time to pay her another visit.'

'What mother wouldn't alibi her son if he was in trouble?' Alison said. 'Apart from his cousin, that's all he's got going for him. Remember the CCTV outside the club? I said it was him all along.'

'And then Chang had the other two killed.'

'We still don't know why. Amy Bailey had only just auditioned. It doesn't add up.'

'Perhaps we'll find something when we go into her background.'

Alison turned the car into Mrs Pelegino's street. As she began to reverse into a parking space, Banham cast his mind back to her thirtieth birthday, when he had bought her a set of advanced driving lessons. As she banged the pavement for the third time, he thought he might ask for his money back. How could anyone make such a mess of a simple job like parking in a side street? There wasn't anything much behind or in front of her, yet her bonnet stuck out and the wheels were at an angle. He decided to say nothing, but propped a Police sign in the front window. At least that that would save them from being towed away.

Mrs Pelegino opened the door before they had time to ring the bell.

'Now what?' she said desperately. 'He's not here, and he's a heartbroken man. Why can't you leave us alone?'

'Can we come in?' Alison pushed past her, giving her no chance to refuse.

'Do you know it's an offence to obstruct a murder enquiry?' Banham said flatly.

'I haven't done anything,' the woman objected. She was dressed shabbily in grubby trousers, and soil clung to her boots.

'Have you been digging something up,' Banham asked her.

'Or burying something?' Alison added.

'I've been helping a trapped badger,' she snapped. 'I run a wildlife ambulance and I nurse wounded animals.'

'Where was Bruno last Friday evening?' Alison asked

'This again? How many times must I tell you? Last Friday evening my son was with me. He came home here after work, soon after midnight. I cannot say the exact time.'

'Have you got any at the moment?' Banham asked her.

'What?' Mrs Pelegino looked puzzled.

'Wounded animals?'

'No. The cat has had a litter. I have the kittens in the kitchen.' She brushed her hands down her trousers and

220

narrowed her dark eyes. 'That's how she was, that wife of his. Irresponsible. Didn't even get her cat neutered. Thank God she didn't have my grandchildren.'

Banham walked past the woman into the kitchen. The cat lay on its make-do bed with half a dozen pink-skinned Burmese kittens sucking on her. Alison knelt beside the creatures.

'Guv, look at this.'

Banham knelt down beside her.

The cat lay on a pillow, discoloured and yellowing, with a bright red stain on one corner.

Banham looked up at Mrs Pelegino. 'Where did you get this?'

'I found it,' she snapped. 'It was in a skip at the end of the road. Is it a crime to take an old pillow for a needy animal?'

'Where exactly did you find it? And when?' Banham stood up and moved away, leaving Alison to relieve the spitting, clawing cat of its bed.

Mrs Pelegino pushed Alison her to one side. 'Let me do that.' She pulled the pillow and some ragged clothing from under the unhappy creature, handed them to Alison and took off her own cardigan and pushed it into the basket. 'I found it on the corner of the street, Saturday morning I think, as I walked to the news-agents. The cat was about to have the kittens. It was all there, on top of the other rubbish in the skip. So I took it.'

'Sadie was murdered in the small hours of Saturday morning, and you didn't think to tell us.' Alison was rapidly losing patience.

'Why would I think it had anything to do with Sadie?'

Alison pushed the pillow into an evidence bag and the

remnants of muddied clothing into another. 'I'm going to have to ask you to accompany us to the station to make a statement,' she said formally.'

'What about my kittens?' the woman asked quietly.

'Call your son,' Banham said acerbically. 'He lives here, doesn't he?'

CHAPTER FIFTEEN

Isabelle was on her break. She sat down at a table near the bar and kicked the red stilettos under the table. She hated them, and the tacky red dress that the Marilyn lookalikes wore like a uniform. She was much happier in jeans and trainers. She had to keep reminding herself that there was only one more day to put up with being told how to wiggle her arse and hold a cocktail tray simultaneously. As soon as CO19 entered the building, the shoes were coming off. She'd work the raid barefoot, and never, ever would she put her feet through this kind of punishment again.

She scratched at her thigh, where her change purse was embarrassingly sewn into a fluffy marabou garter. It rubbed her skin and made it itch. It was still early evening, and hardly anyone was around; she had only served two customers since she arrived, and one of them was Andrew Fisher. He was propping up the bar, gazing at Millie up on stage miming to *I Wanna Be Loved By You*. The man looked genuinely besotted.

Eddie Chang seemed pretty enthralled with Millie too. His smile spread from ear to ear, stretching his crooked scar in a really creepy way. The man definitely had a screw loose, Isabelle thought. Marilyn Monroe was the only thing he showed any respect for.

Isabelle didn't like Millie much; she thought she had got too big for her boots because of her affair with Crowther.

But her talent as an impersonator was without doubt; Millie had the full bust and curvy hips, and she could do the wiggle and the famous Marilyn pout. Most important of all, she knew how to command Eddie Chang's full attention; that would be a big plus when the raid kicked off.

Millie seemed to enjoy doing it. Isabelle would have kicked Eddie Chang in the balls long before now, if he'd looked at her like that. Bad enough he tried to teach her to pout and stick her arse out. This cocktail waitressing was more than enough to put up with.

She swallowed a mouthful of her lager. The temperature was just right; it slid down her throat and calmed her edginess. She was waiting for the opportunity to get into the cottage; she needed to learn the geography of the place to give CO19 the upper hand tomorrow. She scratched at the nylon wig; the hairpins securing it were stinging her scalp. One more day and they'd wipe that smile off Eddie Chang's ugly face and see him finally behind bars where he belonged.

She cast her eyes around, mentally checking all exits and entrances to the club again. Andrew was still watching Millie with that besotted look on his spotty face; at least he would look out for her tomorrow: one thing Isabelle didn't need to worry about.

She downed the rest of her lager and went back to the bar. Her mobile chirped. She pulled it out from the change purse and checked the caller screen; the word Mum had appeared, code for Crowther.

Andrew was by the bar. She threw him a look and he picked up on it, ordering another drink to hold the barmaid's attention while Isabelle took the call. Eddie

Chang was talking to Millie, and Terry King wasn't around; only a couple of other customers were in the place, both too far away to notice. She tucked herself into a corner and put the phone to her ear.

Crowther brought her up to speed. The pillow and clothing from Mrs Pelegino's had gone to Forensics; Penny had just rung back. The red stain was lipstick, and it contained Sadie Morgan's DNA. This was the pillow that had suffocated her. According to Mrs Pelegino's statement, the pillow and clothing had been dumped a skip between the park and the club.

Penny had also found foreign fibres on the clothing, and was in the process of testing them against Sadie's DNA. Penny had said the pillow was filled with goose feathers, which accounted for the hair found on the first two victims. This blew a hole in Banham's theory about two murderers; it suggested that the first and second murders had been done by the same person. If they could link the pillow with Ray Adams, it would look as if he had killed Sadie too, despite the lack of DNA evidence.

Crowther hoped the pillow might come from the cottage at the club. 'Can you get into the cottage?' he asked Isabelle. 'Confirm if the Ukrainians are already there, and then find a pillow and throw it out into the alleyway? We've got a couple of uniforms out there – they'll drive it over to the forensics lab.'

'Will do. What about the Gladmans? Have you let them go?'

'Well, Johnny did write the *Your Turn* notes like he said. And the one Bobby Banham got was Otis – turns out he's left-handed. The guv doesn't reckon they were in on the murders, but we're keeping them here anyway. They don't seem to mind much!'

Isabelle looked around the club. It was quiet and everyone was occupied. Now was as good a time as she'd get.

'I'll go out to the cottage now.'

'Good girl. We've got a warrant, but we don't really want to use it. If those Ukrainian girls are in there, we want them to stay put so we can catch Chang red-handed. A warrant would only make him suspicious. We can't afford any slip-ups this time.'

Isabelle clicked her phone off and slipped it back into the purse.

'Cover for me?' she asked the barmaid. 'I need the loo. My stomach's giving me gyp.'

'No pra-h-blem,' the girl replied in a mock-Bronx accent that irritated the hell out of Isabelle. She caught Andrew's eye then glanced at Eddie Chang, hoping he got the message and would keep Chang from following her.

The Ladies was next to the changing room, and there was another door to the courtyard from there. She prayed Terry King wasn't in the changing room; he spent most of his time there, dressing wigs and sewing and maintaining the lookalike costumes.

The cottage would be in darkness, and she couldn't risk turning lights on. Terry had a torch; as long as he wasn't around she could borrow it. She might have to climb in through a window, maybe even on the first floor; that would mean clambering up on to the outside wall. In this outfit she was wearing it wouldn't be easy. If Terry wasn't in the changing room, perhaps she could slip her jeans and trainers

226

back on.

The fates were on her side; Terry wasn't there. Quick as lightning she grabbed her jeans and scrambled into them. She kicked the high-heeled shoes under the steel rail and grabbed her comfy trainers. She had a foot in one and was rummaging in Terry's box for the torch when a voice behind her made her jump out of her skin.

'Have you been dismissed?'

Terry King.

She had it planned. 'My mother's just phoned. She's not well. She has the beginnings of Alzheimer's, and she's locked herself out.' She started unpinning her wig. 'She needs her medication. I'm the only one with a spare key. I'm just going to pop home, let her in and give her the pills, then I'll be straight back. She doesn't live far.'

'Leave the wig on,' Terry snapped. 'I don't want to have to dress it again, it takes far too long. You're not a natural at all. Just take the dress off.'

Isabelle didn't argue. She stopped pulling at the hairpins, zipped her jeans up and wriggled into her tight black t-shirt, grabbed her leather jacket and headed for the door to the courtyard. 'I'll be as quick as I can,' she said, looking over her shoulder at Terry's face. It gave nothing away.

When she reached the door he was still staring at her. 'My car's the other side of the alleyway. It's quicker if I nip out this way. I'll be back before anyone knows I'm gone.' She tried to look coy. 'Please don't grass on me. He'll dock my money and I need it badly.'

Terry made no reply. He bent down and scooped up the dress she had purposely dropped on the floor to play for time.

227

In the courtyard she stood for a moment trying to suss the CCTV. If she stayed close to the wall, she was out of range. She stepped quickly around the edge towards the cottage. She reckoned she had ten or twelve good minutes, as long as no one followed her out.

She sprang nimbly up the wall, and had one foot on the window ledge when something moved below her.

She took her foot off the ledge and stood on the wall, keeping very still, ready to jump into the alley on the other side if she had to. Time was ticking away; she had a precious few minutes before the CCTV turned to face her. After an endless few seconds of silence, she raised her foot again and was about to hoist herself on to the drainpipe when she heard another noise. It was definitely footsteps this time.

Millie Payne was in the courtyard, in her long red dress and stiletto-heeled shoes. She was pressed up hard against the wall, and it looked as if she had just managed to duck the CCTV.

Isabelle whispered angrily and urgently, 'What the hell are you doing here?'

'Andrew's keeping Eddie and Terry King talking. I've come to help you.'

Isabelle closed her eyes. Dressed in stiletto heels and an ankle-length dress! Where was the woman's brain? Other considerations aside, Eddie Chang wouldn't think twice about having them both shot if he caught them.

But she didn't have time to waste arguing; she needed to get up on to the ledge and through that window.

'Stay out of sight of the CCTV,' she snapped. 'And keep a lookout.'

Fortunately her phone was easily accessible. She quickly tapped a text into it, to let Alison know she was about to go into the cottage with Millie on lookout, and would need back-up if she didn't make contact again within half an hour. She decided texting Crowther was a bad idea; his involvement with Millie had seriously skewed his judgement.

She pressed Send, stowed the phone, and braced herself to climb up on to the first floor window ledge. With horror she saw that Millie was already there, crawling on all fours, still wearing the stiletto-heeled shoes. The long red dress spilled over the side of the ledge and looked worryingly as if it might trip her up any second.

'For Chrissake!' Isabelle tried to keep her voice to a whisper. The woman was a complete liability. 'How the hell did you get up there?' She checked the CCTV; it hadn't swung round in their direction yet, but time was ticking on. She probably had about seven minutes left. 'Get down! I can't be responsible if you fall.'

'No chance.' Millie had reached the window, and was prising it open. 'I'm brilliant at climbing.' She swung one leg over the sill. 'I've got a dog that climbs trees and gets stuck. I'm always having to rescue him. I'll go down and open the front door for you, shall I?'

'You can't turn any lights on.' Isabelle warned her. 'And I couldn't get hold of a torch. You'll have to feel your way in the dark.'

Millie pulled a tiny pocket torch from her garter. 'I was a girl guide,' she said.

Isabelle was impressed against her will. 'Just be careful,' she hissed.

She checked the CCTV camera again; it wasn't moving as fast as she'd thought. They could do this, as long as no one came out of the club. If someone had come out a few seconds ago, they couldn't have missed seeing Marilyn Monroe disappearing through the window with her bum in the air.

Alison clicked her phone off. 'Isabelle is outside the cottage. Millie is with her, and Andrew is inside the club,' she told Banham. 'She said to send back-up if we don't hear from her within half an hour; my feeling is she's in trouble if we hear nothing in fifteen minutes. I think we should get over there, pronto.'

Banham nodded agreement. 'You said Millie Payne is with her?'

'At the moment she's all the back-up Isabelle's got.'

Crowther was shrugging into his coat. 'You keep underestimating Millie,' he said. 'She's a lot cleverer than you give her credit for. She knows how to look after herself.'

Alison glared at him. 'I've got two words for you. Ray Adams. After that little bit of misjudgement, I think you'd better stay here and wait for the results from Forensics.'

Crowther subsided into a chair, glowering at her.

'Have CO19 been brought up to speed?' Banham asked.

'They're standing by,' Crowther replied.

'Then let's go.'

It took Millie less than a minute to get the front door open. Isabelle slipped inside and quietly closed the door behind them.

The only light was the tiny circle from Millie's pocket torch.

'Good thinking,' Isabelle said, pointing at it.

'Never go anywhere without it.'

'We need to find a bedroom; Forensics need a pillow. Then we have to check everywhere we can for those poor girls. We haven't got long. Can I take the torch?'

'Course. What's the pillow for?'

'I'll explain later. You stay by the door. We've got five minutes, max; we need to get back before anyone knows you're missing. Terry King has already got a stopwatch on me. Did he see you come out?'

'I don't think so. Andrew got him and Eddie Chang talking.'

'Let's get a move on, then. You stay down here and look around. As soon as I've got the pillow and checked upstairs, we're out of here.'

She quickly made her way up the stairs and on to the landing. There was a glint of metal in the torchlight: a brass doorknob. She opened the door, and the tiny shaft of light picked out a basin and toilet. On the floor between them was a huge box of Tampax and an even bigger box of condoms. If the girls weren't here, they were on their way.

She shut the door and shone the light along the wall until it revealed another door. That was a bedroom; she dived in and grabbed a pillow. It smelt of lavender, and appeared to be new.

The next door she tried wouldn't open. She pushed it again; it gave slightly in the middle, but the top and bottom didn't move. It was bolted from the inside.

Then the bolt scraped back.

As the door creaked open a ray of light from another torch hit her in the face. She found herself facing a young girl. About a dozen more girls, all fair-haired and pale-faced, crowded behind the first one; even in the dim light the terror on their tear-stained faces was heartbreakingly evident. Isabelle swallowed the lump in her throat. They weren't more than about twelve or thirteen. That bastard was selling someone's children to perverts for sex.

'It's all right,' she whispered to the terrified girl. 'I'm your friend. I won't hurt you. Shut the door, bolt it again and don't open it to anyone except me. I'll be back soon to help you.'

The girl looked at her wide-eyed. There was a blood-crusted cut at the side of her mouth. A hard slap from a hand wearing a ring would have done that, Isabelle thought. One of her eyes was almost closed too, and her cheek was swollen. The girl had taken a beating. She caught a whiff of faeces, and lowered her torch; the girl's legs were streaked with dried excrement. She forced down the fury, told herself to keep her cool. Tomorrow the girls would be safe from Eddie Chang and his kind.

'Do any of you speak English?' she asked

No one answered.

This was getting more difficult by the minute.

She took her phone from her pocket and pressed the short cut to Crowther's number. As he answered with his familiar, 'Yup,' the landing flooded with light and a strong hand slid around her neck and clamped over her mouth. Her phone dropped to the floor.

As it landed she heard Crowther's voice. 'Isabelle? Izzy,

what's happening?' Then a heavy foot ground it into the floorboards. She tried to turn her head but felt something cold and hard nudge the side of her head. The hand around her mouth wrenched painfully at her face, and she found herself staring at Eddie Chang.

Alison pulled out of the side road from the police station. Banham clicked his phone shut.

'There's essence of lavender on the pillow at Forensics,' he told her.

'Some people use it to help them sleep,' Alison said.

He gritted his teeth. Why did she have to turn to face him? Couldn't she talk and keep her eyes on the road?

She floored on the accelerator and he grabbed the door handle and shut his eyes, feeling sorry for the instructor he had paid to give her advanced driving lessons. She simply wasn't a natural driver.

Now she was driving straight across an amber light. He didn't say anything. It wasn't worth the row.

He suddenly thought he might invest in a lavender pillow to put over his face when he was in the car with her. But no; she'd only breathe in the lavender herself and fall asleep at the wheel.

'What was Chang doing with lavender pillows?' he wondered, trying to distract himself as she pulled out to overtake.

'To keep the girl prostitutes quiet,' she explained. 'I suppose it's cheaper than Valium.'

He nodded. 'He gets a better price if they are completely free of drugs when they start out.'

Alison put her foot down again. 'So whoever killed Sadie

Morgan probably used a pillow from the cottage.'

'So did Ray Adams when he killed Lily Palmer,' Banham added.

'Hm. That was a turn-up, wasn't it? Adams, I mean. Not like Know-all Col at all.'

'It happens,' Banham defended him. 'He's a brilliant cop, but he's human. He's allowed an occasional mistake.'

'Makes them all the time with women,' Alison said pointedly. 'Let's hope Millie Payne isn't another one.'

Banham ignored that remark and continued to ponder the possibilities opened up by the new forensic result. 'Ray Adams killed the two women and left his DNA over the scene. That's what Chang would have wanted – it incriminates Adams and keeps him in the clear. But why kill Adams? Unless he found out he was working for us...'

He fell silent and allowed the thoughts to run around his brain. Sometimes if he just threw everything in, a pattern emerged.

Did Chang have Sadie killed to stop her bringing in the knife and the gun which incriminated Otis Gladman?

Did Otis or Johnny Gladman kill Sadie and fabricate the Chang story because she was planning to give them the proof that Otis did stab Felix Greene?

And what about Bruno Pelegino and his mother? Surely they were in the clear if the pillow came from the cottage.

Alison must have read his mind.

'You know, I think I believe Mrs Pelegino's story. I think she did find the pillow with those clothes in the skip. It's just odd that uniform missed it.'

'We all make mistakes.'

She skidded round a parked car and swore. Banham

234

winced but didn't comment. 'Just a matter of time now,' he said. 'The DNA on that pillow belongs to our killer. We just have to wait.'

Alison started reversing into a parking space large enough for a herd of elephants. Banham took a sharp breath as the car hit the kerb.

'So we're saying the Peleginos are out of the frame? That was my mistake, wasn't it?'

Banham decided it was best not to answer that.

'What about the Gladmans?' Alison went on, knocking the kerb for a second time. 'Say Sadie found that Johnny was involved in Chang's under-age women enterprise. Even if they really were close friends, she'd have shopped him. She was a nurse, and she'd worked with children.' She angled the car and started to reverse again. 'He might have killed her to prevent that. And if Otis stabbed Felix Greene, well, blood is thicker than water. We already know Johnny will go to any lengths to protect his brother.'

'Otis is quite capable himself,' Banham pointed out. 'I know he's only a kid, but he's mixed up with that gang on the estate. Who knows what he might have done?'

But he was far from sure he believed that; the lad had crumbled in the interview room, and Banham didn't think he'd been faking.

There was a small crunch of metal as Alison's bumper met the car behind.

'Oh, for God's sake,' he exclaimed. 'Get out. I'll park it for you.'

'You have got to be kidding!'

All Crowther heard when he answered his phone was a loud

235

gasp. Isabelle's name was on the screen. When he pressed redial, a shrill buzz sounded in his ear.

He grabbed his coat and pressed Banham's number. 'Guv, I'm on my way too. Isabelle's in trouble.'

'We're outside,' Banham told him. 'What's up?'

'I heard her gasp, then the phone cut off.'

'Call CO19, tell them to meet us here,' came the reply. 'We're going in.'

Terry King pulled Isabelle's hands behind her back. 'I got lost,' she said weakly. 'I was trying to find my way back.'

'Shut up!' Eddie Chang took the gun away from her temple and relief flooded through her. Not for long, though. He cracked it hard across her face; she staggered and battled to stay upright. 'You think I'm stupid?' he snarled. 'You thought I didn't know you were the Filth? No one plays me for a fool.'

The room spun around her. 'My colleagues are on their way,' she said breathlessly. 'Your game's over. You may as well give it up.'

'Killing you won't matter then, will it?' He put the gun to her head again, releasing the safety catch. The soft click echoed around her brain. She closed her eyes and took what she thought was her last breath.

But a boot in the base of her spine sent her flying into the room with the terrified girls.

Her first thought was *have they killed Millie*?

She stood up and turned to face the gun.

Eddie Chang's eyes told her he couldn't wait for her brains to burst out of her head. But Terry King pleaded, 'Not yet, dear. We might need her, to get us out of here.'

'Where's Millie Payne?' Isabelle asked Terry. 'The girl who was singing earlier? She's not a cop, nor is her boyfriend. There's no need to hurt them.'

Eddie's only reply was a push with his free hand and a kick in her crotch. She doubled over in pain, and as she straightened up he hit her again, this time across the head with the butt of the gun. She stumbled forward and he smashed the door into her face, sending her reeling backwards seeing stars. She felt warm, sticky blood bubble from her nose and drip on to her hand. One of the girls held out a filthy scrap of blanket; it stank, but she took it to stem the bleeding.

Her eyes flicked around the room. The window was tiny and covered in bars. No chance of escape there.

Isabelle's heart hit her boots as the door opened again. Eddie was holding Millie in front of him; he shoved her into the room and closed the door behind her. Now, as well as a dozen young eastern European girls whose lives probably depended on her keeping her wits about her, she had to worry about an inexperienced PCSO dressed as Marilyn Monroe.

She could only see out of one eye and her whole face was so painful she wanted to pass out. But she had to hang on. Crowther knew where she was, and he had never let her down. Not professionally anyway.

The girls were wailing and she had to raise her voice so Millie could hear her. 'How many did Chang have with him when they found you?' she asked.

'Terry and Eddie and the two doormen,' Millie told her.

'That's four. We'll wait for back-up.'

Not that they had any choice, but she wasn't going to tell

237

Millie that.

'What about Andrew?' Isabelle asked. 'What do you think they've done with him?'

'I left him at the bar. He knows we're in here.'

Isabelle was dizzy, but she fought to stay upright.

'I'm so sorry,' Millie said. 'I really thought I kept out of range of the camera. Eddie must have seen me. Next thing I knew Terry and Eddie were coming in from the courtyard with those two doormen. Terry grabbed me and started hitting my head against the wall. Eddie took out a gun, I tried to shout out to warn you, but Terry put his hand over my mouth and said he was going to kill me.'

Isabelle took the smelly blanket away from her nose. The bleeding seemed to have stopped. She shook her head. 'Crowther knows where we are, and I texted Alison just before we came in here. They'll be here any minute.'

'Colin will come,' Millie said. 'Know-All Col. He'll get us out of here.'

'Course he will.' Their eyes met, and Isabelle could see Millie understood.

Millie opened her mouth to speak but an explosion shook the building.

The Ukrainian girls started screaming and banging at the door.

'Try and keep calm,' Isabelle started to shout, but stopped in mid-sentence. She smelled petrol.

Millie's blue eyes widened with fear. 'We're on fire,' she said.

CHAPTER SIXTEEN

As Alison got out of her car she smelt smoke. She called to Banham, but he was already phone to his ear calling emergency assistance.

'Stop them!'

Andrew Fisher ran out of the club in pursuit of Terry King and Eddie Chang, who were heading for the red BMW Alison had just jammed in while parking her Golf. 'Stop them,' he shouted again.

Alison ran across to the BMW, and reached it just ahead of them. 'Police,' she said. 'Hold it.'

Terry King pulled a hand-gun from his pocket and pointed it at her. Banham froze. 'Put it down,' he barked. 'Armed police are on the way.'

Terry flicked a glance at Banham. Alison used that moment to point her key and unlock her own car. Terry noticed. He swung the gun round and put a bullet in each of the Golf's front tyres.

Andrew Fisher was edging himself round towards Banham. Terry's other arm shot out and grabbed the PCSO; he pulled Andrew in front of him as a human shield and pointed the gun at the side of his head.

'Move away from the car,' he ordered Alison.

The sirens in the background grew louder. Alison reckoned they were less than two minutes away. Her best bet was to keep them talking.

Terry fired at the ground in front of Banham's feet, then pointed the gun at Andrew's head again. 'Hands in the air and drop your keys and bag,' he ordered Alison.

She obeyed.

Eddie Chang pulled his car keys from his pocket and flicked his head to one side to tell Banham to move. He did.

'You won't get far,' he told him.

'Shut your fucking mouth,' came the reply.

Terry opened the car door, holding Andrew in front of him. The gun was still pointed at Alison and Banham. 'I won't shoot you if you keep out of my way, but if you try to stop us, I'll shoot you both.'

'You won't get far,' Banham repeated.

'Shut the fuck up, before I do it for you,' Terry snapped moving the muzzle closer to Andrew's head.

Andrew was standing upright, and showing no fear. Alison felt quite proud of him; experienced police officers quivered and turned to jelly in the same predicament.

Terry opened the back door of the BMW for Eddie.

'Don't try to follow us,' Terry warned them. 'I'll kill this guy if I have to.'

'Please do as they ask,' Andrew pleaded.

Banham had no intention of arguing with a gun. He stepped clear.

As if on cue, three armed response vehicles speeded round the corner and screamed to a halt a few yards away. Over a dozen armed CO19 officers jumped out, their guns pointed at Terry and Eddie.

'Better drop it,' Banham told Terry calmly. 'They'll kill you.'

The sound of guns being cocked echoed around the

240

marks-men.

'I'll kill your officer,' Terry said.

'Last chance,' Banham replied.

Andrew Fisher closed his eyes. His whole body was shaking visibly.

Terry King dropped the gun and put his hands in the air. Eddie Chang followed his example.

Andrew's knees almost gave way as he joined Banham and Alison on the pavement. Banham patted him on the back. 'Good lad,' he said.

'Are you all right?' Alison asked.

'Not really. But I will be.'

Alison walked slowly towards Chang. With her face inches from his, she in a low voice, 'If anything – *anything* – happens to either of my officers in that cottage, I will kill you myself.'

She turned and ran into the club, and straight out of the back towards the cottage. Five blaring fire engines had pulled into the alleyway, and a team of firemen were pulling out water hoses.

Banham was close behind her. 'It looks bad,' she called, watching great billows of black smoke snaking towards the sky.

'Isabelle! Millie! Don't worry! Help is on the way.'

Isabelle's heart hit her boots. The window was tiny, no more than a foot wide, and covered in bars. Through it she saw the courtyard filling with smoke.

Then she heard Alison shouting.

'We're here,' she yelled, banging frantically on the glass.

But a series of small explosions like gunfire sent tremors

through the cottage and drowned her out.

The shots alarmed the girls. They started screaming and running around, shaking at the bolted door, some shouting in their own language, others just wailing.

'Don't panic,' Millie soothed them. 'Help is coming. Stay calm and we'll get out.'

Isabelle's vision was still blurred from the beating Chang had given her, but Millie's grim expression told her the other girl knew what the explosions meant. The fire had hit the Mac 10 ammunition store; the whole place could explode at any moment, and if it did the chance of any of them surviving was one in a million. The rescue team would have to work fast.

Millie was amazingly calm. She passed stained blankets to the girls, wrapping them around the ones too scared to do it themselves. She talked to them reassuringly – 'Be brave,' and 'It's going to be OK, we're going to get out of here.' Though Isabelle knew they didn't understand a word, it seemed to be working; they stopped screaming and running around.

Isabelle threw herself at the locked door. 'Help me,' she shouted to Millie. 'We've got to break this down.'

A deep male voice cut across the screams of the sirens. 'Isabelle, can you hear me?' She didn't recognise it. 'My name is Jamie,' it continued. 'I'm the fire chief. Can you get to a window?'

Millie ran to the window and banged on it. 'Up here, up here!' she shouted. 'We're trapped. The window won't open and the door's locked.'

'Can you force the door and get to the upstairs landing?' That was Banham's voice.

'There's a wide window there, with a ledge below it,' Jamie added. 'If you can get to it, we can reach you.'

Then Alison's voice. 'Hang on, girls. We're going to get you out.'

'There are children in here too,' Millie shouted back.

Another series of small explosions shook the walls around her.

'I can't get the fucking door open!' Isabelle was banging and kicking it, half-hysterical. 'The lock's too strong – I can't break it.'

'Hairpin!' Millie exclaimed.

'What?'

'You mean you don't know how to pick a lock?' Millie pulled hairpins from her wig and ran to the door. Her fingers moved swiftly and adeptly, jiggling one pin after another in the lock.

Within a few seconds the door opened. Black smoke filled the room, and they all gasped for breath.

Then there was an enormous bang, and everything went quiet.

'Go!' Millie was suddenly in charge. She handed Isabelle the last blanket. 'Where's yours?' Isabelle put a hand over her mouth to keep the smoke out.

Millie pushed her towards the door. 'Just go.'

Isabelle swallowed a mouthful of smoke and started to cough. 'I've got a jacket,' she wheezed, pushing the blanket back at Millie.

Millie lifted her red sequinned dress over her head, revealing tiny red knickers and a suspender belt and black stockings. Through the smoke Isabelle glimpsed a hand-gun sticking out of the top of her garter bag.

243

Some of the girls ran through the door and into the black smoke. Others cowered, trembling and crying.

Isabelle pointed to the gun and frowned.

'Later.' Millie waved her hands. She turned towards the girls and began to coax them out. Isabelle was last on to the smoke-filled landing.

Millie grabbed Isabelle's hand. 'We can share this blanket,' she said, 'and when we get out of here, we'll share Colin Crowther. Not that there's much to share.'

'Please don't make me laugh,' Isabelle warned. 'I'm trying to hold my breath.'

The first Crowther thing saw was the crowd of people in the street. Then he spotted the row of fire engines, and last of all he saw the flames licking the sky. The emergency vehicles had blocked the road to keep cars out. He parked as close as he dared and started running. He ran past the CO19 vehicles without seeing Eddie Chang and Terry King, handcuffed and under armed guard. He ran into the empty club, flashing his warrant card at the uniformed officer standing outside, and carried on running until he reached the courtyard. That was when he stopped, held back by a couple of hefty firemen.

He tried the warrant card approach again, but the firemen were adamant. 'The place could collapse at any moment,' one told him.

A series of explosions went off inside the cottage. 'That's firearms,' he shouted, trying to force his way past. 'There's a shipment of Mac 10 sub-machine guns in there. And I need to get to my colleagues.'

Banham and Alison rushed over to him. 'Let them do

their job, son,' Banham said.

'Isabelle and Millie! Are they in there? Are they? Isabelle!' he yelled at the top of his voice.

The two fireman held his arms. 'Please, sir. Let us do our job.'

'Crowther! Stand away!' Banham shouted. 'That's an order.'

Another series of small explosions sent an array of sparks like miniature fireworks into the air. 'Get back,' the fire chief shouted above the din of gushing hoses. 'Everyone back,' the chief repeated.

'The building's going to go up,' Crowther shouted. Two uniformed police moved in and took over from the firemen.

Alison ran towards the building, but a fireman stopped her too.

She heard a fire officer shout, 'Jump!' There were two parallel ladders up to a first floor window, and a very young blonde girl, reed-thin and smoke-blackened, was being helped to safety.

Banham squeezed Alison's hand. 'There, I said it would be OK,' he said.

They watched as eight young blonde girls appeared one after another on the scorched window sill. A fireman helped them down the ladder, and another handed them over to waiting paramedics.

'The Ukrainian girls,' Crowther said. 'They were here. Gladman wasn't lying. There was no Wednesday pick-up.'

There was a loud explosion, and the window ledge burst into flames. The last of the eight girls had just reached the bottom. Screams from the cottage tore at Alison's heart.

Crowther began to shout almost hysterically. 'Isabelle!

Millie! Millie! Izzy!'

Another fireman hosed the flames, and others put another ladder up close by.

'There are police officers still in there.' Banham shouted. 'You've got to get my people out.'

'We're doing all we can, sir,' came the reply.

Blue and yellow flames rose from the building. There was a bleeping sound, like a small alarm going off. The fire chief 's calm demeanour began to show cracks. 'That's Roger's alarm,' he said. 'He's in trouble in there.'

It was like battling through thick, black, burning fog. Isabelle couldn't see a thing. She struggled to keep her one working eye open against the sting of the smoke. She was in a lot of pain, and it was making her disorientated. She and Millie had managed to get the young girls to safety, but the last sudden explosion had sent everyone flying and she had completely lost her bearings.

She could hear Millie's voice, but she had no idea if they were still near the window. She fought the urge to cough; her throat was burning and she wanted to throw up, but that wasn't a good idea. Crowther's voice called her name, and that stiffened her spirit. She would get through this; he wouldn't let her down.

'Isabelle?' said Millie's voice, croaky and distorted. 'Where are you?'

'I don't know.' She stopped and held the stinking blanket over her mouth for a moment, but it did nothing to stop the burning in her throat. 'I can hear you. You must be close.'

'Can you see anything?'

'Nothing but smoke.' She felt weak again as she breathed

more of it in.

'I'm by a window.' Millie's voice sounded breathy and hoarse.

'Millie.' Crowther. He sounded a long way off. 'I can see you. Open that window and climb out. We'll catch you if you jump.'

'Go,' Isabelle urged. 'I'm right behind you.'

The truth was she had no idea where she was.

'Millie!' Crowther watched the firemen secure another ladder. One climbed up, lifted Millie out through the window and carried her to safety. She still wore the scorched remains of her red sequinned dress. Her feet were bare, and she looked as if she was about to lose consciousness.

The flames had temporarily subsided and the firemen started to assemble more ladders into a climbing frame to get to Isabelle and Roger.

Two more ambulances shrieked to a halt in the alleyway, and four paramedics jumped out with oxygen and blankets. The Ukrainian girls were being supported through the gate by firemen.

'Keep all the girls at the hospital,' Banham told the paramedics. 'They will all need to be interviewed.'

Alison and Crowther both had tears in their eyes as a para-medic ran over and put an oxygen mask over Millie's face.

Andrew Fisher pushed past them and bent over her to cuddle her close. She tried to push the oxygen mask off, but passed out before she could speak.

More explosions shot through the roof, and black smoke

and flames billowed into the sky. It was like a grim Bonfire Night party.

'Back!' the fire chief shouted again. The firemen obeyed without question.

The building began to crack, and flames shot in all directions. Black smoke swept down to fill the courtyard, and everyone starting coughing and retching, as the cottage roof building collapsed and burning debris flew in all directions.

'Retreat!' the fire chief commanded loudly. 'Everyone clear! Clear this area NOW!' There was desperation in his voice.

Banham and Alison dragged Crowther back. He was hoarse from shouting Isabelle's name. He pulled free and ran towards the bright orange flames. His foot was on the ground floor window sill and he was about to haul himself on to a wobbly drainpipe when a fire-fighter turned a hose on him.

The fire chief was taking no chances. He threw a net over Crowther, and it took two of the biggest firemen to pull him to the ground. Banham and Alison watched in fascinated horror as the window sill he had been about to step on collapsed into the courtyard.

Crowther struggled like a salmon caught by an angler.

'Clear the fucking area!' the firechief shouted, but his voice was lost in the crackling and roaring that followed the next set of explosions.

Crowther put his hands to his head and cried like a lion in pain. 'No-o-o-o-o!'

The fire had rampaged out of control, spreading in all

directions. More engines skidded into the street and nearby buildings were being evacuated.

Banham and Alison used all their strength to drag Crowther into the street. The three of them stood side by side, a safe distance from the blazing centre of the fire: the cottage.

Crowther said very quietly, 'Please God, don't let it end like this.'

Alison swallowed back tears. Banham touched her shoulder, and they walked around to the police cars where Eddie Chang and Terry King were sitting handcuffed. She saw Millie Payne climb out of the ambulance and stumble along the pavement shouting hysterically. She was barefoot and wrapped in a thick blanket, and her face was starting to blister. Her voice was hoarse with smoke, and it was impossible to make out what she was saying.

Andrew Fisher was standing on the pavement. He held out his arms as she approached him, but she stopped a few yards away.

'Don't let him near me!' Alison heard her croak.

'She's a bit delirious, sir,' Andrew said to Banham. 'I'll stay with her, and wait for her at the hospital.'

Millie pointed at Andrew. 'He's working for Eddie Chang!'

'She's delirious,' Andrew repeated. 'She needs to go to hospital – '

'He's got a gun.'

Andrew's mouth opened and closed like a goldfish. Alison grabbed him and began to pat him down.

Millie lurched to the ground in front of him and scrabbled around his ankles. She pushed his trouser leg up and held up

249

a hand-gun identical to the one Sadie Morgan had been carrying. An Astra Cadix .22.

Banham held out his hand for the gun, but Millie staggered to her feet and pointed it at Andrew. 'It was you, wasn't it?' she rasped.

Banham was suddenly aware of two armed CO19 officers moving toward her. 'Millie, give me the gun.'

She ignored him. 'It was you! You killed Sadie.' Her voice cracked and her hand began to shake.

'Millie, you're delirious...'

'You came to the club with me. I gave you an alibi, I lied for you. You're a murdering scumbag and I'll...'

Banham took a step towards her. 'Give me the gun, Millie. Andrew didn't kill Sadie.'

Alison could only watch, horrified at this new turn of events. Where had this come from? If Millie was right, why hadn't any of them worked it out?

Millie steadied the hand holding the gun. 'He did. He killed her. And he just set fire to the cottage and tried to kill us all.' She was swaying on her feet, but she managed to stay upright. 'Ask him where he got this gun. Go on, ask him.'

The CO19 men closed in on each side of her.

'Tell them you're a murderer. Tell them you killed my friend.'

'That's enough, Millie. Give me the gun.' Banham tried to speak calmly. If he didn't get the gun off her, he couldn't be responsible for the armed response men's actions. They were trained to do this job.

'Tell them!'

Andrew looked terrified.

'Millie, you have to give DCI Banham the gun,' Alison shouted urgently.

The young PCSO shook her head defiantly and took a step nearer Andrew. She extended her arm so that the gun almost touched his head.

A warning shot from one of the armed response team hit the ground next to her. Everyone else jumped; she only flicked a glance down at the pavement.

Her aim didn't falter. 'Last chance,' she said.

Andrew's pinched face betrayed his terror but he said nothing.

Alison yelled, 'Millie, for Chrisake, give the gun to...'

Millie pointed the gun at Andrew's foot and pulled the trigger.

The armed response unit took aim.

'Don't shoot her!' Banham leapt in front of Millie.

Andrew was hopping up and down in agony. 'You bitch, you've shot me.'

Banham faced Millie and held out his hand for the gun. *Alison's fragile hold on her temper snapped. 'You stupid girl, give DCI Banham the gun, or someone will shoot you.'*

But Millie had become hysterical. 'I don't care!' she shouted, pointing the gun at Andrew's crotch. 'He killed Sadie, and he started the fire. *Tell them*, or I swear I'll shoot your bollocks off.'

'OK.' Andrew put his hands in the air. 'You win.'

Alison closed her eyes. She wouldn't have seen this coming in a million years.

Millie's arm dropped slackly to her side and Banham waved the armed officers away. Andrew Fisher began to speak.

'I had to kill Sadie,' he said dully. 'Eddie Chang made me. He'd have had me killed.'

'I wish he had,' Millie screamed hoarsely. 'And the fire. Tell them you started the fire.' She began to raise the hand with the gun in it.

'That as well,' Andrew said. 'Chang made me.'

Eddie Chang's head appeared at the police car window. 'What a liar,' he shouted. 'He killed Sadie because he wanted her and couldn't have her.'

Alison couldn't move. She felt as if she'd stepped into a parallel universe, and could only observe what was happening. And none of it made sense.

She heard Banham arrest Andrew Fisher and read him his rights. Two uniformed constables walked past her, and Banham handed Andrew over to them. 'Go with him in the ambulance, and bring him back to the station when the hospital releases him.'

Millie waited until they had walked away before handing the gun to Banham. As she did, CO19 dropped their aim, and Banham said quietly. 'Millie Payne, I'm arresting you for being in possession of a dangerous firearm.'

'What? I was helping you. I'm on your side!'

Alison suddenly found she could move again, and ran towards Millie. 'Get in the ambulance,' she shouted, fighting the urge to smack the girl. 'Before we do anything you're going to hospital.'

Millie looked at her, closed her eyes and swayed gracefully. Next moment she was lying on the pavement in a dead faint.

A couple of paramedics moved in to deal with her, and at the same moment Crowther appeared at the corner of the club building, fighting off a uniformed constable who was trying to restrain him.

'He tried to get into the cottage,' the fresh-faced young officer said apologetically to Alison. 'It's not safe, ma'am. I tried to tell him, but…'

'It's OK, I'll take it from here.' At least this was straight-forward, she thought.

The young man looked relieved, and disappeared in the direction of the alleyway behind the club. Alison stood face to face with Crowther. 'Get a grip, Colin,' she told him firmly.

Banham was behind her. 'We know how it feels,' he told Crowther. 'We're as worried about Isabelle as you are.'

'If I'd got here sooner…' Crowther muttered, desperation roughening his voice.

Alison took a deep breath. 'We're all going to hold it together,' she said firmly. 'We don't know where Isabelle is. Do you hear me, Colin? *We don't know*. She could come walking round that corner any minute.'

'But…' Crowther waved a hand at the glowing sky.

Alison slapped his hand down. 'There are four teams of firemen dealing with that. Leave them to do their job and we'll do ours. We've got all the evidence we need to put Eddie Chang away for a very long time and we couldn't have done that without Isabelle. So let's do what she'd want us to – go back to the station and throw the bloody book at him.'

CHAPTER SEVENTEEN

When Millie woke up she was lying in a hospital bed. She felt as if a swarm of bees had made their home on her body. Her arm was bandaged, and when she touched her face she found that was bandaged too. In fact, an awful lot of her was covered in bandages, some of them leaking orange cream with a vaguely antiseptic smell.

She turned her head cautiously, and to her surprise found Colin Crowther sitting by the bed. As their eyes met, the compassion and concern on his face melted away, to be replaced by one of his mischievous Mr Irresistible smiles.

'Don't worry,' he said. 'The doctor is pretty sure there won't be any scars. They got to it quickly.' The smile dropped away, and she saw sadness in his eyes. 'You've been very brave.' He looked down at his interlaced fingers. 'I told you it was a dangerous job to take on.'

'Just as well.' Her throat was still sore, but she could talk normally now.

'Just as well what?'

'Just as well my face won't be scarred. I'm going to need it to get acting work. I think I've got the sack from the police.'

Crowther didn't answer. He locked and unlocked his fingers. 'Where did you get that gun, Millie? Not the one you took from Fisher. The one in the little bag hanging on your garter.'

She sat up and pushed the blanket away, and slowly swung her legs to the floor. 'I stole it from Terry King's sewing bag before I followed Isabelle to the cottage. I was looking for his torch, but when I saw the gun I took that too – for evidence, I thought, but I did think it might come in useful.'

A sob welled up in her chest and she fought it down. Crying in front of Colin was not an option.

His eyes hadn't left her.

She shivered and grimaced, cautiously touching the large bandage across her forehead. 'It's an Astra Cadix, the same as Sadie had in her bag. That has to prove that Eddie Chang was dealing them.'

'So it wasn't the only one?'

'There were guns in the cottage. That's what caused the explosions. I just hope there's something left for evidence.'

'There will be.' He lifted her bandaged hand and screwed up his nose at the smell of burns ointment. 'Do you regret getting involved?'

'My only regret is not shooting Andrew.'

'You're lucky no one shot you! What was all that about? The guv's going to have some tough questions for you.'

'I know.' She raised her bandaged hand to her eyes to mop the tears. 'What's the news on Isabelle?'

Crowther lowered his eyes and scratched the back of his neck. 'There isn't any. Yet.'

She bit her lip. He was obviously upset, and desperately worried. 'Can I be discharged?' she asked him.

'Yes. I'm here to take you back to the station. You're under arrest for possession at the moment – and Terry King will deny all knowledge of that gun. You'd better get yourself a brief.'

The coffee machines had been drunk dry, and morale in the incident room was at rock bottom.

The DNA tests were in on the pillow and remnants of clothes Banham had taken from the Pelegino's house. They proved beyond doubt that Andrew Fisher had killed both Raymond Adams and Sadie Morgan. He had been officially arrested after being treated for the bullet wound in his foot. No one yet knew why he had killed them, but it looked increasingly likely that had been one of Chang's men all along.

The fire was finally under control, and two bodies had been brought out, both burnt and unrecognisable. One was confirmed as male: almost certainly Roger Atwood, the fireman who went in to help rescue the trapped women. The other was female, but too badly damaged to identify. It could be the last unaccounted-for Ukrainian girl.

Or Isabelle.

A Ukrainian interpreter had spoken to the all the girls. None of them could say who drove them from Dover; their only contact was a man called George. A picture of Eddie Chang drew a blank, but they all recognised one of Johnny Gladman. He had been kind to them, they said, and so had a woman they described as big and broad, and a little odd-looking.

One of the girls spoke a little English. She had told Alison how Millie had opened the door with a hairpin and led them to safety through the black smoke. She said Millie had gone back twice to try to find Isabelle and the missing girl.

Most significant of all was that the same girl had witnessed the scene between Millie and Andrew as she sat in the ambulance. 'That bad man,' she told Alison. 'He is not kind to us.'

The six-month surveillance operation on Doubles and Eddie Chang had been disbanded. They were waiting for further news, but as it stood they still had no evidence to link Chang directly with the Ukrainian girls or the Mac 10 firearms which were currently going up in smoke.

That could change. Johnny Gladman, his brother Otis, Andrew Fisher, Eddie Chang, Terry King and Millie Payne were locked in separate cells awaiting interview.

The only coffee left in the department was in Alison's office. Banham heaped sugar into his own and Crowther's, and handed Alison hers.

'Well, who would have put money on Andrew Fisher?' he said, flopping down in the spare chair.

Crowther perched on the edge of the desk looking thoughtful. He turned his head as Banham handed him the strong, sweet coffee. 'Millie shouldn't be locked in a cell,' he said. 'She's been to hell and back, and you heard what that girl said about her.'

'She was carrying a gun,' Alison pointed out. 'And she took the law into her own hands in front of witnesses.' But she softened when she saw the look on Crowther's face. 'We'll sort it,' she assured him.

'We'll let her off with a warning,' Banham said.

'Better make it a stern one,' Alison advised. 'She could have got herself killed.'

'She deserves a medal, not a dressing down,' Crowther

257

said angrily.

'The press are outside waiting for her,' Alison told him. 'She'll get a lot of publicity out of this.' She tilted her head. 'She might even get some acting work, then we won't need to sack her – she'll resign.'

Alison could hardly bear to look at Andrew Fisher. He sat the other side of the table, slouched untidily in his chair, hair falling over his eyes.

'We know you killed Sadie Morgan and Ray Adams,' Banham said. 'What we don't know is why. Do you want to enlighten us?'

Andrew shrugged and shook his head.

Alison felt a strong urge to punch him. 'You thought you could get away with it, did you?' she said. 'You made out you were the big hero, when in fact you were just a snake. You started a fire in a building with two fellow officers and a dozen children in it.'

She swallowed hard as an image of Isabelle jumped into her mind, fighting to get out and choking on the oily black smoke.

She leaned across the table. 'I've got an officer still not accounted for, and I am holding you responsible for her life.'

Andrew bowed his head.

She sat back. 'You are all I loathe in a human being and believe me I am going to throw the book at you.' Her eyes burned into him. 'They hate our kind in prison.' His eyes flicked nervously; that clearly worried him. She rubbed it in. 'You'll be there for a very, very long time.'

Banham's tone was softer. 'Try to help yourself,

Andrew. We know Chang is behind this, and you can help us put him away. Why did you agree to kill Sadie and Ray?'

Andrew sat in silence for a long moment. Alison's eyes never left him. 'Up to you,' she said. 'But you've a chance here to help yourself.' Isabelle's face flashed back into her mind. 'Not that I'm making any promises.'

Andrew looked at her for the first time. 'I owed Chang a lot of money,' he said quietly.

'Speak up please, for the disc.' She wasn't about to make it easy for him.

'What for?' Banham pushed.

'I was in debt. I was a gambler. The loan sharks moved in on me. They would have killed me. I had no choice.'

Alison didn't trust herself to speak. She turned a pencil over and over again to occupy her hands. She wanted to hit him so badly.

'Go on,' Banham said.

'Eddie Chang turned up on my doorstep one night, and made me an offer I couldn't refuse.' He paused. 'I'm not proud of myself.'

Alison felt Banham's eyes on her but she dared not look at him. Isabelle's desperate face was in her mind again, along with her own voice shouting reassurance.

Andrew continued, 'He said he would pay my debt and make me rich if I came to work for him.'

Alison held on to the corner of the desk, still clutching the pencil in the other hand. She hadn't completely dismissed the idea of poking him in the eye with it.

'What did he want you to do?' she asked tightly.

'Get a job here as a PCSO. It's not hard to get in. He wanted me to find things out for him.'

259

'What things?'

'Who was grassing on him.'

'Is that why he had you kill Ray Adams?'

Andrew nodded reluctantly. 'I shot him. I didn't do the... other things.'

'You mean you didn't cut his penis and tongue off?'

Andrew winced as Banham spelled it out. 'Yes, that. It wasn't me.'

'You killed Sadie Morgan though.'

'Yes, but not the others. I didn't kill the other Marilyn looka-likes or the boyfriend. Ray Adams killed them.'

'Why did Chang want Sadie Morgan killed?' Banham asked.

'I don't know.' He flicked his hair from his eyes and scratched at one of his spots.

'I think you do.' Banham wasn't letting go.

'Something to do with Otis Gladman. That boy that got stabbed – that was Chang. One of his men, anyway. Sadie found out.'

'How?'

'She and Johnny Gladman were friends. Really good friends.'

'So Chang ordered you to kill her.'

He nodded.

Alison wasn't making it easy. 'For the disc please.'

'Yes.' He rubbed his spots again. 'I didn't want to kill her. She was a nice girl. But he gave me no choice.'

Alison folded her arms. 'There's always a choice.'

'He wrote off my debts, and he paid me thousands. I've been able to get full-time carers for my parents. Mum has bad arthritis – she used to be a dancer – and Dad has had

260

two strokes. If I didn't do what Chang wanted I was a dead man, and they were back to square one.'

'So the CCTV of you in the club at the time of Sadie's murder was rigged?' Banham asked. 'By Chang, for our benefit – was that it?'

Andrew nodded. 'Chang realised you were suspicious the morning after, when you asked him about me visiting the club. Terry King fixed the DVD timer to show me in the club at the time Sadie was killed. Terry got me a coat identical to the one I was wearing when I k-killed Sadie – 'He swallowed hard and blinked several times. 'And a Tesco bag to make it look like I'd been shopping, but all that was in it was the other coat. He told me to dump that.'

'And you dumped it Saturday late morning, after the search, near the park where you killed her,' Alison prompted.

'Yes.'

'And gave us the coat Terry had given you, which didn't have Sadie's DNA on it.'

'We knew you'd ask for it.'

Banham blew out a long breath. 'What about the other two Marilyn lookalikes?' he asked. 'Why did Chang want them dead? What did they do to upset him?'

Andrew looked miserable. 'Nothing. Nothing at all. He had them killed to throw you off the scent. He got Ray Adams to do it for an armful of heroin. He said you'd think you had a Marilyn Monroe serial killer, and I'd be off the hook. He wasn't far wrong, was he?'

Alison wanted to kick someone, but wasn't sure if it was Fisher or herself. 'At the expense of two innocent lives,' she said.

261

'So Lily Palmer, Amy Bailey and Joshua Timpkin were just victims of a cold-blooded plan to throw us off the scent?' Banham repeated.

'Partly. Chang knew Adams was the grass by then.'

'Because you'd told him.' Banham said flatly.

'Yes. He got Adams to kill two of the lookalikes, it didn't matter which two, then to tell you the girls and the guns were being picked up Wednesday, but they were already here. Then he said I had to shoot Adams, at the garage where they kept the crystal meth. He had arranged a meet with Adams there, to pay him for the killings, but I went instead and… and shot him.' Andrew looked pleadingly at Banham. 'I shot him in the head. I didn't cut his...' He put his hands over his face. 'Oh God, what have I done?'

'Where did you get the gun?'

'Chang.'

Banham sat back. It was all starting to fit, at long last.

'OK, what about last night? It was you who you set fire to the cottage?'

'Only because Chang told me to.'

'But you knew Millie and Isabelle were in there,' Alison said through clenched teeth.

Fisher started to cry.

'Oh, spare us the theatricals!'

'I've been a real idiot. I'm so sorry.'

'Not half as sorry as you'll be if Isabelle Walsh doesn't make it.' Half to herself she added, 'And to think I put you in the club to look after Millie.'

'You don't know what Eddie Chang is like.'

'Oh, don't I?' Banham said the black flecks in her eyes shone when she was angry. The way she felt right now, they

262

were about to break into flames. 'What about those poor girls? You knew they were in the cottage. Some of them are only twelve years old, and they hardly speak six words of English between them.'

He hung his head.

She raised her voice. 'And the guns. All those Mac 10s. Didn't you realise they'd explode?'

Banham leaned towards him. 'Do you have any idea what damage those sub-machine guns could cause? Chang doesn't care who they're sold to. They would cause carnage on the streets.'

Andrew shook his head vigorously. 'I didn't know the guns were in the cottage. Please, Mr Banham, you've got to believe me. He didn't tell me a thing about that. Or the crystal meth. '

'But you know where he kept it.'

'Not until he told me to shoot Adams, I swear.'

Banham's eyes held his. 'Don't fuck with me, Fisher. You knew what his business was. Guns, girls and drugs. You're Chang's boy. Of course you knew.'

Andrew cowered back in his chair.

Banham raised his voice. 'You knew. Didn't you?'

Fisher closed his eyes. A tear squeezed past his lashes, and he began to whimper. 'Yes,' he whispered. 'I know all about him. What do you want to know?'

Ten minutes later Banham and Alison were back in the incident room. There was no more news from the fire, but the building was safe enough to allow a search for the remaining victim.

Banham played the disc of Andrew's confession for the

team.

'We've got a confession,' he said when it ended, 'but we still can't prove Chang's involvement with the Mac 10s or the girls, or even the drugs. It's Fisher's word against Chang's. It's just not enough.'

If Eddie Chang thought he could wind Banham or Alison up today, he was wrong. He sat opposite them and beside his middle-aged, mouthy brief, who always turned up in a brightly coloured bow-tie whatever the time of day. His name was Toeman; in the force he was known as Toerag. Banham was waiting for an excuse to throw the book at him too.

'You have been arrested for the possession of firearms and illegal substances, trafficking illegal immigrants, and the instigation of the murders of Sadie Morgan, Lily Palmer, Amy Bailey, Joshua Timpkin and Raymond Adams,' Banham said formally. 'And the instigation of a fire that has so far resulted in the deaths of two people, including a fire officer.'

Eddie Chang smiled. 'What Johnny Gladman does in his house is nothing to do with me,' he said. 'And there are witnesses who say Andrew Fisher started that fire. I am the victim here. I have lost my club, my memorabilia, everything.'

'Why did you have Sadie Morgan killed?' Alison asked him.

'I didn't.'

'Do you have any proof of that?' Toeman demanded.

He was ignored.

'You had Ray Adams killed by Andrew Fisher,' Banham

persisted.

'No.'

'He killed Lily Palmer, Amy Bailey and Joshua Timpkin.'

'If you say so.'

'It was you that said so. You paid him to kill them.'

'Certainly not.'

'Using the illegal substances that you trade at the club as a lure.'

Chang smirked. 'You've been watching too much television.'

'Inspector, my client has had an emotional…'

Alison cut across Toeman's intervention. 'Are you saying you didn't know there were a dozen young Ukrainian girls locked up in your cottage?'

'I had no idea.'

'You never go in there?'

'No.'

'There's CCTV everywhere. How could you miss them?'

'There's no CCTV in the cottage…'

'If you know that, you must have been in there.'

'As I was about to say, Inspector, there's no CCTV in the cottage unless Gladman has installed it. I certainly haven't. I own the cottage, but I rent it to Johnny Gladman. It's his home. I don't intrude.'

'How did the firearms get in there?'

'I've no idea. Ask Johnny.'

'Why were you running away?'

'I was afraid.'

'Your friend had a gun.'

'Yes, he had. I had no idea he possessed a dangerous

265

weapon. That scared me too.'

'Good at passing the buck, aren't you?' Alison said, staring in to his eyes.

'Not enough,' Banham said, pacing up and down the corridor.
'Not nearly enough. Toerag will get him bail and we'll lose him.'

'We'll have to crack Terry King, then,' Alison suggested.

'That'll be a hard battle,' Banham said. 'They've been lovers for twelve years.'

'We could tell him Chang is dropping it all on him, and see how he reacts.'

Banham looked dubious.

'Don't we owe it to Isabelle?'

Banham stopped pacing. 'Take Crowther with you,' he said. 'Tell him to frighten the life out of him.'

Terry King's indignant face reminded Alison of the pet goldfish she'd had as a child. The spiteful hazel eyes sneered at Alison.

'Where did you get the gun?' Alison asked him.

'Andrew Fisher gave it to me. He suggested I shoot you, but I refused, of course. I wouldn't do that. We panicked, that's all. Andrew had started a fire, and we realised Johnny Gladman had firearms in the cottage when the explosions started. We didn't want to get dragged into it – we wanted to get away.'

'What about the gun that was found in your sewing bag?' Crowther asked him.

'If there was a gun in there, someone planted it.' He

plonked an elbow on the table and wiggled his fingers as if he was drying his dark maroon nail varnish.

Crowther leaped up as if he was about to lose it. Alison pulled him back.

'You've already been charged with threatening a police officer with a loaded gun,' Alison told him. 'We know you have access to firearms.'

Crowther cut in. 'Make it easy for yourself, Terry. You know what they do to your kind in jail.'

Terry shifted uncomfortably.

'Tell us where the guns came from.'

'Andrew Fisher gave me the one I pointed at you,' Terry said, opening his eyes innocently. 'And of course I don't keep one in my sewing bag. Whoever says I did is lying.'

'Who do you think the judge will believe? You – or the police officer who found it?'

'Why don't you be sensible?' Alison said.

'For your own good,' Crowther added.

Alison piled on the pressure. 'We know Chang is behind all this. If you help us, we'll put in a recommendation to the CPS. You really don't want to go back to prison, do you, Terry?'

'Chang won't be there to protect you this time,' Crowther added. 'The likes of you wouldn't do well in there.'

There was a few seconds silence. He's thinking about it, Alison thought with a little rush of relief.

Then he took his elbow off the table.

'Why don't you go fuck yourselves?' he said calmly.

'They're going to get away with it,' Alison said, slumping into her office chair. 'Toerag will help them load all the blame on to Johnny Gladman and Andrew Fisher, and he'll get a nice fat fee for it.'

'Have you spoken to Millie yet?' Crowther asked Banham.

'No. I went down to the cells, but she was fast asleep. She's had a rough time – she needs to rest. We'll talk to her again when she wakes, and then send her home with a warning. You got her statement at the hospital.'

'Any news?' Alison asked.

Banham shook his head. 'Isabelle's a survivor,' he said, but he didn't sound convinced.

'Let's talk to the Gladman brothers,' Banham said with a sigh. 'At least they tell the truth sometimes.'

'Chang has given us enough evidence to have you charged with importation of women for prostitution, possession of enough firearms to wipe out South London, and accessory to murder,' Banham said, settling back in his chair.

'He's fitting me up again like he did with the drugs.' Johnny Gladman sounded resigned. 'I've told you, Mr Banham. Chang killed my mother and set my brother up for that stabbing.'

Neither Banham nor Alison said anything.

'Felix Greene was stabbed as a warning to me.' There was desperation in his eyes. 'It's Otis's turn next, that's what he was telling me.' He glanced at his brother, who was hunched in the chair beside him, twisting his hands together. 'Sadie lost her life for trying to help us. Chang has had me over a barrel for months because my mother owed him money – and now I'm going down for this.' He shook his dreadlocks and covered his face with his hands.

'Why would Sadie want to help you? Alison asked him.

He shook the dreadlocks again. 'She was kind. We was friends. You understand about friends? Her ex-husband was a bully and I stuck up for her. That's what friends do. She was the first real friend I ever had.'

Otis started to cry. Quite different from the boy on the estate, surrounded by a gang armed with knives and meat cleavers, Alison thought.

'Johnny, I'd really like to believe you,' Alison said. 'But we need real evidence if we're going to put Chang away. Help us get it and you can walk away. If you don't, he'll be the one who walks.'

Johnny shook his head. 'No way. Even if I could help you, I wouldn't. Chang's got contacts everywhere. Even from prison he'd have us shot.'

'We can sort that,' Banham assured him. 'We'll put you in witness protection. We can change your identities and send you somewhere far away.'

Otis sat up. 'Can you do that?'

'We certainly can. And we will – if you help us.'

Otis looked at his brother. 'So we can live together, and go somewhere new?' he asked again.

'If you help us, we'll help you,' Alison said. 'That's a promise.'

Otis and Johnny exchanged another look. There was doubt in their eyes, as if they still weren't sure who they could trust. Banham sat back and tried to look relaxed. This could be the break they needed, but if he pressured the brothers any more, it might go the wrong way.

'Do it, bro. Put the bastard away.' Otis spoke quietly, but his tone conveyed the strength of his feelings about his

269

brother's boss.

'Yeah?' Johnny still wasn't sure, but he was softening. 'Mr Banham, what happens when we get outa here? How long before we can, like, disappear?'

It took Banham a few minutes to explain the witness protection procedure. 'It'll mean another couple of nights in the cells,' he finished, 'but at least you know you're safe there!'

The brothers consulted in whispers, then Johnny raised his head and stuck out a hand. 'Deal, Mr Banham. Shake on it?'

Banham suppressed a smile as he shook Johnny Gladman's hand. 'You'll be our star witness,' he assured him.

'OK.' Johnny took a deep breath and launched in. 'When Sadie left the club on Friday, I gave her the key to Ray Adams's garage on our block. The knife with Felix's blood on it and the sample of crystal meth was all at her flat. She was going to go home and fetch it all, then come to you and hand it in with the key.

'She looked a bit odd when she left the club, like she'd been drugged. I think maybe Terry had given her something in a glass of water. I know Terry keeps some stuff in his room – he gives it to the girls from abroad to make them sleepy. Maybe you'll find that?'

Alison nodded. 'Toxicology report has gamma hydroxybutryate in Sadie's system at time of death. It's a date-rape drug.'

'How did Chang find out that Sadie had taken the gun and knife?' Banham asked.

'That was your man – Andrew Fisher. When Millie came

270

to work in the club, she introduced Sadie to him. None of us knew he was one of Chang's men, that's the truth, Mr Banham. Sadie found out he was a copper – people talked to Sadie, told her things, she was a real nice person – and she told him she was going to go to the police station and asked him who she oughta talk to. Next thing Sadie was murdered.' He looked Banham in the eyes. 'I was worried sick for Otis's safety so I told him to keep away from the club, to stay at Mum's flat, out of sight. He's had to fend for himself.'

'Otis fends for himself quite well, from what I've seen,' Alison said.

'The estate gang have been looking out for me,' Otis protested. 'If I had gone against them, they would have been my enemy and carved me up.'

No arguing with that, Alison thought. 'Do you know who actually killed Sadie?' she asked Johnny.

'Andrew Fisher.' Johnny spoke very quietly.

'You knew all along?'

He lowered his head. 'Yes. Eddie told me. He warned me it would be Otis's turn if I tried anything stupid.'

'What about the other three victims?' Banham asked gently.

'Chang liked the idea of a serial killer after his Marilyn girls. It was Lily made him think of it, when she said she was being followed. He decided to have a couple of Marilyns killed to make you think there was a stalker. He got Ray Adams to smother Lily with a pillow, same as Andrew…' He stopped, and his throat worked as if he was swallowing down a sob. When he continued, his voice has risen in pitch. 'Same as Andrew killed Sadie, then Chang

271

told him to kill any girl he liked, just to throw you off the scent. Man, that is one sick bastard.'

'And Adams? Alison asked, already knowing the answer.

'Chang had him killed.'

'Who by?'

'Andrew shot him. Chang wanted his tongue cut out for being an informant, but Andrew wouldn't do that. So Chang did it himself after he was dead. Cut his cock off too – sorry, miss, but that's what he did. That was for the pervy things he did to the two girls.'

'Chang actually told you this?'

'Yeah, told me himself. I think he wanted to frighten me. It worked.'

He fell silent, and sat with his hands in his lap, staring at the floor. Otis's eyes flicked uneasily from Alison to Banham and back again, and he nibbled at the skin around his thumbnail.

'What happens now?' he asked nervously. 'When do we go to the new place?'

'Not for a little while,' Banham said, hiding a smile. 'I'm afraid your brother will still have to face a charge of withholding evidence.'

Otis's face fell. Johnny didn't move.

'We'll talk to the Crown Prosecution Service,' Banham continued. 'When we tell them everything that's happened to you both and who you're helping us to put away, I wouldn't be surprised if they decide not to pursue the charges. Then we'll get you into witness protection, give you new identities and send you a long way away. You'll be safe.'

Now it was Johnny's turn to look nervous. 'That's what

the social worker said after Mum died, when she came to see about Otis. *You'll be safe*, she said. In care, she meant.'

'Better in care than with that gang on the estate. If he stays in with them, he's heading for a criminal record.'

'I want to take care of him myself! He's my brother, man!'

'You'll get your chance,' Banham told him. 'Now, I have another job for you. I'm going to arrange bail – don't worry, it's only for a few hours, and there'll be an officer within yards of you all the time. I want Otis to go and talk to his friend Felix. If he'll give us a statement, we're home and dry. As it stands it's still your word against Chang's.'

Otis looked like a frightened rabbit. 'He'll do his best,' Johnny said.

As they walked back down the corridor Banham spoke on his phone, making arrangements to have Johnny and Otis put under surveillance.

'You reckon they're on the level, then?' Alison asked him.

'I think so. But I'm still not a hundred percent.'

'Better make sure the surveillance on Lottie and the kids stays put, then.'

In the incident room, Millie Payne was sitting next to Crowther. A warm, fleecy, pink tracksuit top covered the top half of the red Monroe dress's charred remains, and the rest of her was huddled under a hospital blanket. Her arms, legs and much of her face were lost under gauze bandaging the hospital staff had applied to her burns, and a strong aroma of antiseptic cream surrounded her.

'You should be resting,' Alison said gently. 'You're

probably still in shock.'

'I thought I was under arrest for possession of a firearm.'

Alison looked over her shoulder at Banham. 'Actually you're quite a hero,' Alison told her with a glint in her eye. 'Though you did behave irresponsibly and disobey your commanding officers.'

Millie's attempt at a smile didn't quite succeed. 'Any news?' she asked with a sadness in her eyes that brought a lump to Alison's throat.

'Not yet. The fire officers are still searching the building.'

'What's happened to Andrew?'

'He's been charged with murder,' Banham told her. 'That's ninety percent down to you.'

'We've got evidence that he killed Sadie Morgan and Raymond Adams,' Alison added.

'It's not down to me.' Millie said unhappily. 'I gave him an alibi. If I hadn't gone to the club during my shift… I'll never forgive myself for that. One mistake, and look what it leads to.'

Alison nodded. 'I will have to put that in my report. And to be honest, Millie, I'm not sure you're cut out for PCSO work.'

'I've been so stupid. I'm truly, truly sorry.'

'We won't be bringing any charges,' Banham said. 'You need to get some rest. I'm going to get a car to take you home.' He moved away and took out his phone again.

'Crowther took a statement from you at the hospital, didn't he?' Alison checked.

'Yes. I told him about taking the gun from Terry's sewing bag.'

'Terry refutes it. He said he'd never seen it before. So it's your word against his, I'm afraid.'

Millie looked puzzled. 'What about all the others?'

Alison held her breath. 'What others?'

'There was a box of them in the corner of the dressing room. Under the box of red shoes. I thought you'd found them.'

'Is that in your statement?'

Millie shook her head. 'Nobody asked about them. I assumed you knew.'

Alison had already picked up the nearest phone.

'We'd better take another statement,' she said to Millie when she had finished giving the instruction. 'Then you can go home. You really do need to rest.'

Banham reappeared. 'Did you know there's a whole lot of press photographers and reporters outside?' he asked Millie. 'They want to talk to you. I expect they want to get your picture for the paper. That'll be good for your career, won't it?'

'Can I go out the back way?' Millie asked.

Alison couldn't believe her ears. 'Well, yes,' she said. 'But don't you want the publicity? I thought actresses never missed a chance to get their names in the papers.'

'Not any more,' Millie said firmly. 'This is my real job now. I'm taking it seriously from now on.' She paused, looking Alison in the eyes. 'I want to do this full time,' she said. 'I'm applying to be a WPC.'

No one spoke for a moment, then Banham said, 'Good for you.'

'But you've got one hell of a lot to learn,' Alison added quickly.

'I know that,' Millie said. 'But I've already learned a lot from my mistakes. Don't you learn from yours?'

Alison was aware of Banham's eyes on her.

'Yes,' she said. 'I try to, anyway.'

Millie nodded. 'I made a big one, and I've owned up to it.' She handed Alison an unsealed envelope. 'This is my application, asking if I can train to be a full-time WPC. It needs to go to Human Resources, but you can read it first. I hope you don't mind – I've put you both down for a reference.'

CHAPTER EIGHTEEN

The fire was out at last, and forensic police and fire teams were in the building, searching among the debris and trying to determine how it started. Part of the cottage roof had collapsed and nearby buildings had caught the odd flying spark. The road was still cordoned off and its residents remained in temporary accommodation.

Most of the squad had been sent home, but Banham and Alison hadn't left the office. Neither of them had slept; Alison had dropped off for less than five minutes in her tiny office, but Banham had paced the floor of the incident room willing the phone to ring.

After the interviews, Crowther had spent what remained of the night travelling between the station, the scene of the fire and the forensics lab. Tests had proved without a shadow of doubt that the unrecognisable female body belonged to the only Ukrainian who hadn't managed to escape the fire.

Isabelle was still unaccounted for.

When Crowther arrived back at the station, he almost collided with Banham at the front door. Banham had been waiting outside the bakery on the corner when it opened, and was carrying a bag of warm croissants and a bacon roll.

In the almost deserted incident room, Alison was brewing yet more hot coffee. She poured a cup for Crowther, and Banham handed him the bacon roll, but the smell turned his stomach over. He managed to swallow a few mouthfuls of sweet coffee as he flicked through the witness statements.

'Guv, you realise we've got nothing concrete,' he said, flinging the folder down on the desk. 'The whole CO19 op was a joke; Chang was on to us all along. That toerag Fisher gave him regular updates. He probably knew Millie was with the police before he even took her on as a lookalike. Look how he played us over the gun shipment delivery and the girls. It'll be his word against theirs. The CPS may not even bother taking it to court.'

'He's right,' Alison said. 'Chang's bent brief will get him bail and even if he doesn't skip the country and we do get to court, he stands a good chance of getting off.'

Crowther slammed his empty coffee cup down. 'What do we have to do? Shoot the bastard ourselves?'

Banham laid a hand on Crowther's shoulder. 'We'll get him,' he said, with a lot more confidence than he felt.

Alison's mobile rang.

She checked the screen. It was the DC detailed to report back from the fire scene as soon as there was any news. She switched the phone to speaker.

A team of twenty strong of forensic officers were in the building, and they now had proof that the fire had been started deliberately.

The officer took a deep breath before continuing.

'Guv,' he said. 'They've found the third body.'

The coffee and croissants were all cold. The phones in the incident room were ringing constantly with the press asking for comments; no one obliged. Nobody had spoken for about half an hour.

The charred body was confirmed as Isabelle from the watch she wore with a photo of her mother in the back; one of the forensic officers had recognised it.

The internal line rang, and this time Banham picked up. It was one of the surveillance officers detailed to keep watch on Lottie and the children. Some people had arrived at the house.

'I'm on my way,' Banham said, guiltily relieved to have something positive to do. 'Keep me informed.' He clicked off him phone and looked at Alison. 'Come with me?'

Lottie lived less than a mile from the station. They arrived to find her on the doorstep, with Bobby and Madeleine close behind her. Lottie was talking to Johnny Gladman, his brother Otis, another young black youth, and a tall Caribbean woman. Johnny introduced her as Mrs Greene, and the second boy as her son Felix.

'What are you doing here? Banham asked them.

Bobby pushed past his mother and looked up at his uncle. 'Otis has come to say sorry for frightening me,' he said importantly. 'A bad man made him write me that note. He had to do it, or else Felix would get hurt again. He said he didn't want to do it. He doesn't like hurting people.'

Banham put his hand on Bobby's shoulder and looked at his sister. 'Lottie, do you mind if we take this inside?' he asked. 'I'm sure you can do without the neighbours taking an interest.'

Curtains were already beginning to twitch along the road, and Lottie didn't demur. She led the way inside and closed the door behind them.

In the lounge, Lottie motioned Mrs Greene into an

279

armchair and sat down herself, pulling Madeleine on to her knee. Everyone else stood, and Banham looked expectantly at Otis Gladman.

But it was Bobby who spoke again. 'Otis said it's going to be all right, and the bully boys will leave me alone now. He says he's really sorry, Uncle Paul, and I believe him.'

Banham's eyes were still focused on Otis. Bobby touched his uncle's hand. 'Felix says he'll tell you all about the bad man, isn't that right, Felix?'

'Felix is going to make a statement against Eddie Chang?' Alison asked, looking from Banham to Felix Greene and back again.

Felix's mother stood up and held out her hand to Banham. 'Detective Inspector, my son told me today that he has known all along who stabbed him, but he was too afraid to say anything. He also told me the reason someone tried to kill him; he was there when Otis's mother was shot last summer.' She sat down quickly, as if the effort of divulging all this was too much effort. She put out a hand to her son, and he went to stand beside her, a protective arm around her shoulders. 'He used to be a strong boy,' she said quietly, 'but he has become very nervous. He has nightmares and sometimes he even sleepwalks.'

There was a pause. Felix stared at the carpet looking slightly embarrassed. After a few moments his mother continued. 'The man who stabbed my son told him he would kill me if Felix uttered a word.' She took a deep breath. 'Felix didn't tell me that until today, when Johnny and Otis came to our house. Detective Inspector, I will not have my son persecuted. I want that man behind bars where he belongs. We are God-fearing people – we go to church

280

regular. Johnny and Otis too, before their mother died. They're good boys like my Felix – they got themselves mixed up with the wrong sorts.'

Johnny was standing by the door, but Otis had moved to the other side of Mrs Greene's chair. A tear rolled down his cheek and he knelt on the floor beside her. She put a motherly hand on Otis's head and rubbed his dreadlocks; he didn't seem to object.

'I have told them all that the only way forward is to tell the truth,' she said with a note of defiance. 'Somebody has to stand up to this demon. He killed Letitia Gladman, and but for the grace of God my son would be dead too.'

Felix gripped his mother's hand. She sat upright in the armchair, the embodiment of calm and dignity.

'Felix? Can you tell us who stabbed you?' Alison asked him gently.

He looked at his mother and she nodded. 'Go on, son. Tell the lady the truth.'

'That policeman.'

Alison's heart hit her boots. They should have known; Eddie Chang didn't do his own dirty work. They still didn't have him. Banham's expression was stony.

'What was his name? Do you know?' she asked the boy.

'Fisher. He's not a real policeman – he's one of those, you know, support people. But he's not the... what my mum just said. The demon. The bad man.'

'OK. Can you tell us about the bad man? You said you wanted to give us a statement. What was his name?'

She held her breath, sending up silent prayers to any god who happened to be listening.

'Chang. Eddie Chang.'

Relief flooded Alison's veins and she started to breathe again.

Felix went on, 'He came to visit me in hospital. He told me I should be dead, and I was a very lucky boy. I knew that already – I thought he was another doctor, at first anyway. But he gave me some money, quite a lot of money, and doctors only give you medicine. And 'sides, I remembered I seen him before – he wasn't no doctor. Then he said I should keep quiet. I asked him about what, and he said if I talked about who stabbed me, my mum would die.'

'Eddie Chang said that to you?'

'Yes, miss. He said he would kill my mother just like he killed Otis's.'

'Was anyone else there when he said it?' Alison asked.

'No, but I believed him. He shot Otis's mother for sure. I seen him do it. That's why I didn't tell no one who stabbed me.'

The boy was obviously in distress, but Alison had no choice; they were so nearly there. She pushed on. 'You were there that day? You actually saw him shoot Otis's mother?'

'Yes, miss. I took a photo. That's why that policeman stabbed me. He wanted my phone with the picture.'

'Before he stabbed you, did you tell anyone else you had a photo of the man that shot Otis's mother?'

'No, I didn't tell no one. That is one scary dude, man.' Felix was trembling. 'You gotta understand, I thought he would come after me – and then the next day I got stabbed. I didn't tell no one who did it because I was afraid for my mum.'

'It's all right,' Banham said gently. 'You've been very

282

brave. Nothing will happen to you now. We will make sure it doesn't.'

Janet Greene patted her son's hand. 'You're a good boy,' she said. 'Sometimes it's hard, but you're a good boy.'

'It's over now,' Banham told him. 'Eddie Chang will go to prison.'

Alison and Banham exchanged a look. It was still touch and go; even if Felix could be persuaded into court, all they had was the testimony of a fifteen-year-old boy. Without more solid evidence, Chang was still capable of wriggling out of their clutches despite everything he had done.

Then Felix changed everything.

'Miss?' he said to Alison. 'Do you want the photo I took? It's here.'

He dug in his pocket and drew out a mobile phone.

Alison could hardly believe this was happening. 'I thought you said Fisher took it?'

'That was my mum's. I didn't know what to do with the photo. Otis's mum was dead, but that man scared me even before the hospital. So I gave my phone to Mum, and took hers to school that day.'

Mrs Greene looked as flabbergasted as Alison felt.

'Did you know about this?' Alison asked her, knowing the answer. The other woman shook her head and stared in disbelief at her son. 'You never said why you wanted me to have your phone,' she told him. 'Why didn't you say?'

'That's not important any more,' Banham intervened. 'What matters is Felix has still got the picture. Can I see it, please?'

Felix flicked some buttons and passed the phone to Banham. 'It's not that clear, but that's Mrs Gladman lying

283

on the pavement, and you can see it's the bad man. He's still holding the gun, look.'

Alison and Banham looked at the picture and then at each other. The boy had described exactly what was on the tiny screen.

'Felix, this is brilliant,' Alison said. 'Are you are willing to stand up in court and tell the judge and jury what you've just us?'

Felix opened his mouth to speak, but his mother hushed him. 'You have to protect us,' she said urgently. 'That Mr Chang has many men working for him and we don't want to be looking over our shoulders for the rest of our lives. What kind of life is that for a growing boy?' She paused and looked at Johnny and Otis. 'Johnny said you told him about a scheme – I think he said it was witness protection, where they get new names and a place to stay a long way from here, somewhere nobody knows them. But two boys on their own... This time they broke the law because they were scared of that man – but who knows what kind of trouble will find them if they have no one to look out for them? When poor Letitia passed over, I made a promise that I would do that, look out for them I mean, and I haven't been able to keep that promise yet. Detective Inspector, if I look out for them, will you look out for me and Felix? Can we all four go away somewhere new as a family?'

She spoke to Banham, but Alison answered. 'We'll put you under police protection right away. You'll need to stay close by until the trial, but afterwards all four of you can go into the witness protection programme. I'll get someone to explain what it means, but you're right about moving away and having new identities. And I'm sure we can make sure you stay together.'

The atmosphere in the room had changed, as if a heavy weight had been lifted and the air had cleared. Alison looked at Banham. They had him. They had the evidence that they'd been trying to get for five years to put Eddie Chang away. Felix Greene had simply handed them the picture, totally oblivious that he had finally allowed them to nail the most dangerous criminal Greater London had known in a long time.

So why wasn't she jumping for joy?

Lottie was standing in the doorway, with Bobby and Madeleine holding fast to her hands. 'This probably feels like a champagne moment to you,' she said to her brother, 'but I think I'd rather have a cup of tea.'

Banham grinned and nodded, and Lottie headed for the kitchen. Otis Gladman was still on his knees beside Mrs Greene's chair.

'You have to get away from the gang on your estate,' Banham said to him. 'They're bad news, and you'll end up in big trouble if you hang around with them.'

'He's already in big trouble,' Johnny said sharply. 'You think I want my brother stealing, and being a delivery boy for drug dealers?' He cuffed the side of Otis's head. 'I've been too busy trying to stop Chang hurting him to take proper care of him. He was going the same way as Mum and I didn't even see it.'

Janet Greene squeezed Johnny's hand. 'Not any more. Our flat is small, but we'll find room for both of you, till we move away.'

'Good idea,' Alison said. 'It's easier to protect you if you're all under one roof.' She held up Felix's phone. 'And you don't need to worry about Eddie Chang. He's going to prison, and when he comes out he'll be a very old man. If he ever does come out.'

'I have to be honest,' Banham said to Johnny and Otis. 'There are still charges you two will have to answer. But you were coerced and taken in, and that's what we'll be telling the CPS. Whether or not they proceed is up to them – but we'll do all we can.'

The photo was grainy, but it was clearly Eddie Chang holding a gun. The CPS were now confident they would win the case – but then Penny Starr played another blinder. The Astra Cadix gun Terry King had waved around on the night of the fire had gone to Ballistics. The report was back – and it confirmed that this was the gun which had shot Mrs Gladman. Eddie Chang's prints were on it as well as Terry's, and some careful enhancement of Felix Greene's photo revealed that it was identical to the gun Eddie Chang was pointing at Mrs Gladman's head. The CPS were now so confident they would win their case that they sent the investigation team a case of champagne.

No one felt like drinking it.

Banham had gone out, and Alison was sitting at Isabelle's desk sorting through the paperwork the young DC had left behind. Crowther was at his desk in front, writing his report.

Crowther's words were ringing round inside Alison's head. 'If you want to succeed you have to take a few chances.' He had said it when he was persuading her to let Millie work undercover at Doubles. She had taken those chances, and they had solved four murders and gathered enough evidence to put a dangerous criminal away.

But it had cost her a friend and the police a good officer.

Alison still believed a newly qualified PCSO shouldn't have been allowed in on such a dangerous mission. It was her decision, and her heart had said a firm no. It had been a mistake to give in. If she had stuck to her guns, Andrew Fisher wouldn't have been in the club, and Isabelle might even be alive.

And what about her affair with Banham? Was that another mistake? They still hadn't resolved their disagreement about his emotional involvement in the case, and at the moment she didn't know if they had a future. She just knew she wanted time to think things through.

Crowther had also made mistakes, first in his choice of informant, then by having an affair with Millie. As things had turned out, they had all underestimated Millie; not only could she look out for herself, but she possessed useful skills and a degree of courage that had saved the lives of eleven young eastern European girls, and come close to saving a fellow police officer.

Isabelle had made a mistake too. Falling for Crowther meant she had missed out on the promotion she coveted; and since going into the club had almost certainly been a way of impressing him, it ultimately cost her her life.

Alison buried her face in her hands. Was the job worth all this?

A tap on the shoulder broke into her thoughts. It was Banham.

'I've just been on the internet,' he told her. 'I've booked us on a plane leaving for Venice tomorrow morning.'

'Is this a good idea?' She heard herself speak, but wasn't

at all sure what she'd meant to say.

'You need a break. It's only for three nights.'

She couldn't look at him. Why did he have to keep pushing her?

'It's a present from me. A fabulous hotel.' There was a pause. 'And it comes with no strings attached.'

Now she looked at him. 'I'm not sure I want a commitment.'

'I know.' His expression was unreadable. 'You can go on your own if you want.'

For a moment she was tempted. Then she realised that wasn't what she wanted at all. She shook her head. 'Just don't push me.'

'I won't.'

She still had a report to write. Banham sat down at the next desk and started writing his. The tickets lay next to the computer Alison was using. Neither of them spared the white envelope a glance.

Crowther was at the desk in front, quietly tapping the keyboard. Ten minutes later Penny Starr walked in and sat on the corner. 'Colin, I know how hard this has been for you. You and Isabelle were very close.'

Crowther lifted his head and looked at Alison.

Compassion and love were written across Penny's face. She had no idea exactly how close, Alison thought.

'I thought you might enjoy a few days away,' Penny was saying. 'So I've booked us a few nights in Venice.' She handed him an envelope.

Alison's eyes met Banham. Neither of them dared look at Crowther or Penny.

'Shouldn't you have consulted me first?' Crowther said

288

to her.

'No.' Penny's grin made her look like a mischievous imp. 'I'm your girlfriend. I know what's best for you. Don't argue!'

Suddenly Alison saw the funny side. She picked up the envelope on her own desk and opened it. 'Where are you staying?' she asked Penny.

'Hotel Kette,' Penny told her. 'It's lovely, right by the water, near the shops and very close to St Mark's Square.'

Alison looked down at the booking form she had just slid out of the envelope. It said in unmistakeable block capitals: HOTEL KETTE – TWO SINGLE ROOMS.

'I hope you booked a room the other end of the building,' Banham said to Penny.

'Pardon me?'

Crowther lifted his eyebrows questioningly.

Alison held up the booking form so they could both read it.

'Oh well,' Crowther said. 'We can drown in passion in the city of love, or drown our sorrows with the best Italian wines. Or we can just drown ourselves – there's no shortage of water!'

'And we all need a break,' Banham added.

Discover more from Linda Regan . . .

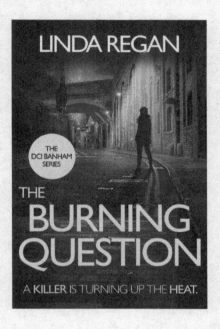

When an arson attack strikes in south London, leaving three
people dead, it quickly becomes clear that the youngest victim,
Danielle Low, was the intended target.

With no clear motive, and the killer at large, DCI Banham
must act fast. But working with his partner, DI Alison Grainger,
has its own challenges that threaten to stall the investigation.
Then another body is found in similar circumstances and he
knows that there is someone far more sinister at work.

As they begin to unravel a dark web of secrets,
the case unexpectedly leads close to home and with time
of the essence, and the killer always one step ahead,
can DCI Banham and his team work together to put a
stop to the depravity before another life is lost?

Available to order now